The new Zebra Regency ... ne
cover is a photograph of ... e
fashionable regency lady ... a
satin or velvet riband arou... ...y...g...... nose-
gay. Usually made of gold or silver, tuzzy-muzzies varied in design from the elegantly simple to the exquisitely ornate. The
Zebra Regency Romance tuzzy-muzzy is made of alabaster
with a silver filigree edging.

(91)

AFTERNOON DELIGHT

Brandreth drew off one of his gloves and touched
the white ruffle edging the brim of Evanthea's bonnet,
then gently stroked the curls about her face and fingered her eardrops.

"Damme," he whispered enigmatically, and gave a
strong tug on the bow of her bonnet. Afterward, he
pushed the hat away from her chestnut curls and her
face, then placed a light kiss on her forehead and a
gentle one on her lips. "Why is it whenever we are
alone I experience the most overwhelming desire to
take you in my arms?"

"I don't know," she murmured, searching his eyes
and feeling warm with deep affection for him. Somewhere in the back of her mind she knew she ought to
draw away from him, even a little, lest he assault her in
earnest as he had before. Thus far, an innocent kiss
upon the lips was truly nothing, but if he were to grab
her and hold her . . . well then, she would have to begin wondering whether or not the manner in which
they had begun conducting themselves in recent days
was not leading to something as serious as *love*. . . .

A Memorable Collection of Regency Romances

BY ANTHEA MALCOLM AND VALERIE KING

THE COUNTERFEIT HEART (3425, $3.95/$4.95)
by Anthea Malcolm
Nicola Crawford was hardly surprised when her cousin's betrothed disappeared on some mysterious quest. Anyone engaged to such an unromantic, but handsome man was bound to run off sooner or later. Nicola could never entrust her heart to such a conventional, but so deucedly handsome man. . . .

THE COURTING OF PHILIPPA (2714, $3.95/$4.95)
by Anthea Malcolm
Miss Philippa was a very successful author of romantic novels. Thus she was chagrined to be snubbed by the handsome writer Henry Ashton whose own books she admired. And when she learned he considered love stories completely beneath his notice, she vowed to teach him a thing or two about the subject of love. . . .

THE WIDOW'S GAMBIT (2357, $3.50/$4.50)
by Anthea Malcolm
The eldest of the orphaned Neville sisters needed a chaperone for a London season. So the ever-resourceful Livia added several years to her age, invented a deceased husband, and became the respectable Widow Royce. She was certain she'd never regret abandoning her girlhood until she met dashing Nicholas Warwick. . . .

A DARING WAGER (2558, $3.95/$4.95)
by Valerie King
Ellie Dearborne's penchant for gaming had finally led her to ruin. It seemed like such a lark, wagering her devious cousin George that she would obtain the snuffboxes of three of society's most dashing peers in one month's time. She could easily succeed, too, were it not for that exasperating Lord Ravenworth. . . .

THE WILLFUL WIDOW (3323, $3.95/$4.95)
by Valerie King
The lovely young widow, Mrs. Henrietta Harte, was not all inclined to pursue the sort of romantic folly the persistent King Brandish had in mind. She had to concentrate on marrying off her penniless sisters and managing her spendthrift mama. Surely Mr. Brandish could fit in with her plans somehow . . .

Available wherever paperbacks are sold, or order direct from the Publisher. Send cover price plus 50¢ per copy for mailing and handling to Zebra Books, Dept. 4139, 475 Park Avenue South, New York, N.Y. 10016. Residents of New York and Tennessee must include sales tax. DO NOT SEND CASH. For a free Zebra/ Pinnacle catalog please write to the above address.

Captivated Hearts
Valerie King

ZEBRA BOOKS
KENSINGTON PUBLISHING CORP.

ZEBRA BOOKS

are published by

Kensington Publishing Corp.
475 Park Avenue South
New York, NY 10016

Copyright © 1993 by Valerie King

First Printing: April, 1993

Printed in the United States of America

*To Carol, whose Greek birthname,
Evanthea, I borrowed for my heroine*

Love looks not with the eyes, but with the mind,
And therefore is wing'd Cupid painted blind.

— William Shakespeare

Chapter One

Evanthea Swanbourne watched her great-aunt's ear trumpet of burnished mahogany glimmer in the dancing firelight. She was amused, as she always was, by her aunt's preoccupation with invisible guests across the room, but withheld her smiles out of love and respect for her elderly relation.

The early summer night was cool for Lady Elizabeth's old bones and a fire had been ordered to warm the drafty drawing room where the two ladies were currently seated, opposite one another, in worn red velvet wing chairs. Evanthea was struggling with a grueling piece of cutwork, while Lady Elle extended her ear trumpet as far as she could toward the east side of the chamber, which housed an unpolished harp, a dusty pianoforte, and an antiquated bust of Zeus. She was smiling, an occasional chuckle erupting from between wrinkled, rouged lips.

Though loving her great-aunt dearly, Evanthea thought in this moment that the old woman, with her blue eyes narrowed and twinkling spritely and her thin shoulders shaking with mirth, appeared rather like a half-wit instead of the aristocratic daughter of a long-since deceased marquis. For some years now, Lady Elizabeth had suffered the strangest delusion that she had gained audience to the various daily occurrences of the inhabitants of Olympus. So absorbed did she become in the antics of the gods and goddesses of the ancient, forgotten religions of Greece and Italy that she frequently offended her earthly guests by ignoring them entirely, until such a time as her Olympian players returned at last to rest in their respective palaces.

Evanthea had for so long been an inmate of her great-aunt's dilapidated manor house in the heart of Bedfordshire that she was never offended by Lady Elizabeth's frequent lapses into a world filled with the petty rivalries of an Aphrodite or a Mars or a Vulcan. Indeed, she took some delight in watching her aged relative take pleasure in her imaginary world.

The odd thing, however, was that Lady Elle, as she was fondly known to those who loved her, was otherwise perfectly sound of mind and did not in any manner give the usual impression of one who has grown into an addled state. On the contrary, she could be quite wise in her observations, pointed in her criticisms, and witty in her conversation. She only appeared the bedlamite at the curious moments when she *saw* her Olympian friends actually enter the room and, instead of partaking of the society of the real world, gave the whole of her concentration to her more exalted, ghostlike company.

There were also occasions upon which Evanthea doubted the need for the ear trumpet, for while Lady Elizabeth could be deaf whenever she chose, there were moments when her hearing was painfully acute!

Evanthea, who had by now lifted her gaze several times from her embroidery for the sole purpose of observing her great-aunt in her preoccupation with the east portion of the chamber, finally let her restless fingers sit quietly on her lap. What was the dear old woman seeing? she wondered.

Pushing her spectacles up to the bridge of her nose, she decided to find out. "My dearest Lady Elle," she began softly. "Do not tell me your Olympian guests have come to call again? How many times have they visited with you this sennight alone, and so late at night?"

Lady Elizabeth, an aged widow of some seventy years, bid Evanthea to be silent with a lift of her hand and a quick shake of her head. She appeared as though she were afraid the smallest interruption would prevent her from hearing all that was going forward. After a moment, she whispered, "At first I was quite amused, but now I am concerned. You see, I have never heard Her Majesty Aphrodite so incensed. It is her daughter-in-law, Psyche, you know—Eros's errant wife—who has caused all the mischief! Not that I blame her one whit, poor child. But wait! I'll tell you more in a moment. It is the most amazing thing!" And with a childlike, impish hunch of her shoulders, she resumed listening.

Evanthea would have likewise resumed her needlework, but on this occasion, she was struck by the agitated expression on her great-aunt's face. "What is it?" she could not restrain from querying.

Again she was hushed with an imperious hand as Lady Elle leaned toward the east and extended her ear trumpet as far as she was able without breaking its connection to her ear. Her mouth then dropped wide and she let out a startled, "Good heavens!"

"What?" Evanthea cried, now caught up entirely by the intensity of Lady Elle's words and demeanor.

"I find it most remarkable! Indeed, I do. And it has all come about because Psyche stole her mother-in-law's famous cestus—a belt which possesses the power of turning a man's heart toward the wearer! At all events, Venus—that is, Aphrodite—has taken a pelter and all because of—of you!"

"Me?" Evanthea burst out laughing. This time, her aunt's fierce imagination had spun off on quite a ridiculous turn.

"You don't believe me?" Lady Elle queried, some-

11

what taken aback. "But it is true. It would seem Psyche has come to champion your cause!"

"My cause?" Evanthea queried, bemused. Then with a traitorous smile, she continued, "Do you mean the bust of Zeus? Oh, I do hope she intends to see that I am granted my father's most prized acquisition instead of your horrid nephew."

Lady Elle shook her head. "Brandreth's interest in purchasing the bust of Zeus from me has nothing to do with it. It would seem Psyche has not come to champion your desire to possess the statue your father gave me, but rather your heart! Psyche has come here to champion your heart—even braving Venus's wrath to do so! I am greatly astonished!"

Evanthea tilted her head slightly. She could feel the frown creasing her brow as she gently drew her spectacles from her eyes and folded them carefully together, lying them upon her lap. "Why ever would she wish to do that," she returned quietly, "when I haven't a heart?"

Chapter Two

"Only do but look at her, my dearest mama-in-law!" Psyche pleaded intently, her large blue eyes filled with sympathetic tears, her hands clasped to her breast.

"I have looked at her!" Aphrodite retorted, an angry scowl between her brows. "And do stop sniveling! How was it possible my son—*my son* fell in love with you, nonetheless wished to be leg-shackled to you, for a more hen-witted widgeon I have never known! Always poking your nose where it doesn't belong. These mortals are hopeless! How many times have I told you as much? Come! It is far better that you return to Olympus and leave these hapless creatures to their own, quite absurd devices. As for Evanthea, I *am* looking at her, and what I see is a plain-faced female of uninteresting proportions! Only look at her gown! Why, it positively hangs upon her bosom and—"

Psyche interrupted her, "But wouldn't you agree she has a pretty bosom otherwise?"

"Yes," Aphrodite agreed reluctantly. "But that is hardly the point. Of what use are such advantages if one willingly slights them? She mocks *me* in the way she dresses and cares for herself. And as for her hair! Good God! Though the color is a commanding chestnut, why in heaven's name has she wound it about her head in coils? She looks like Medusa! Most unattractive! Her features are not intolerable, but the specta-

13

cles which are usually drooping to the tip of her nose give her the air of a complete dowd. Why, even Lady Elizabeth here has more charm of person, however much she looks like a wrinkled fig at present, than this unfortunate young woman! Why ever do you concern yourself with one such as she? If I am not mistaken, one refers to a lady of her age as an *ape-leader!* She has certainly earned the appellation. I daresay she's been on the shelf for *years!*"

"Oh, not years," Psyche retorted hopefully. "Well, perhaps just one or two."

"More like a dozen, I've little doubt."

Psyche looked at Evanthea and sighed deeply. "I suppose you're right. She is nearly eight and twenty. That's almost a dozen years . . . well, ten at least since she first came out. I admit it is quite bad. Usually a young woman of her day is married before she attains her majority."

"I won't support you in your efforts here and that is my final word. And if my common sense is not enough to persuade you, need I remind you of the events which transpired when you interfered last?"

Psyche felt a blush creep up her cheeks. Even though the memory was some thirty years old, she could still be overset by how near to grief her project had come. She had been involved in bringing Evanthea's mother to Greece — surreptitiously, of course — in order to introduce her to Hiram Swanbourne, when her sailing vessel was fired upon by Algerian pirates. The ship miraculously did not sink and limped its way to Greece.

"But all of this," Aphrodite concluded with a wave of her hand toward Evanthea and Lady Elle, "I could easily forgive, except for the truly horrendous fact that you actually stole my cestus from me! What possessed you to do so? You know how I abominate thievery, deceit, and cunning!" To emphasize her displeasure, she slapped her hand upon the rosewood pianoforte and a roll of thunder promptly resounded through the chamber.

Psyche quailed beneath the lightning flashes in Aphrodite's exquisite eyes. From the first, she had been overawed by the woman's abilities, by her beauty, by the terrible strength of her will. And once crossed, no one could be more formidable than Aphrodite. She was truly a goddess by every Olympian standard, and not more so as the goddess of love and of beauty. In her eyes were all the colors to be found, slivers of violet and brown, hazel and blue. Her hair seemed to change shade with the shifting of her majestic head beneath the sun or the moon. Her figure was stately and full, completely feminine, evident even beneath the floating gossamer robe she wore of spun gold. On her head was a crown of gold, her hair falling richly back in Grecian waves, bound by gold braided ribbons. When she walked she swayed delicately, her beauty found as much in her countenance as in her face.

At the same time, for all Aphrodite's beauty of person, Psyche found her mama-in-law to be wanting in some of the attributes more nearly ascribed to mortals, such as kindness and compassion. In these, Aphrodite paled.

Psyche bit her lip. "I know it was very wrong of me, but I was *compelled* to come to Evanthea's assistance, particularly when the marquis slighted her so unbecomingly. You see, I suspect were he not so arrogant and she so seemingly disinterested in love, they might be well suited."

"I don't give a fig for any of it!" Aphrodite responded at last, extending her hand toward Psyche and commanding, "Now give me the cestus."

Reluctantly, Psyche handed the intricately worked belt to her. It was an exquisite creation embroidered with pink roses and green leaves on a bed of gold velvet and laced with an occasional diamond, which

15

appeared like dew on the petals of the flower of love.

"Much better," Aphrodite said, nodding firmly. "And now I suggest you return at once, or—"

Whatever threat might have followed her *suggestion* was left forever hidden, because in that moment a familiar fluttering of wings was heard, instantly bringing Aphrodite's speech to a halt.

"Eros!" Aphrodite cried, her voice softened and affectionate as she turned toward the gently slowing sound. "My darling boy. But whatever are you doing here?"

"I received your message, Mama! Mars was quite beside himself. It would seem you had somehow given him the impression that you meant to do some great injury to my wife, though I now perceive he was greatly mistaken!"

"For heaven's sake!" Aphrodite exclaimed. "I merely said I meant to wring the child's neck!"

"How can you call me a child," Psyche responded, stung, "when I am nearly two thousand years old!"

Aphrodite further exacerbated Psyche's dislike and ill temper by rolling her eyes in a familiar and quite irritatingly *patient* manner she was used to employing strictly in her son's presence.

"If you must know," Aphrodite began with a beleaguered sigh, ignoring Psyche completely and addressing Eros instead, "your *charming* little wife stole my cestus!" Since she followed this up by waving the offending object beneath his nose, Eros had little choice but to turn astonished eyes upon Psyche.

"Butterfly!" he cried, making use of her Olympian nickname, his tone clearly expressing his disappointment. "Don't tell me what Mama says is true?"

Psyche hung her head and nodded. She could not immediately speak because when he had uttered the sweet word *Butterfly,* her heart had jumped clear to her throat, preventing speech. Taking two deep breaths, she finally began in a small voice, "I know it was wrong of me, terribly so! If you only knew to what ends I meant to employ the magical garment, you would not be so unhappy, I'm sure of it." She then lifted her gaze to meet his and saw an expression of hurt glint in his rich brown eyes.

"Nothing, Psyche, absolutely nothing can justify stealing. Surely I do not need to remind you of that!"

Psyche looked at her famous husband, who was also known as Cupid, and felt her heart turn over several times. She loved him so much and wanted nothing more than to please him, yet she had no words with which to answer him. He was right, of course, she should not steal, but what could she do? She needed the cestus to help Evanthea attach Brandreth to her side, and for reasons she could not comprehend it had become of supreme importance to her to see the young woman happily married.

As she looked at her husband, Psyche found herself torn between a desire to beg his forgiveness by casting herself at his feet and an intense sensation of despair. The mere sight of Eros, even after so many centuries together, still caused her knees to weaken in an ominous fashion and her heart to throb almost painfully in her breast. Yet as one decade had surmounted the next, as they lived together in the same palace since time out of mind, rubbing against one another as husbands and wives are wont to do in the daily business of life, Cupid had come to that extraordinary place of taking his wife completely for granted, ignoring her presence three years out of four.

But Psyche's gentle spirit and loving heart were not meant to be treated with disinterest and disaffection. Why, in the past century alone, he had taken up the truly dreadful habit of uttering monosyllables at the breakfast table, all the while ensconced behind the latest scroll from Zeus's establishment at the very pinnacle of Mount Olympus.

"Will you be seeing Vulcan today?" she had asked

him only this morning. "I understand he has fabricated some new arrows for you of a superior metal than the last?"

"Yes, dear."

"Did you hear the latest rumor from Hades?"

"Mmm," was his eloquent response.

"I see grapes have begun growing out your ears," she stated coldly.

"Yes," he said absently. "Very interesting, isn't it? I love grapes, especially in ambrosia."

She had stormed away from the table at that moment. The only satisfaction she gained from it, however, was the look of surprise on his fair brow, the monster!

It was not to be borne! Did he believe she had no pride? Did he think for one moment that she could countenance such horrendous indifference without—without making a life for herself apart from him? No. A thousand times, a million times, *no!*

Eros's voice interrupted her despairing reverie. "Mama," he queried, his attention riveted to the wall just beyond the pianoforte, "is that not the bust of your father, of Zeus, which you mislaid . . . let me see . . . twenty-five years now?"

Psyche felt her cheeks pale to a blue coldness. It was bad enough that she had been caught with Aphrodite's missing cestus, but what if the terrible goddess recognized the offending piece of statuary that she had stolen from her apartments some three decades earlier?

Jupiter's beard! She would be in the basket, *indeed!*

Chapter Three

Evanthea had stopped listening to Lady Elle at the moment her great-aunt was remarking that the stolen cestus was made of gold velvet, green leaves, pink roses, and dotted with diamonds. She continued to nod absently at the descriptions Lady Elle put forth regarding the interesting trio, since Eros, Aphrodite's beloved son, had suddenly joined his mother and wife in what sounded like a familiar familial quarrel. However much she might find it fascinating to hear her aunt repeat an imaginary conversation, her own agitated thoughts had quickly cut off the old woman's ramblings.

As she set her stitches and rethreaded her needle with white silk floss, she glanced up at the bust of Zeus. Her heart became filled with a deep pain, which frequently took strong hold of her and which she simply had not been able to convey to Lady Elle. The small marble statue, quite beautiful yet ancient in appearance, was all that was left of her father's labors and therefore the only tangible relic of all the many hours they had spent together some years ago digging through the ruins of Greece. She cherished the bust in a way she could not easily explain, as though it held some inexplicable magical power for her. When she was near it, she felt warm and comforted, the loneliness that her papa's death had imparted to her three years earlier assuaged, if but for a mere whisper of time. When she awoke with night terrors, she had but to descend to the drawing room, candle in hand, and approach the bust in order to be eased from her sore distress. The thought that Lady Elle's great-nephew had offered her a fortune for the statue so filled her with anxiety that her heart seemed at times to stop beating. How would she live if she were separated from the only remaining treasure of her father's work? She felt, quite irrationally so, that if she were parted from the antiquated statue, some integral portion of her own heart would die.

Unfolding her spectacles and placing them carefully over each ear, she returned to her embroidery. The delicate white work, lying in folds upon her lap, required the greatest of patience as she picked out and edged small spaces in white floss, the whole of which created a lacy, elegant effect when completed. She tried to ply her needle, but when her thoughts turned unhappily to Lord Brandreth, her fingers began to tremble and again she let her embroidery rest on her lap.

And why the Marquis of Brandreth, knowing full well the extent of her interest in the statue, still insisted upon offering her aunt a figure that the impoverished woman could not possibly refuse was beyond her comprehension. Save, of course, that his exalted lordship was all that was contemptible in mankind and pursued his intention to possess the bust out of a misguided desire to do her injury.

She jabbed the needle into the fabric with a quick thrust, wishing only that it were the marquis's thick, obstinate hide instead of her embroidery. Oh, what pleasure she would surely receive from lancing his flesh even but a trifle. It was considerably less than what he deserved, after all!

She held the needle up before her and struck at the air several times.

"Whatever are you about, Evanthea?" she heard her aunt query.

"I am practicing," Evanthea responded forthrightly. "If your darling great-nephew should ever dare to come near me while I am at my embroidery, I shall jab him thoroughly with my needle, though I daresay he has so little sensibility he will not even notice he is bleeding. Now that I think on it, perhaps I ought to take up a fencing sword instead!"

"Good heavens!" Lady Elle responded with a scowl. "Such a speech, Evanthea. And you, gently bred!"

"I was not gently bred at all, ma'am, as you very well know. Papa did not believe in coddling his daughter."

Lady Elle shook her head and set her ear trumpet on a table beside her chair. "I wish you hadn't quite so much spirit," she sighed. "How on earth do you expect to enslave a man's fancy if you are not more demure and flirtatious, especially if you begin speaking of blood and swords as though they are merely commonplace? It is no wonder the gentlemen of your acquaintance back away from you so politely, giving you ground as though—as though you have the pox! They fear you! Do you wish to remain a spinster to the end of your days? Is this your design, your intention, your hope?"

Evanthea did not wish to enter into what was a very old argument between them. She knew she had disappointed her great-aunt and therefore responded quietly, "I know you wish I were a different sort of creature than what I am. But I assure you, I heartily enjoy those peculiar freedoms which are part of my unwedded state. Besides, I fear I am a great deal like my father and ever shall be."

"Well, I wish you would make an effort, my dear," Lady Elle continued, her tone kinder. "I know there are some females who can be quite content without the companionship of a husband and children. But

21

not you. Don't look so surprised, Evanthea. I know you cherish the illusion that you are content, but how do you account for the many hours you spend staring at nothing in particular and sighing in that truly unhappy manner of yours?"

"I was not aware I did so."

"Precisely so," Lady Elle said. "I have not lived to be such an ancient creature without having learned a lesson or two. If you would only appear less of an intellectual turn—why, even Brandreth thinks you are a blue stocking!—you would have no difficulty whatsoever in fixing your affections on whatever man you chose. Though I daresay it would do you no harm to unloosen your braids a trifle." Her attention became suddenly diverted by events she saw transpiring near the pianoforte. "Good heavens!" she cried, apparently startled. "Venus is preparing to leave. Pray ring for Meppers and have him fetch my nephew. I must see him at once!"

"Whatever do you want with Brandreth at this late hour? He will undoubtedly be in his cups and speak reproachful words as he was wont to do last night. Even to you, aunt, he said the most lamentable things!"

"And you are by far a great deal too sensitive for one who is determined to set up people's backs. I find his humor quite charming. He merely teased me about not being as deaf as I pretend to be! Now do as I bid you! Send Meppers to find him. He is probably in the billiard room."

"Undoubtedly," Evanthea responded with a disapproving lift of one brow as she dipped her needle into the fabric and set the whole of it aside. Rising to her feet, she removed her spectacles and afterward withdrew a lace kerchief from the long sleeve of her pale green gown of embroidered muslin. As she moved toward the door, she carefully cleaned the thin, round lenses. "Brandreth is always seeking after some pleasure or other. He never applies himself to serious matters. I can't see why you must needs invite him to the drawing room when he is certain to disrupt our contentment."

"Oh, Evanthea, for once, must you be contentious? You are always fretting and brangling."

"I am not!" she cried, replacing her spectacles over her ears.

"There! You argue even now. You are very much like your father, indeed! Now, your mother wasn't anything like you. She was the most biddable, adorable, lively child that ever existed. You would have done well to have garnered even one of her qualities."

Evanthea gave a tug on the tapestried bellpull and returned to her seat. "I don't remember her very well," she responded wistfully, unoffended by Lady Elle's disparaging remarks on her character. "And I certainly will not disagree with you where she is concerned. Papa even said I hadn't but a spark of my mother in me."

"She was quite short."

"And I am a long Meg."

"Her eyes were the clearest, lightest blue I have ever seen."

"Mine are just like Papa's, a deep brown to the point of being almost black."

"She had the prettiest, curliest blond hair one could ever imagine."

"And mine is straight, brown, and dull."

Lady Elle glanced at her, a little startled. "Your hair is the color of chestnuts, my dear. A rich brown with just a hint of red. You have beautiful hair. Have I not told you as much? I merely think you keep your light under a bushel by wrapping it about your head in that silly, antiquated fashion! Why, you do not even sport a fringe of curls upon your forehead, which would go a long way to softening your habitually severe expression. No, no! Your hair is not at all dull, just your manner of dressing it."

Evanthea touched the coils atop her head. "Do you think so, indeed? Papa was used to saying I looked horsey if I let it down."

"Your father, for all his excellent qualities, was quite ignorant in his care of you and knew nothing at all of females. It is only a wonder he ever fell in love and married, nonetheless to your charming mama." A scratching on the door interrupted the interesting discourse on family resemblances. "There you are, Meppers," Lady Elle cried, ignoring her order to have Evanthea discharge her errand. "I am glad you were close at hand."

"I was conferring with Mrs. Brown regarding tomorrow's dinner, when I heard your summons. If you don't mind my speaking, my lady, we are in a bit of quandary." Meppers was a short, balding man who, when particularly nervous as he was now, scratched his shiny pate with complete disregard to the decorous requirements of his post as butler. "Mrs. Brown is needful for James to go into the woods on the morrow. We are . . . er . . . a trifle short of provisions, as you probably already know."

"Of course we are," Evanthea interjected hotly, addressing her great-aunt. "And all because Brandreth must come and make his home here for several weeks, never once considering what a burden he is upon your purse!"

"Hush!" Lady Elle cried. "As though I give a fig for that. He is my beloved great-nephew, and the day I cannot offer him my home as his own . . . well! . . ." She pursed her lips and swallowed hard, her blue eyes filling quickly with unwanted tears.

Evanthea immediately regretted her words. However much cause she had to dislike Brandreth, her ill feeling toward the marquis was no reason to bring grief to her aunt. She winced when Meppers turned

24

his small brown eyes upon her, frowning her down. She quickly begged Lady Elle's pardon.

Only five staff members remained at Flitwick Lodge, a mere quarter of the once-burgeoning tally of servants who had formerly kept the ancient manor in its prime. Ever since Lady Elle's beloved Henry had broken his neck on the hunting field and left the Lodge under an enormous weight of debt, Flitwick had literally gone to rack and ruin. But times were hard everywhere, and those servants who remained, besides feeling a loyalty to their mistress, stayed simply because they had nowhere else to go. Lady Elle could not afford to pay them, owing each at least two year's back wages, but a home garden, a home wood, and James's unerring shot kept the entire establishment fed. Beyond that, everyone relied on the combined stitching skills of the female inhabitants in order to keep the linens repaired, knitted garments mended, and the fading draperies of the principal rooms transformed into winter cloaks.

Lady Elle addressed the larger issue. "I suppose Sidlow has flown into the boughs."

"He has never quite accustomed himself to having only one groom underfoot, and when James spends a day in the home wood, Sidlow's duties encompass those tasks better left to one of . . . let us say, lesser sensibilities when it comes to tending to the horses."

"We must have meat," was Lady Elle's response.

"Sidlow is likely to resign his post if James picks up his rifle."

Lady Elle was quiet for a moment, well acquainted with her head groom's fastidious sense of the dignity of his office. "You might suggest to him," she said with a half-smile, "that if he does decide to leave us, James will simply have to take over as head groom."

Meppers tried not to smile but failed. "I wish I had thought a' that afore, my lady. It will answer, indeed it will. Sidlow wouldn't take to the notion above half, since he's convinced he's the only one that knows how to properly keep the stables in order. And now if it pleases you, how may I be of service to you?"

When Lady Elle had dispatched Meppers on his errand to fetch Brandreth, her attention was again drawn back to her Olympian guests. "Thank heavens Aphrodite has not left!" she cried, lifting her ear trumpet to her ear. "But I didn't suppose she would quit the field just yet. She is still considerably overset. Did I tell you she insists that the bust of Zeus belongs to her? She has even gone so far as to accuse Psyche of stealing the statue from her chambers. How very odd. Good heavens, she is moving toward it as though she means to remove it from my house! She can't mean to take it!" Lady Elle dropped her ear trumpet on the floor and rose from her chair in apparent anticipation of preventing the deity from robbing her of the handsome bust. After a moment, she fell back into her seat and sighed with relief. "Thank heavens. She fears her father, Zeus, would discover she has been conferring with mortals were she to bring the bust home. Did I tell you that it is quite unusual for Venus to make an appearance? She dislikes her daughter-in-law immensely. I have for some time suspected that Aphrodite has poisoned Eros against his wife, but I cannot imagine how she did it. Oh my! I do wish you could see her, Evanthea — both of the women, really! I have never in my entire existence witnessed such elegance and beauty combined — and Psyche was once a mortal like you and I."

"Lady Elle, really!" Evanthea exclaimed, feeling that her great-aunt's flight into a fanciful world had gone quite far enough. "Of all the absurd starts. And what is this nonsense about Aphrodite and the bust of Zeus? Papa found it in one of his digs in Greece. You know he did!"

"Someone from Olympus could have put it there, I suppose," she responded somewhat absently, glancing toward the door. "Oh, dear, I hope Brandreth does not dawdle. You see, I am hoping that if Aphrodite could *see* my great-nephew, Psyche's plans might yet succeed."

Evanthea felt vaguely uncomfortable by this last remark, knowing that Psyche's plans—at least according to her aunt's imagination—involved her own heart. "I don't understand," she began. "Why do you think it would make a difference in Psyche's schemes if Aphrodite *saw* Brandreth?"

Lady Elle's blue eyes twinkled. In a whisper, she said, "Aphrodite has a great weakness for beautiful men, and you know how handsome Brandreth is—for a mortal, that is. I am persuaded that were she to see him, she might take a personal interest in Psyche's schemes and permit her to make use of the cestus after all. And the cestus would answer all our dilemmas!"

Evanthea regarded her aunt askance. "What charm did you say the cestus possessed?" she asked, trying to remember what her aunt had mentioned earlier. "And what does Psyche wish to do with it?"

"She means for you to wear it, of course, and as for its powers, the wearer can enslave the heart of the first man she sees once the belt is tied securely about her waist."

Evanthea hid her smiles and could now ignore the whole of what her poor, misguided aunt was saying. Was anything more ridiculous than the notion that the wearing of a belt could attach a man firmly to one's side? As she again resumed plying her stitches, it occurred to Evanthea that in recent days Lady Elle's sometimes diverting, sometimes exasperating treks into the Olympian world had become more and more directed toward her own unwedded state. Now Brandreth was being drawn in as well, but to what purpose? Was it possible that Lady Elle, in her own peculiar manner, was attempting to encourage a match between herself and the marquis?

Evanthea could not prevent a chuckle from escaping past her lips, for a more unlikely pair one could never find. She spent her days usefully employed, whether taking extractions from Greek and Latin translations or copying the latest poems to send to her various acquaintances or helping Mrs. Brown in her housekeeping chores, whereas his lordship delighted in only the most useless of activities, such as hunting and billiards and gaming. Only last season he had been known to lose a thousand pounds at Watier's—in one night! Though Lady Elle had tried to tell her that a thousand pounds was nothing compared to what some had lost—some having forfeited an entire fortune in a single night's gaming—Evanthea could not be moved from her opinion that his lordship was a hopeless gamester, caught up in naught but his own pleasure while his enormous staff slaved to keep his estates and his fortune in good order. No, she had no great opinion of Henry Staple, Marquis of Brandreth, Lord Brandreth! He might be a vision fit for the goddess Aphrodite, but for her part, he could go to the devil!

No, a more unlikely pair one could never find.

"Is Annabelle due to arrive tomorrow, or will it be Thursday?" Evanthea asked, changing the subject. Annabelle was Lady Elle's great-niece on the marquis's side of the family. She was a second cousin to the marquis, whereas Evanthea had no blood relation to his lordship whatsoever. Annabelle was pretty, lively, wealthy, and had set her cap for his lordship since time out of mind! For as long as Evanthea could remember, she had found much enjoyment in watching the singularly foolish young woman make a complete cake of herself in her pursuit of the elusive marquis.

What she could never comprehend, however, was why Brandreth seemed to be pleased with all the fulsome compliments Annabelle was wont to shower upon his arrogant head. He could not be such a sapskull as to actually believe everything Annabelle said, particularly when he could not help but be aware that his cousin had set her cap for him.

But then, there was no comprehending his mind. Nor could it be said he lacked the perception to properly discern Annabelle's tactics. However much Evanthea might despise his seemingly endless need for pleasures of all sorts, she was not deceived into thinking that he was an unintelligent man. The truth was, he displayed remarkable acumen, which only increased Evanthea's disgust of him. A man so blessed with such a fine capacity for knowledge and learning, yet to exploit it only in determining just how he should hedge his bet in a game of hazard was a man she could not admire! His existence was a complete waste of his life and the gifts bestowed upon him from the heavens above!

"She is here already," Lady Elle responded, interrupting the rapid train of Evanthea's thoughts. "Did not I tell you? She was arrived this afternoon when you were in the vegetable plot with Cook. She complained of the headache, though I saw nothing in the brightness of her dancing green eyes to indicate illness. . . . You know what that child is! I suspect she wished to retire early to bed in order that she might appear to advantage on the morrow."

"I expect you are right. Only the other day I had a letter from her explaining her intent to bring Brandreth at last to heel. She was busy purchasing a bevy of gowns from New Bond Street and—" Evanthea was cut off from expressing her opinions by the arrival of the marquis, who knocked loudly upon the door and then gave it a hearty shove.

He stood framed in the doorway, twirling his quizzing glass and smiling his laziest of smiles. One fine, arched brow was lifted arrogantly as he caught Evanthea's gaze.

"Ah, cousin," he said, provoking her by speaking in his most infuriatingly *bored* voice.

"Oh, do shut the door, Brandreth," Evanthea responded curtly. "You are causing the fire to smoke with the draft you create by just standing there. And I am not your *cousin,* for the hundredth time. I wish you would cease taunting me by addressing me as such."

Chapter Four

When Evanthea, her gaze fixed on her busy needle, realized after a time that Brandreth not only was silent but had failed to move into the chamber as she had commanded him to, she turned to look at him and asked baldly, "What? What is the matter? What do you mean by staring at me in that infernal manner!"

"You are out of sorts. I'm sorry for it. I did not know you were ill. Have you the headache?"

Evanthea rolled her eyes. "You know very well I have no such thing. Now pray, leave the doorway, close the door behind you — though I would much prefer that you shut the door in front of you and go away — but if you must remain, spare us a chill to our bones!"

"I know what it is!" he continued, turning at last to close the door. "You are sadly out of temper because I called you cousin." With mock innocence, he placed a hand against an apparently wounded breast and faced her. "I fear I have angered you. Then, I will beg your pardon at once! I beseech your forgiveness. A thousand times, I beg your pardon, my dearest cous — oh, oh, dear. I should say, *my dearest acquaintance!* But you know, I had no real notion you didn't wish for me to call you cousin. Besides, I had always considered the appellation quite affectionate. Zeus! Had I known such a form gave you offense, I most certainly would

31

have made every effort to discontinue what can only be—"

"Oh, do stubble it, simpleton!" Evanthea cried, amused in spite of herself, yet trying desperately to appear otherwise.

He must have seen something in her eyes, however, or perhaps a gentle twitch of her lips, because he was not deceived. Sauntering into the room, he continued, "I suppose I simply felt that calling you cousin would add to the general contentment of the house."

"And are you content?" she asked, blinking several times up into his face, feigning interest and devotion in a similar manner as Annabelle had done since time out of mind.

The expression on her face seemed to give him pause. Smiling softly, he inclined his head to her. "In this moment, I profess to be content. You see, I forgot how deuced pretty you were—that is, when you are being civil."

"When I am being civil!" Evanthea cried, offended. "But I see what it is. You expect me to be flattered by your remark. But do you realize you have completely overlooked the fact that I was facetiously pandering to your vanity when I begged to know *if you were content*."

Her words pulled the smile from the marquis's mouth. His nostrils flared in irritation and his gray eyes sparked. To his credit, however, he did not give voice to the angry sentiments exposed on his face, but bowed to her ever so slightly from the waist in recognition of her hit and let his quizzing glass drop to dangle upon its long, black silk riband.

Evanthea found a droplet of respect for him in this moment. She knew his temper was decidedly choleric, and though she was fully aware he longed to rage at her, the fact that he controlled himself was worthy of at least a tuppence of her esteem.

He was an extraordinary creature, if the truth be

32

known, tall, handsome, regal of form, impeccably groomed. He was dressed in formal evening attire, sporting a coat of black superfine, black pantaloons, and black silk slippers. It was said that Beau Brummell himself had guided the marquis in the construction of his coat, which Weston had fitted admirably to a pair of broad masculine shoulders. His figure was near to perfection, angling from fine shoulders to a small waist, narrow hips, and strong athletic thighs. Above a crisp neckcloth, folded intricately *à la Brandreth,* as it was known amongst the *beau monde,* starched white shirtpoints touched cheeks that drew inward from a clean line beginning at high, marked cheekbones and lancing downward to a firm chin. His thick black hair was cut and styled in the fashion known as *à la Brutus.* But beyond every excellent aspect of his person, one feature commanded the rest: In Brandreth's gray eyes were combined his intelligence and his strength of will, so that no matter how much one would admire him, his eyes demanded that more be given.

It was no wonder, Evanthea thought with a begrudging smile as her gaze swept over his person, that he was by far the most sought-after Matrimonial Prize on the Marriage Mart. Where else had nature brought together such a startling configuration of wealth, rank, and excellent good looks as the Marquis of Brandreth?

Having noticed her scrutiny and her smile, he queried coldly, "What is your judgment, Miss Swanbourne?"

Evanthea, used to his directness, responded, "What you probably expect. You are a considerably handsome creature, you dress to perfection, and you have a unique ability to sway the opinions of an entire assembly merely by directing your gaze where you will. One cannot help but venerate your combined attributes."

He seemed startled. "Have I heard you correctly?"

Brandreth asked with a laugh of disbelief. "Did you, just then, compliment me, or are you again being facetious?"

Evanthea lifted her brows purposely, hoping to appear indifferent. "No, of course I was not. But I did not compliment you as you suppose. I am not one of your fawning admirers. I was merely speaking the truth as I see it and"— here she smiled and inclined her head to him—"as most of the women of my acquaintance perceive it."

"I'm not sure what to make of this, Evanthea, but I have the worst fear you are still mocking me."

"No. If I were mocking you, I would have smiled sweetly and batted my eyelashes while telling you how truly beautiful you are."

He stared at her for a long moment, during which Evanthea returned his gaze candidly. "For the life of me," he said at last, "I do not make you out! I never have!"

"Now you have made me content, so we are at liberty again to despise one another freely."

He shook his head as though utterly confounded and turned to greet his great-aunt, taking her hand in his and placing an affectionate kiss upon her crooked fingers. Lady Elle told him not to pay the least heed to what Evanthea said, then thanked him for responding to her summons. She was quite bored, she said, and wished for a little piquet if he would oblige her. Brandreth was nothing if not gracious and, setting up a table between them, took a seat on the sofa situated next to his great-aunt's chair and immediately engaged her in a lively game of cards.

Noting that the candles had begun to melt away almost to nothing, Evanthea set aside her needlework and began refurbishing the three candelabra set about the drawing room. In other households, where funds and servants were plentiful, the chore of snuffing, replacing, and lighting the candles would have been assigned to one of the footmen. But given the state of affairs, Evanthea was glad to be of service in this small way.

Settling candles into the various candelabra, however, served to remind Evanthea of the penury of Flitwick Lodge. She passed behind Brandreth and scowled at him. Lady Elle could solve all her monetary difficulties, which were quite numerous, merely by accepting his incredible offer—ten thousand pounds for the bust of Zeus! He had but to press their great-aunt even a trifle and Evanthea was convinced Lady Elle would be persuaded to accept. She certainly had need of the money.

Only this morning, her aunt had told her that she had received yet another correspondence from Messrs. Thomas & Riley of Hanover Street, moneylenders known to cater to the upper classes. This firm charged exorbitant rates of interest and had been in the habit of lending her deceased husband his gaming funds—little of which he had repaid before his untimely demise.

And Brandreth had come to Flitwick with the solution to her difficulties.

How could Lady Elle possibly refuse ten thousand pounds, and worse, how could Evanthea even wish to prevent her from availing herself of his more than generous offer?

Chapter Five

"By Jupiter, by Zeus!" Aphrodite cried, then clamped a hand over her mouth. She glanced first at her son and then at Psyche, an admonishing scowl furrowing her pretty brow. "If either of you dare to mention to the *Exalted One* that I have used his name as the mortals do, I shall banish you both to Hades—for a decade or two!—and don't think for a moment I won't." Her features softened suddenly as she slowly transferred her gaze, as one instantly smitten with love, back to the brow of the Marquis of Brandreth. "Who is that exquisite creature?" she breathed at last.

Psyche informed her of the marquis's identity, whereupon Aphrodite turned to her daughter-in-law and, with an accusing finger leveled impolitely at Evanthea, spoke sharply, "Do you mean to tell me that you want that—that singularly unfortunate excuse for a *woman* to fall in love with this incredible ensemble of the very best parts of humankind?"

Psyche held her ferocious mother-in-law's gaze steadfastly with her own. She knew that to cower beneath Aphrodite's stern expression would prove fatal, so she straightened her shoulders and answered her with as much confidence as she could summon. "Indeed, ma'am, that is precisely the notion which has obsessed me for these many weeks and more. I am convinced they are well suited, however much they brangle."

Aphrodite, in a rare moment, tossed her head and laughed. So pretty was the sound that Psyche was convinced if the inmates of Flitwick Lodge heard the delicate trills and tremolos of the goddess's amusement, they would sob. After a moment, when Venus's singular laughter had abated and she had wiped several tears from her alabaster cheeks, she caught Psyche beneath her chin with her hand and gave her, what from any other relative would have been recounted, a gentle, almost affectionate tug. But Psyche was not misled.

"What a silly little ninnyhammer you are," Aphrodite cried. "Eros, however do you tolerate this absurd simpleton? When I have reached a million years in age, I will still not understand the ridiculous turns of her mind. . . ."

"Mama," Eros responded, chiding. "I believe you've quite said enough."

"I've hardly started! For anyone to think that such a grand gentleman as this one" — here she placed her fingers to her lips and blew a kiss toward Brandreth — "should in any fashion be attracted to that one" — and with the same fingers she flicked them toward Evanthea, as though flipping an insect from her gown — "could only be the fitful starts of a weak mind."

Eros again appeared to wish to defend his wife, much to Pysche's pleasure, but she placed a gentle hand upon the soft, white cambric sleeve of his tunic and stayed the impetuous words readied upon his tongue, words that more often than not threw Psyche in a worse light than before. "Cupid, my love," she began tenderly, using the Roman form of his name, "your mother speaks only the unhappiest of truths. I do not have your genius or hers. I do not pretend otherwise. But this I know: Beneath Evanthea's quite rigid demeanor and her disinterest in fashionable attire lies a passionate woman waiting only to be awakened to love. As for Brandreth"—here she glanced slyly at Aphrodite—"he is prevented from loving well by a degree of pride which I have never before encountered."

Psyche could see that she had chosen her words well. Aphrodite's curved brows rose in an intrigued arch over her glittering eyes. "His pride?" she queried. "Well, of course he has pride. He has every right to feel satisfied with his appearance. Zeus must have had a part in the shaping of his features, his shoulders, his well-turned leg."

Psyche gave the appearance of perplexity as she wrinkled her brow and responded, "Perhaps you are right. I do not deny he is everything that is beautiful nor that he should be proud of his appearance, but I heard him boasting to one of his acquaintance only yesterday that he could win any female he desired by the mere crooking of his finger. Was I wrong to believe, then, that his pride has transformed into that greater evil—arrogance?"

Aphrodite pursed her lips and turned her gaze to watch Lord Brandreth with penetrating eyes. Psyche hid her smiles. How easily her mama-in-law rose to the fly! The beautiful deity could never resist giving an arrogant male a setdown whenever the occasion required it.

Psyche also shifted her attention to the ensuing conversation between Evanthea and Lord Brandreth. It appeared the unlikely pair was fully engaged in a dispute, the subject of which caused Psyche's knees to begin trembling. They were arguing over the bust of Zeus, and above all things she did not want Aphrodite's attention diverted again to the statue. Her mother-in-law had already rung a peal over her head where the bust was concerned, even though Psyche pretended that she hadn't the least notion how it had come to reside at Flitwick Lodge.

It had been at least three decades since Psyche had stolen the small marble statue from her mama-in-law's lavish apartments in Olympus. The furor that had resulted had so frightened Psyche that she had permitted Evanthea's father to uncover it quite by accident some few years ago in Greece. At the time she had been convinced that if a mortal were made guardian over the offending object, then Aphrodite would never learn of its whereabouts.

But how doggedly that terrible menace Nemesis had kept at her heels, so that here she was, with Aphrodite in tow—not to mention her critical husband, Eros—and the bust a mere ten feet away! If she lived to be fifty thousand years old, she would never comprehend the complicated manner in which Fate kept the whole of the Olympian circus in an uproar. One simply could not keep one's secrets for longer than a decade or two, for someone was bound to discover the truth, and all because Fate would keep bringing the wrong person to the wrong place at the wrong time and because that horrid Nemesis would not let any sin go unnoticed, or even unpunished.

She bit her lip and thought ruefully of the many objects hidden in her own wardrobe that she had stolen from all parts of Zeus's glorious kingdom. She didn't know why she took the things she did, but she rather suspected it had begun the day some two centuries earlier when she had found Cupid flirting with a tavern maid in Gloucestershire. She hadn't known until then that he could transform himself for a time into the shape of mortal man, nor had she realized she could stand amongst the mortals herself, remaining unseen, of course, and be-

come involved in their lives as well. Eros had not realized that it was she who had brought the maid's
father charging from the kitchen of the Oak Inn to
rescue his daughter from the questionable advances
of a stranger.

She smiled suddenly. How shocked her husband
had been. He had even been startled into changing
back to his true form right in front of the astonished
mortals, one of his wings escaping from the confines
of his velvet tunic, the sight of which caused the
poor maid to drop into a dead faint. Psyche had
laughed herself into stitches at the expression of
shock and confusion on his face. But later, when she
had reflected upon the true nature of the disaster
that had befallen her, she realized that her darling
spouse, upon whom she had doted for more than
two millennium, had begun wandering in his affections.

That night she had stolen one of his arrows from
his workshop, the point recently sharpened with the
blood taken from a lamb, and had kept it beneath
her pillow. She had cried herself to sleep, and afterward their relationship had suffered a severe strain.
She had not known what to do then, and now she
hadn't the least notion how to rekindle his ardor for
her.

But she was not one to dwell upon her misfor-
tunes, seeking instead consolation by turning to the
task of helping mortals fall in love. One of her more
recent projects had been Evanthea's father, and now
his daughter had need of her.

But how was she to keep Aphrodite from learning
that it was she who had stolen her adored statue?
Clearly her mama-in-law suspected her, particularly
since she had just been caught with the dragon's cestus in hand.

Glancing at Cupid, her next thought sent her spirits plummeting further. Would she ever know her husband's love again?

Evanthea slapped the silver candlesnuffer hard against the palm of her hand, her cheeks aflame. "How dare you, Brandreth, accuse me of any such thing! I have not ensconced myself in Flitwick Lodge for the wretched purpose of ingratiating myself with Lady Elle. Those who know my character are fully conversant with the fact that I would never reduce myself to such a heinous stratagem. On the other hand, anyone knowing you as I do could readily believe *you* capable of following such a course in order to achieve *your* ends. But not me! My devotion to my great-aunt is well known. And you may ask the good vicar whether or not I am capable of such horrendous cunning, artifice, and shameless misconduct as you suggest."

Evanthea never hesitated to lock horns with the marquis. She had no fear of him as did a large number of her acquaintance and the *beau monde* in general. By most he was considered a formidable adversary, but her dislike of his entire person and character made it a simple feat to place herself between the wretched marquis and the bust of Zeus, thrust the snuffer toward him as though it were a sword, and continued forcefully, "Though why you must choose to make this insignificant statue the object of your greed—the only article in this entire house, indeed in the entire world, which holds for me a sentimental connection—I shall never comprehend. You know my father discovered that statue in one of his earliest excavations in Greece—"

"—and bestowed it upon Lady Elle—"

"—who has since expressed her wish at least a hundred times that I come into possession of it,

41

which I undoubtedly would have by now save for your outrageous offer for it. If I didn't know better, I would suppose you had dangled your ten thousand pounds beneath her impoverished nose out of pure spite for me. But that won't fadge, not by half, for I cannot imagine what I could possibly have done to have set you so steadfastly against me."

She watched in surprise as Brandreth's gray eyes became suffused with a cold, steely glint. He opened his mouth to speak, then with a strong effort clamped his lips shut. She was convinced he had longed to say something to her of no mean order but that he resisted strenuously the notion of doing so. What was he thinking? she wondered, blinking her eyes rapidly, as was her habit while in the midst of serious mental cogitations. Evanthea swiftly dissected every critical encounter she could remember having had with him, in an attempt to discover the source of his ill will, but she could find nothing that might have cause to bring such a hateful expression to his eye. And why didn't he immediately enlighten her?

"I beg you will speak," she encouraged him at last. "Say what you will to me. How have I offended you? If you are reluctant to tell me, I beg to remind you that nothing you might say would injure me. Now tell me what you are thinking, for your satyrlike appearance does not in the least hide the nature of your ungenerous thoughts."

"I would not give you the pleasure," he responded bitterly, his eyes narrowed to challenging slits.

"Then you admit you harbor a grievance against me."

"You have but to examine your heart, your conscience, and you will discover it. Though I even wonder if you possess a conscience. And you certainly don't have a heart, at least not one with a shred of tender feelings, else you would not have—"

He broke off as though aware he had nearly revealed the injury he wished left unsaid. His habitually cool, arrogant smile overtook his chiseled features as he amended smoothly, "Else you would not have fought me so hard where the bust was concerned."

"That is not what you meant to say."

"That is all I *will* say, however."

Silence reigned in the formal room for a moment as Evanthea held the marquis's gaze firmly. She could think of nothing she had ever done to have earned his reproaches or his venom. She shook her head and, after a moment, moved away from the statue toward the rosewood pianoforte, where she sank down into a hardwood chair beside the dusty instrument.

"I am very sorry, Brandreth," she said quietly. He was wrong about her. She might not have a heart, but her conscience was such that she was sorely distressed when she unwittingly wounded others. "But I can think of nothing—nothing!" She lifted her gaze to him. "Do tell me how I have hurt you, that I might beg your pardon."

To her surprise, she watched his features soften a trifle. "Almost, I believe you," he said.

At that moment, Lady Elle called to her. "Evanthea!" she cried. "I have just remembered a most stupid matter I must attend to. Brandreth, forgive me if I leave you to . . . er . . . *entertain* my greatniece for a few minutes. Mrs. Brown has need of a— a bit of sticking plaster. Cook mentioned it to me before dinner and I quite forgot until this very moment. I believe she cut her finger rather severely, and I only hope she has not bled nigh to death! I mean, of course she hasn't, or Meppers would have informed me! I shall return in but a few minutes."

43

Evanthea nodded absently to her great-aunt as she watched her go, her mind too full of the marquis and the matter that lay heavily between them to properly assess Lady Elle's disjointed speech. Her gaze was fixed on the frayed Aubusson carpet beneath her own worn slippers, as she tried yet again to ascertain precisely what she had done or said to have made Brandreth so unreasonably cross that he must provoke her by attempting to purchase the bust of Zeus from Lady Elle.

"What is the meaning of this?" she heard him query, an astonished note in his voice.

When she looked up from her contemplation of the red, black, and purple carpet, she saw to her surprise that his expression was decidedly suspicious. "To what do you refer?" she asked, curious.

"Come, come!" he cried. "Don't play the innocent with me. Of all the absurdities! Does Lady Elle actually believe if she leaves the drawing room, I shall make violent love to you, win your heart, and beg you to marry me?"

"Good heavens, Brandreth! Whatever are you rattling on about? Make violent love to me? Now who is speaking of absurdities? And as for winning my heart, I believe you rather had the right of it when you mentioned earlier that I haven't one. I was telling Lady Elle as much not an hour ago. I have never sought the married state and so far as I know I have never been in love, except once with a Greek boy when I was but eleven and he played near the Acropolis, where my papa was busy with his delicate brushes and minuscule shovels. He spoke only a dozen words of English and had the most beautiful laughing eyes — large, brown, dancing eyes. I felt my heart would break when we returned to England. But that is the last of love I ever experienced. What's more, Brandreth, I think it highly conceited of you

44

to think that Lady Elle should suddenly decide we ought to make a match of it. And as for your ability to change my inclination, I laugh at the thought of it. I could never be persuaded to marry you by your entreaties, though I must admit the notion of your making violent love to me does have a certain amusing ring to it! Don't you agree?"

Evanthea was a little surprised that the Marquis of Brandreth did not immediately concur. In fact, she mused uneasily, there was that familiar look in his eye, which he would get when the fox had gotten past the gate and the pack of hunting dogs was set in strong pursuit. Brandreth barely waited for the sounding of the horn before his spurs were set deep into the flanks of his black horse, and man and beast were flying as one across the fields. Whatever did such an expression mean?

Pushing the spectacles back up to the bridge of her nose, Evanthea shook her head and said, "Brandreth! Why are you leering at me?"

Chapter Six

Having followed the interchange closely, Psyche leaned forward, waiting with suspended breath to hear, to see, to learn what would next occur. She felt a tingling of anticipation spread throughout her entire person. Her heart began pounding in her breast. She had waited several weeks, indeed years, for this moment to arrive, and here it was at last when she was so certain one or the other would discover a budding of love. Oh, if only Evanthea's heart were better prepared to receive Brandreth's quite rakish advances, all would be as good as settled between them! She, of course, realized that the marquis intended to attempt to bowl Evanthea over with a kiss or two, and for quite contemptible reasons, but what did that matter?

And what a strange female Evanthea was to throw down such a gauntlet at Brandreth's feet and not understand the effect she would have upon him. The marquis was precisely the sort of man who must, by the sheer force of his nature, pick it up directly. At the same time, however naive Evanthea was, nothing was more perfect than the series of rejoinders with which she had answered his lordship. What better to say to a conceited, prideful man than, *And as for your ability to change my inclination, I laugh at the thought of it.*

What inspired words!

She could not have proposed a better response than that herself!

He will kiss her, she thought, biting her lip, ignorant of what was transpiring next until she heard her husband cry out, "I will not!"

"What is wrong?" Psyche cried, turning to find Aphrodite with a sure hold on her son's bow and arrow. "Whatever are you doing, ma'am? Eros, why does your mother try to steal your weapon?"

He scowled at Psyche over his shoulder. "She is of the opinion that his lordship ought to be struck deep in the chest with one of my darts, but I want none of it! I haven't engaged in such interference for over two centuries and I shan't begin now!"

"Give me the bow, Cupid!" Aphrodite commanded. "At once! Have you no respect for your own parent?"

"Don't tempt me to give answer to that one, Mama!"

Psyche, fearful that Eros should relinquish the weapon to Aphrodite, said, "Pray don't wound Brandreth, my love. I am persuaded more harm than good would be accomplished. If you must inflict your charms upon someone, pray shoot Evanthea. Her heart is so unprepared for love that I fear if Brandreth were to become suddenly enamored of her, his passionate advances would cause her to run from him."

"Do not pay heed to your wife!" Aphrodite countered. "Brandreth needs to be taught a lesson. He ought once in his existence form a passionate *tendre* for a female who does not return his regard. Do but listen to your mother! Am I not the one who gave you life? Oh, for heaven's sake, Eros, do stop striving with me!"

47

"I will shoot neither of them," Eros responded through clenched teeth as he tried to wrest his bow from his mother's tenacious grip. Because Aphrodite had it carefully wrapped about her elbow and held one of her son's arrows in her free hand, Eros was having some difficulty extricating the delicate bow from her without ruining it.

Psyche watched with dismay as Aphrodite settled the arrow into the taut string and even with Eros wrestling with her was able to draw it back.

"No!" Psyche cried, throwing herself into the fracas. At the very last moment, she was able to turn the offending bow.

With a sharp ping, the arrow flew through the air, accompanied by a pretty musical cacophony, like the erratic tinkling of small bells. Psyche stepped away from her husband, watching the feathery spear shoot straight and clear as it wounded Evanthea at the base of her neck.

"Oh!" Psyche cried, delighted. "Evanthea has been hit!"

"Imbecile!" Aphrodite retorted. "It was Brandreth who needed to be inflicted, not that stupid female. I wanted him to become besotted with the girl and make a complete cake of himself before the *haut ton*. Now all that will happen is that this poor simpleton will tumble head over ears in love with him, foolishly cast herself at his feet and, when he rejects her, succumb to the exigencies of a decline."

Psyche stared at her for a moment, then with a lift of her chin stated, "Not Evanthea. She has a great deal more spirit than that!"

Brandreth was almost upon Evanthea when she

felt a strange heat at the base of her neck, followed by a delicious chill that traveled all the way down her back. She wondered vaguely why her body felt so strange suddenly, but her thoughts were too consumed with trying to discern the marquis's intent to concern herself with a mere spattering of gooseflesh.

What was Brandreth about? she wondered as he planted his hands firmly on the rosewood pianoforte and leaned over her. She had never seen such a look in his eye before, thinking with horror that he gave every appearance of intending to kiss her!

"So you don't believe I could persuade your heart toward me," he stated softly, his voice a whisper, his breath warm in her hair and upon her forehead.

Evanthea opened her mouth to tell him to stop behaving like a buffleheaded clunch, but when her lips parted to speak the words, his mouth was swiftly upon hers, a tender assault that not only robbed her of the ability to speak, but also caused the most peculiar sensations to begin pouring over her in delicate, somnolescent waves. A heady warmth had begun spreading to every part of her being, through her mind and heart, down the lengths of her arms to the tips of her fingers, even to her toes, flooding her soul with a curious mixture of desire and hope. She felt whole and new.

But what ridiculous sentiments these were!

Yet how tender were Brandreth's lips upon hers, so gentle and kind, so unlike the beast!

But why was she permitting him such a liberty, except that she could not seem to move? His kisses held her captive. She felt his hand touch her neck, in the very place where that strange shiver had first occurred. Another chill coursed through her.

She began rising from the chair, without even having formed the thought to do so, and literally slid into his arms. He pulled her tightly against him, his lips becoming a fervent search of her own, a pleasure so intoxicating as to make her head reel. Again, without actually having commanded her body to do so, she suddenly found her own arms slipping about his neck as she returned kiss for kiss, embrace for embrace.

Evanthea had never known such delight as this. But what startled her most, and forced her to continue submitting to his kisses, was the wonderful sensation of safety that seemed to belong exclusively to the strength of his arms about her. Not since she was a child had she been held so closely and loved so warmly. The feelings that his embrace engendered were too sweet, too profound, to be believed. She wanted the moment to last forever.

What was he thinking? she wondered.

"Oh, good grief!" Aphrodite sneered. "I knew this would happen if you shot the girl! Do but look at her! She is clinging to him already. I had forgot how potent your arrows were! Well, I will not permit this terrible farce to continue."

She drew apart the strings of her elegant reticule, shimmering with thin shells of mother-of-pearl, and removed a vial of dark, amber liquid. Within the depths of the small glass bottle, the potion swirled lethargically as though it had a life of its own. "No, pray do not, ma'am," Psyche cried. "I beg of you! Evanthea would benefit greatly from knowing what it was to be madly in love with Brandreth. Stay! Let her remain in this state for a day, or even an hour. Then if you should

50

choose to remove Cupid's spell, some of the memory will remain with her, and she will begin to despise her spinsterhood and seek love as she ought. I am convinced of it!"

Venus rolled her eyes. "I never heeded the advice of mortals!" was her only response as she moved in her graceful, fluid manner toward Evanthea. Standing directly behind her, she rubbed a dot of oil upon the place where the arrow had first wounded her neck. She then retrieved the arrow from the top of the pianoforte, where it had fallen after having smitten Evanthea, and tossed it gently back to her son. To Psyche, she said, "Now you will see the power my potions wield, even against Cupid's arrows."

Psyche wrung her hands. She feared that if Evanthea were to become empty of feelings, which she strongly suspected would be the results of her mother-in-law's famous oil, she would be even less inclined than before to stretch her heart toward others.

Evanthea tried to remonstrate with herself, to remind herself of all the truly dreadful things Brandreth was, but nothing came to mind severe enough to cause her to wrench herself from his arms. Nothing, that is, until she heard him laugh. It was a deep chuckle, which seemed to affect her as mightily as if she had been plunged into a lake of freezing water. She drew back from him and stared in astonishment. "Why did you do that?" she cried.

Brandreth looked at her, blinking slowly. He did not at first appear to hear her, but when her words finally fitted better together in his brain, he queried, "Do what? Oh, you mean kiss you? I—I don't know. I can't remember what prompted me—"

Evanthea felt bitter tears sting her eyes. "Well, I can tell you what prompted you, because there is only one reason why you do anything: to please yourself, of course, to indulge your own vanity. But I think you are a cruel man, Brandreth. First you take extreme advantage of me, and then you laugh—"

"I did not laugh," he interjected quickly. "That is, I don't think I did, but now I seem to recall. . . . But I couldn't have! Evanthea . . ."

"Were you crowing, then?" she queried, humiliated.

"Of course I wasn't! I wasn't doing anything. At least . . ." His gaze seemed liquid as he looked at Evanthea, his speech entirely incoherent. "I just didn't expect . . ." He tried to take her back into his arms but she pushed him away.

"What gammon!" she cried. "And do you think I will permit you to kiss me again? What a fool you are. But don't think for a moment that I am the least affected by your kisses. They were adequate in their way, I suppose, but hardly outstanding in execution. And now, if you please, I have grown excessively fatigued. I bid you good night." She lifted her chin to him and walked unsteadily toward the door. Her knees felt watery and useless, and every step brought her a great deal of trepidation, since she felt at any moment her legs might fail to support her.

But the door was achieved at last, and the moment she crossed the portals, passing into the hall out of his view, she sought the support of the wall and fell against it. How cool the oak wainscoting

52

felt against her cheek, which still burned from the knowledge she had been so indiscreet as to have permitted Brandreth to place his lips on hers. She drew her spectacles from her eyes and dabbed with her fist at the tears that trickled down her cheeks. She could not believe she had allowed him such a gross liberty, and in such a completely roguish manner. Why, she had even flung her arms about his neck and returned his kisses as wantonly as a tavern wench! It was as though she had been suddenly possessed by some mystical charm. Was this Brandreth's power over all the women he intended to tumble in love with him?

She was terribly frightened, but even more so than by the way the experience had left her wanting to do it all over again!

Realizing, however, that Brandreth had no reason to remain within the drawing room, since neither she nor her aunt were present, she suddenly feared that he would discover her in this weakened condition and immediately set her feet in the direction of her bedchamber.

Chapter Seven

"There!" Aphrodite cried triumphantly, addressing Psyche and replacing the vial within the confines of her shell-laden reticule. "You see how easily I am able to reverse the effects of my son's arrows." She continued searching about in her purse and murmured to herself, "Now where *on Olympus* did I put the other vial?"

Eros stood apart from the ladies, polishing the arrow and examining it closely to see if it had been damaged in the fracas. But upon his mother's last comment, he turned toward her, one of his wings twitching in irritation, and queried, "You do not mean to interfere, do you, Mama? To what purpose do you then direct your recriminations toward Butterfly?"

"Oh, do go away, Cupid! I only intend to amuse myself a trifle . . . to see that Lord Brandreth learns a lesson or two about love. You can have no real objection. After all, I am a goddess, and your wife is a mere mortal-become-*immortal*. There is a considerable difference, as you very well know!"

Cupid lifted an ironic brow. "Of the moment," he responded stoically, "I can't say that I see one!"

"Oh, for Jupiter's sake, quit being so high in the instep! Now where is that vial!"

Eros turned toward his wife and extended his hand to her. "Then you, at least, must show some sense. Come, Psyche, do as you are bid and rejoin me in our home. You should not be here in the first place and as your husband, I insist—"

"I can't leave just yet," Psyche interjected quickly. "It is my fault Evanthea was struck by the arrow, and I must remain to see that she recovers from the . . . er . . . mishap!"

Cupid's face turned white and took on a stony appearance. "I see," he said slowly. "Well, I shan't argue with you, only if you come to grief, don't come sniveling to me."

"When have I ever done so!" Psyche responded sharply.

Eros cast her a darkling look and, with a single beat of his wings and a twist of his fine, handsome body, whirled magically upward, disappearing through the first and second floors of the lodge. A gentle sound, like wind through a stand of thick reeds, echoed his flight and left Psyche with a hollow sensation in her heart.

She swallowed hard. She had offended him yet again, and Psyche experienced a profound longing to call after him but could not—especially since her throat was knotted with tears.

Giving herself a shake, she directed her attention fully upon her mama-in-law, who was still searching her reticule and muttering beneath her breath. Aphrodite had two oils, one that ended the effects of love—the very one she had used on Evanthea—and another that initiated profound feelings of desire. If Venus decided to touch the marquis with the second oil, he would tumble in love with the next creature he laid eyes on—which could just as easily be Annabelle as Evanthea.

"Ma'am," Psyche said softly, "I beg you will forget about Evanthea and Brandreth. What are they to you?" When Venus merely scowled at her, she remembered an incident that had occurred just before she left Olympus and that was certain to capture Venus's attention. "By the way," she continued quickly, "did you have tea with Artemis? Or did she wickedly complain of the headache yet again? Oh! I nearly forgot to tell you! When I left my palace not an hour or so ago, I saw her. She appeared in excellent looks, so young and vivacious, and—" Psyche was not disappointed with the expression of astonishment on Venus's face.

"What?" Aphrodite cried, her gaze now fixed intently upon Psyche, her fingers quiet as they gripped the strings of her reticule. "Impossible! You must have been mistaken."

"On the contrary. She wished you well and hoped that her *headache* had not inconvenienced you." All the while she spoke, she drew her mama-in-law gently away by the elbow—away from Brandreth—leading her toward the wall and out of doors.

Aphrodite ground her perfect teeth. "I have no opinion of that platter-faced huntress! I never have! She is all smiles one moment, then scheming and intriguing the next, first telling me she would be *ever so delighted* to pay me a visit, then actually feigning one of her renowned headaches afterward, begging you to congratulate her upon her renewed health."

"Well, she did not precisely say I was to congratulate her—"

"What does it matter! She might as well have.

56

And that ridiculous costume she wears when she goes out to hunt, with a feather in her cap! And—and I particularly despise the way my father calls her *Diana,* in just that tone as to make one want to scream! Why, anyone with a particle of intelligence would know, just by looking at her, that she is little better than a Cyprian. Did you happen to notice her at Bacchus's last fete? I vow she dampened her muslin for all to see, and afterward . . ."

Psyche began at last to breathe, pleased with the manner in which Aphrodite was so easily diverted by the smallest reference to any of her rivals. "Indeed, ma'am, indeed. Yes, I know. Truly dreadful," she murmured soothingly, nodding all the while and trying to appear as sympathetic as possible.

Instead of entering the lodge's east garden, which had a lovely view of Lady Elle's home wood of beech trees, all about Psyche and her mama-in-law was a warm glow of light, visible through the dark night sky, through which could be seen the fringes of Mount Olympus. Never did Psyche approach Zeus's realm without a sense of awe and wonder. A gentle, silvery mist cloaked lush, green hills, majestic with stately cypresses and tall Corinthian palaces. The kingdom was generously endowed with well-planted avenues, terraces, and the quaintest of winding lanes. On every breeze, Apollo's music could be heard in the gentle beautiful strains of the lute, as though he were everywhere at once, plucking the strings and singing.

Over the centuries, Psyche had come to love Olympus and was particularly fond of Zeus, who from the first had shown her nothing but kindness, even though he had the most terrifying reputation for retribution and punishment. And not once had he importuned her, which she had been assured he would. No, Zeus was all that was kindness, and he even listened concernedly to her tales of her mama-in-law's acerbic tongue and her husband's dreadful indifference. He was the one who had told her to find her own amusements, promising that when he was able, he would speak with Cupid and discover the reason for the poor boy's odd behavior of the last two centuries. She doubted, however, that Jupiter had ever found a proper moment in which to discuss such a matter of delicacy with Eros, for no long-awaited alteration in Cupid's affections had ever occurred.

Psyche was drawn away from her reverie when Aphrodite fell silent and sighed. She picked up the original thread of her mama-in-law's discontentment by interjecting quickly, "To own the truth, I could not credit Artemis had actually invited you to sup with her, when she has broken no fewer than eleven previous engagements!"

"That woman is beyond bearing!" she cried. "The last time we were to grace the same table— for the strict purpose of burying all our former grievances, mind!—she complained of an inflammation of the lungs! Can you imagine anything so absurd! Besides . . ." She broke off suddenly and jerked her arm from Psyche's grasp. "Why, you little minx! I have never known you to take up my cause against Diana! What are you about? though I can guess. You've been trying to divert my attention from Brandreth and you almost succeeded, but not quite!"

With that, she dug her hand deep into her reticule which tinkled with the sounds of the shells bouncing together, whirled about and, with a triumphant cry, removed the second vial. Smiling brightly, she twisted the tight glass stopper from the bottle with a flick of her wrist and, moving quickly, as if upon winged feet, floated through the blue brick wall of the manor house.

"Please do not," Psyche pleaded with her, following closely on her heels. "I beg of you! Have you forgotten there are other ladies in the house! What if Brandreth tumbles violently in love with Annabelle or, heaven preserve us, Lady Elle!"

But Aphrodite merely smirked at her daughter-in-law over her shoulder. "It does not matter in the least with whom our arrogant marquis tumbles in love, only that he does."

Brandreth was still alone in the chamber and stood by the fire, where he reposed one elbow upon the mantel and shoved at the logs in the hearth with stiff jabs of a blackened poker. He wore a heavy scowl and muttered, "That curst female, that curst female. She is a Nemesis to me."

"Is Nemesis here?" Aphrodite asked, startled. "She has been very angry with me of late."

"No, of course not. I am certain Brandreth was speaking metaphorically."

"Oh, thank heavens!" she cried, relieved, then sniffed the bottle clutched tightly within her hand. She stepped forward, preparing to place a dot of oil on the marquis's forehead, but Psyche caught her elbow and gave it a hard jerk, hoping to prevent the anointing. Her intention misfired entirely, however, when the bottle fell to the brick hearth and shattered silently all over Brandreth's black silk slippers.

"Oh, merciful heavens, what have you done, you simpleton!" Aphrodite cried, backing away from the hearth and clasping her hands to her bosom. Standing next to Psyche, she continued, "Oh, dear! Oh, dear! I cannot possibly predict what will happen! One dab of my potion is sufficient to bend the heart of the wearer, but an entire bottle?"

Psyche stood rigid and horrified as she stared first at his lordship's slippers and then at his lordship's afflicted face. The marquis had dropped the poker and now stood to his full height, leaning his shoulders back and apparently trying to breathe. An expression of acute misery came over his face. A moment later he weaved on his feet, appearing as though he would topple over. But to Psyche's surprise, not only did he remain upright, but he whispered, "Evanthea, my darling Evanthea. I have been such a fool."

"He has invoked her name," Aphrodite murmured in an awed voice as she pressed her fingers against her lips. "He had only to invoke her name to fall in love with her! He did not even have to *see* her! My, my, my! I am even more wondrous in my arts than I had supposed. Look how his heart swells with thoughts of her. I wonder what would happen if I doused Adonis's sandals with a similar quantity of the oil!"

Psyche, who was greatly distressed by all that had gone forward, could not keep from retorting, "He would probably invoke Persephone's name!"

Aphrodite turned on Psyche with a look of horror in her eyes. "You dare to say such a thing to me! *Me!*" With this last word, shouted as it was, even the air in the drawing room shook.

"I forgot myself," Psyche returned meekly. "I should not have said anything so unkind, but I am very angry. Look what you have done!"

"Why are you flying into the boughs? You always are, you know! And why my son chose you above all the goddesses I had arranged for him to . . . why, where is Brandreth going now?"

60

When Lord Brandreth wheeled on them suddenly, both ladies as one took three quick steps backward. It was clear he could see neither of them. But the wild expression on his face, along with the gleam of perspiration that covered his brow, made him a frightening spectre, and they avoided him when he turned to race from the chamber.

Psyche and Venus exchanged a quick glance, and both followed immediately behind him.

On he flew, down first one hallway, then another, taking quick turns of the jumbled ancient manor house, to finally fly up a steep staircase. The entire time he murmured Evanthea's name. When he reached her bedchamber door, he scratched on it not once but thrice.

"Who is it?" Evanthea queried, the expression in her voice one of surprise.

"Brandreth," was the husky response. "Open the door. I must speak with you."

"Brandreth!" was the shocked reply. "Whatever are you doing? What do you mean by approaching my door at such an hour? Have you taken complete leave of your senses?"

"I must speak with you! I must!"

"No," Evanthea said. "You have done enough mischief for one night. Now I beg of you, go away! What manner of scandal do you mean to create by coming here? Go away at once!"

Brandreth weaved slightly on his feet as did one who had imbibed far too much brandy. "I cannot leave you without knowing if you love me."

"What? If I love you?"

"Yes!" he cried. "Only tell me that you love me, Evanthea. There is no one in the world for me but you! I have loved you ever since I can remember, wildly, passionately. Only what say you? Are you in love with me?"

Silence reigned behind the door. Psyche wanted to shift her position, to move beyond the wall in order to discover what Evanthea was doing or whether she could ascertain what she was thinking by the look on her face, but she found herself spellbound by the sight of Brandreth in an impassioned state.

If he was an exquisite creature before, once caught in the throes of love—or at least in the mystical web of Aphrodite's magical oil—he was utterly magnificent! His face was lit as if with a holy light, his gray eyes glowing with a fervor that seemed to accentuate the clean, handsome lines of his face. Even Eros had only once appeared thusly—the day his mother had finally acquiesced to their marriage. She knew, even as she had known with her husband, that it would be a wonderful thing to be loved by a man such as this and found unexpected tears blinding her eyes. Evanthea would know a wondrous love in the arms of Brandreth, were they ever to overcome their respective prejudices. At the same time, her heart felt shattered at the sight of Brandreth. Cupid had loved her once with as much passion, but no more, it seemed.

Perhaps she could do nothing to rekindle her husband's faltering love, but at least she could help Evanthea, or try to. And she could start by seeing what effect Brandreth's ardor had on the spinster.

But when she moved to enter Evanthea's room, the door suddenly flew open and a heavy sheet of water passed through from the now-empty confines of a painted ceramic basin. A glimpse of pretty bluebells on the side of the basin struck Psyche's eye at the same moment the water crashed through the doorway.

The deluge seemed to pause for a moment before Brandreth's astonished visage, then spread over him with a hearty thump, splashing him from head to toe and drenching the carpet about his feet.

"I certainly hope your head is clear now, my lord, for I have no more water with which to reverse the effects of too many glasses of Madeira or whatever it is you've been drinking. I cannot otherwise account for the ridiculous speeches with which you have been pummeling my poor door. Now do go away before I lose my temper completely and serve you a little of the home brewed, as my papa was used to say. He taught me to box, you know. Oh yes, you may stare! But if you ever choose to mock me again by professing a love as absurd as it is false, I shall see that you regret every word you speak!" With that, Evanthea, her cheeks aflame, slammed the door shut.

Brandreth glanced down at his feet and wriggled his wet toes. "What the devil am I doing here?" he queried aloud. "Good God! Have I just—" He rubbed his head and looked around him, as though trying to gain his bearings. "I've got to stop drinking so much, though I can't remember having partaken of more than one, perhaps two glasses." He rubbed the water from his eyes, hair, and face, then stared for a moment at the door. With a puzzled expression, he took a step toward it and gently touched the smooth, well-grained oak. He released a sigh, which to Psyche seemed laden with feeling, with the unrecognized truth of his heart, then let his hand drop to his side.

"I don't understand," Aphrodite said, clearly bemused. "It was almost as if the water reversed the effects of my potion. How very curious! Well, I shall simply have to contrive another receipt and begin again. But first, I must see what Brandreth means to do next."

Aphrodite followed after her quarry, but Psyche could not leave without discovering the state of Evanthea's heart. She passed through the wall of her bedchamber, and what she found there disturbed her as nothing had for a long, long time. The object of her efforts was lying facedown on her bed and sobbing. She wanted to go to Evanthea and pet her rich chestnut hair and smooth away the tears from her pretty, cheeks, but she could not. In order to do so, she would have to take a mortal shape for a time, and she was not prepared to expend her energies on such a momentous task. The concentration involved in assuming a fleshly human state was quite enormous, never failing to leave her weak and dizzy for hours thereafter. Even now, after such a lengthy time at Flitwick Lodge, she found herself in great need of her chaise longue and a long Olympian sleep, in order to restore her strength.

As it was, she merely let out a coo of sympathy and retraced her steps to the drawing room, where she found Venus standing over Brandreth, who was presently slumped in a chair by the fire, his eyes closed. Oh, why had Venus chosen to involve herself with Brandreth! No good could come of it, of that she was convinced.

"He is a splendid specimen, isn't he?" Venus queried as she placed a kiss on his lips. "Do you think he felt my salute?"

"Perhaps in his dreams," Psyche responded, a terrible weariness and sadness overcoming her. "I am returning now to Olympus. Do you join me?"

Venus shrugged as she turned away from Brandreth. "I suppose I ought to before Zeus discovers what I have been about. I have had so little fun since he commanded us to stop interfering in the lives of mortals. I shouldn't tell you so, but I admire your having broken one of his edicts."

She then glanced at the bust of Zeus, which now lay in darkness, the candles in the pair of wall sconces on either side of it having long since guttered. "And though I can't prove that you stole this bust from my chambers, I believe you are guilty. Finding my cestus in your possession is proof enough of your proclivity to steal. Therefore, I hold you responsible for it, and if you don't find a way to return my statue to me by month's end, I shall tell Zeus of all your activities, and I've little doubt he'll insist you work on that horrid barge on the River Styx and accompany the dead to their respective rewards."

Psyche felt her knees begin to tremble. She looked first at the bust, then at her mama-in-law, and cried out, "You would not be so cruel!"

"Oh, wouldn't I just! I am out of patience with you, Psyche, and what's more, my son is as well. You know it is true. Everyone has been talking and laughing about it for decades, how his love has faltered. Cupid's love! Isn't it a brilliant joke? But I told him how it would be if he married a mortal! But did he listen to me? Of course not. It is the curse of parents to love and nurture their children, only to have the little wretches fail to heed their mothers at the very moment when they ought to listen the hardest. I hope you don't mean to become a watering pot, Psyche. Now, take my arm and support me back to Olympus, where we

65

both belong. I find myself greatly fatigued. I had forgotten how tired one gets when trespassing the Olympian boundaries."

Each word Venus spoke was as a fiery dart to Psyche's tender heart. And worse! There was not one inaccuracy among all the terrible things Aphrodite had just said. The harshness of her mama-in-law's tone, however, had made each phrase all the more difficult to bear. *I will not cry,* she commanded herself, knowing that Aphrodite would simply despise her all the more for exhibiting such a *human* failing. So it was she lifted her chin and begged her mama-in-law to tell her what manner of retribution she had planned for Artemis.

Chapter Eight

On the following morning, Evanthea awoke in her bedchamber with a dull headache and her eyes feeling as though small grains of sand had been permanently embedded in her lids. She slowly opened her eyes and stared up into the faded gold silk canopy of her bed. The smooth fabric had been drawn from all four mahogany posts, gathered in the center and attached to the ceiling. The entire effect must have been quite pretty at one time, when the silk was new, but with several tears and holes in the fabric, she rather thought the whole of the design now had the look of a spider's web — a most unpleasant notion, especially since her spirits were already quite low.

She had cried herself to sleep after closing the door upon Brandreth. She wished the memories that now began flying about her brain, of his lordship standing in a puddle of water, were scenes from a nightmare rather than what had really happened only a few hours earlier. The ache in her head, however, as well as the soreness of her eyes, testified that she had indeed listened to his mocking professions of love and that she had in her anger thrown a basin of water over him.

Evanthea lay still, sighing heavily and trying to

compose her heart. She was grievously distressed in a manner she had never known in the entire course of her life. Perhaps this was why she could not readily adjust to all that had transpired the evening before.

Her mind began to whirl with thoughts she could not run to earth. Why had Brandreth said all that he had said? Goodness gracious, he had actually proclaimed a love for her! Could it be possible that he loved her—*her*—and was only able to admit it when he was foxed?

Impossible!

Or was it? Even if he did love her, she wasn't in love with him. Then why had she flung herself so readily across her bed and sobbed as a child does when something goes awry? What was he to her?

Only the man who had kissed her, and so thoroughly that she knew she would never again be the same. Never.

Remembering his kisses caused Evanthea to first catch her breath in her throat, then to leap from her bed as though someone had just doused *her* with a basin of cold water. She began violently pacing the floor and pulling at the long chestnut curls that had escaped from beneath her mobcap.

If only he had not kissed her, she could be easy. But he had kissed her, and somehow his wondrous embrace had effectually cut up her peace forever.

She stopped in her wild movements suddenly, espying herself in her long gilt-edged mirror. She knew an impulse to look at herself as a woman, something she was not certain she had ever done before. She stepped toward her dressing table, which sat to the left of the looking glass, and picked up her spectacles. She was not hopelessly blind without them, not by half, but she wanted to really see herself, perhaps as others saw her, perhaps as Brandreth saw her.

Placing the spectacles carefully over each ear, Evanthea opened her eyes wide and peered into the looking glass.

What she saw was a distressed frown between thin, arched brows and spectacles that had already begun to slide almost to the tip of her straight nose. Behind the spectacles her eyes were the image of her father's, a deep brown that the vicar, Mr. Shalford, had told her not a fortnight earlier held glints of amber when viewed by candlelight. She had been surprised by his compliment, which he had delivered not without a color rising to his cheeks. She had briefly suspected he was attempting to fix his interest with her, but after a moment's consideration she set down such a notion as ridiculous. Very rarely had any gentleman paid her a compliment, not to mention one delivered with an eye to matrimony. Surely the vicar was not of such a mind.

But did her eyes indeed sparkle with an amber hue? Is this what had prompted Brandreth's passionate madness of the night before? A drunken madness, of course, but still, his words were so intense, so warm with feeling. Had he mocked her, or was it possible that he, too, saw slivers of amber light in her eyes?

Again her heart cried out — *impossible!* — particularly when all she had to do was scrutinize her appearance and know that it was wholly unlikely for a man of Brandreth's stamp to fall in love with one such as her. He was a man about town, one who had acquired a great deal of Town Bronze in his first season and more every season thereafter. He was a noted Corinthian and an expert in ladies' fashion. He was an elegant being who undoubtedly despised her for her careless disregard of her appearance and of the opinions of others.

What, then, had he meant by saying that he loved her . . . that she was the only one he could ever love?

There could be only one answer: He meant to hurt her, to mock her. She knew it was true. In her heart of hearts she knew it was true. She left the condemning reflection in the long looking glass and moved to her dressing table, where she sat down on a stool covered in light green damask. She slowly removed her mobcap, picked up her brush, and began smoothing out her tangled chestnut locks. She thought yet again that he must have wanted to hurt her very badly to have said such things at her door. He had already admitted that he harbored some grievance against her, but she had never believed he would be so cruel as to shame her with his lying words of devotion. She did not understand him.

Another thought spun through her brain and she felt her cheeks burn with embarrassment. How had it come about that she had actually dumped an entire basin of water over his person? However hurt or angry she might have been with his conduct, had it been necessary for her to respond in kind?

She set her brush down and covered her hot, red cheeks with her cool hands. She had behaved very badly and knew she must apologize. The very thought of confronting his lordship, however, and admitting her wrongs set her knees to trembling. At the very best, she would now find it difficult to converse with Brandreth, but to actually beg his forgiveness for her actions made her cower inwardly.

Taking a deep breath, Evanthea again picked up her brush and resumed tidying her hair, this time with brisk strokes as she tore through every recalcitrant tangle. Would he laugh at her if she offered him her apologies, or would he respond with an angry retort? She did not know.

As her hair began to fall into a long, smooth wave over her shoulder, her brush slowed to a gentle pull. She found her thoughts also becoming quieter and less erratic. What Brandreth's true feelings for her were she could not know, but the memory of his lips upon hers washed over Evanthea like the warmth from a fire that suddenly bursts into life.

In all her eight and twenty years, she had never experienced anything so perfect, so wonderful, as the feeling of being held in Brandreth's strong arms. He had kissed her thoroughly and completely.

She closed her eyes, trying to remember in explicit detail how the kiss had begun. She remembered how he had daringly placed his hands on the pianoforte behind her; how his breath on her hair had caused a spattering of gooseflesh to travel down her neck; how gentle his lips had been; how tender, warm, and comforting the kiss was; how easily she had slid into his arms; how audaciously she had wrapped her arms about his neck and kissed him fully in return!

She took a deep breath, feeling strangely as though she were experiencing his kiss all over again. To her horror, the thought came to her that if he were to walk into her bedchamber at this very moment, she would most likely catapult herself into his arms and beg to be kissed again. An odd sensation of pain suddenly gripped her heart as she realized that was probably the first and only time he would ever kiss her. Why he had done so in the first place she could not truly comprehend, but she was quite certain that her clever basin of water had ended any desire on his part to repeat his advances.

"Good grief!" a female voice cried out abruptly, interrupting her reveries. "If ever I have seen a mooncalf expression, it is yours! Evanthea, do not tell me you have finally come to your senses and fallen in love? Oh, do say it is true, and then tell me with whom, how, and when this miracle occurred. Was it the vicar who finally caught your eye? Oh, yes, it must be Mr. Shalford, and a better match I could not have planned myself. I only wish I did not dislike him so very much! But if you are indeed in love with him, then I will hold him in the highest esteem, if only for your sake. Only tell me it is true!"

"Annabelle!" Evanthea cried out, startled by the young woman's sudden appearance and embarrassed at having been caught wearing her thoughts so unabashedly on her face. "Don't be absurd. Of course I am not in love with Mr. Shalford, or anyone else, for that matter."

"Don't play off that humbug to me! Who were you dreaming of just then? Tell me! I insist you tell me! Was it someone you met at the assemblies last month? Oh, but how exciting if it is so! Does Lady Elle know?"

Unable to bear more of Annabelle's teasing, Evanthea rose abruptly from her seat. She knew she would not leave her in peace, so she chose to address the subject with an air of indifference. "If you must know," she began, "I have tumbled wildly, fitfully, disgracefully in love with Brandreth.

There! I expect I have given you a severe shock, but you insisted I tell you, and now you know!" She stole a glance at Annabelle from beneath her lashes and was content with the young woman's reaction. Annabelle stood strangely still, her green eyes unblinking for a long moment, the color draining from her face in quick stages.

"In love with Brandreth?" she queried, horrified. "But you can't be! Just because he is forever dancing attendance on Lady Elle, you can't imagine it is because of you?" The very next moment, Annabelle's quixotic spirits shifted ground. "Oh, of course you don't think any such thing, and of course you are not in love with Brandreth. You are teasing me, dreadful, dreadful Evan!" She rushed to Evanthea's side, slipping her arm about her waist and giving her a squeeze. "And what a bird-witted female I am to have believed you for even a moment. I see what you are about, though. You do not mean to tell me anything, do you?"

"No, I do not," Evanthea answered truthfully. She stood several inches taller than Annabelle and did not hesitate, in a quite motherly way, to put her arm about the beautiful young woman and return her affectionate hug.

Apparently satisfied, Annabelle changed the subject and began drawing Evanthea toward the window. "Speaking of my cousin, have you seen Brandreth racing his curricle up and down the drive?" She sighed deeply. "I have been watching him for this half hour and more. What fine, light hands he has, and yet he is still able to keep his team easily in check. And once or twice he even rode the length of the avenue standing straight up on the floor of his carriage, driving at top speed the entire distance. What do you think of that?"

They had reached the window by the end of Annabelle's speech, and some quarter mile distant, Evanthea could see Brandreth and his team just beginning their next run. "It is because of the stupid race Mr. Shalford challenged him to. They are to drive like Roman charioteers! Could anything be more dangerous or more absurd? He could easily break his neck if anything were to go awry."

"Nothing will, not for Brandreth," Annabelle returned confidently. "I think he is immortal, like the gods of Olympus."

Even as Annabelle spoke these words, Evanthea felt a chill rush down her spine. She remembered something of the night before, which had escaped her entirely until now. When Brandreth had been pleading his love for her through the door, she had heard a deep, rumbling, ghostly laugh—only for a moment—coming from the direction of the heinous basin of water. The laughter had seemed so real, and the thought had struck her that she had begun imagining Olympian guests, just like Lady Elle. The odd thing was, not until she heard the sound had she conceived of the notion that she ought to pour the water over Brandreth's head.

Disengaging herself from Annabelle, she walked over to the basin and touched it as though somehow she expected it to suddenly disappear. But that laughter, she thought, wondering if perhaps a spirit had taken up residence in her bedchamber. It sounded so familiar, not unlike Brandreth's laughter when he had finished kissing her.

"Oh, do come and watch him!" Annabelle cried in her girlish voice. "You must see him! Oh, do come. He is standing up again!"

Evanthea returned to the window and watched, mesmerized as Brandreth rose to his height and en-

74

couraged his horses along at a spanking pace. She felt a rush of fear so strong she became dizzy. "I wish he would not," she whispered.

"Isn't he utterly marvelous?" Annabelle cooed. She suddenly whirled away from the window and fairly skipped to the door. "I intend to join him and beg for a ride before breakfast. Do you think he will admire my new gown?"

Evanthea turned to regard Annabelle, who now pirouetted in the doorway. She was wearing a striped dimity round gown, sporting a joyful row of ruffles about the hem. The stripes were a spritely shade of green chosen no doubt to match her eyes.

Annabelle was a beautiful young woman who had just enjoyed her twentieth birthday. She was short and diminutive in every aspect of her perfect frame: She had small, delicate hands, neatly turned ankles, and the tiniest feet Evanthea had ever seen, particularly for a young woman who claimed to have never sat out a dance in the course of career. She wore her hair in a knot atop her head, from which bounced a hundred perfect blond curls. She was vain about her beauty, yet Evanthea felt no one could fault her for it, since the combination of her large green eyes, bow-shaped lips, and heart-shaped face created an unearthly vision worthy of worship.

Evanthea could not keep from expressing her true opinion. "If Brandreth does not think you a goddess from Olympus, then he must either be blind or a complete idiot."

Annabelle dimpled and ran away.

Chapter Nine

Brandreth stood on the floorboards of his curricle holding the reins firmly in hand. He had only one more day in which to prepare for a race against Mr. Shalford, a tiresome cleric who had insisted the feat be performed while standing instead of driving. How it had come about that he had let the provoking vicar corner him into the race he would never know, except that they had been arguing about his cousin Annabelle.

Mr. Shalford had been complaining about Annabelle's flirtatious demeanor, and Brandreth had responded by saying that at least she was not as stiff-rumped as a certain cleric with whom he was acquainted, who officiated in some forgotten hamlet and who hadn't a particle of spirit in him.

He shouldn't have taunted Mr. Shalford so fiercely. To own the truth, he had been surprised by the hard light that had come into the vicar's eyes. He had half expected Shalford to draw his cork or at least attempt to do so, particularly when he clenched his fists and held them close to his sides as though preparing to plant him a facer.

"I ought to call you out," Shalford responded, "but my position in this *forgotten hamlet,* as you call it, absolutely forbids such a breach of the King's law."

"Oh, I wouldn't let that stop you."

"Of course *you* wouldn't," Shalford returned with a knowing sneer, relaxing his hands and removing a silver snuffbox from the pocket of his bottle-green coat, "since you never concern yourself with the sentiments, opinions, or values of those around you. I am not in so *enviable* a position as to be able to disregard the feelings of others. But if you think for a moment I mean to ignore your accusation, you much mistake the matter. Instead, I challenge you to a race, with the conveyance of your choosing, from the High Street in front of Flitwick Lodge, to the village—a distance I believe to be a mere two miles."

"Done," was Brandreth's quick response, his choler high from Shalford's criticisms of his character.

"You have answered too hastily," the vicar responded, one of his eyebrows arched disdainfully. "In addition, the race shall be conducted *standing.*"

"Standing?" Brandreth had responded, shocked.

"Yes, like Roman chariots, if you've the bottom for it."

"If I've the . . . Why, you insolent . . ." He broke off, holding a curse back with only the severest of efforts. He had never liked Mr. Shalford, nor had he ever quite comprehended the younger man. He knew Shalford had suffered a severe disappointment in the choice of his profession. Though the particulars had never been explained to him, it seemed to Brandreth that the vicar was more suited to the army than to the Church of England. His suggestion, therefore, that a race be exchanged for a duel did not come entirely as a surprise. Shalford might have taken Holy Orders, but he had not given up his athletic Corinthian pursuits and was as fit and as able a man as Brandreth had ever seen. The marquis did not foolishly believe that just because Mr. Shalford composed sermons for the local inhabitants of the village of Old Flitwick, he had forsaken all former interests, not by half. In truth, the only real complaint he had of Shalford was that the cleric was uncommonly critical of Annabelle—and he wouldn't have it! He might not be in love with his cousin, but he had known her since she was in leading strings and thought of her as he would a younger sister. "Of the moment," he stated boldly, "I'd give anything to cross swords with you."

"And I've already given you a gentlemanly reason for refusing and an adequate substitution. What do you say, then? Will you agree to it?"

Brandreth hesitated, but only for an instant. "Of course." Then he smiled. "But I warn you, I won't be easily defeated."

"I didn't expect you would," was Shalford's quite indifferent response. It had been this last remark that caused Brandreth to realize that however much he was himself accounted a nonpareil, it was possible that Shalford might be skilled enough to best him. For that reason, he practiced driving, over and over, the quarter mile that constituted Lady Elle's shady if worn avenue.

As he encouraged his horses to a quick trot and rose to his feet yet again, Brandreth had one consolation: The match might be dangerous, but at least it would help keep his mind occupied for the next few hours. His thoughts had been too full of Evanthea and his bizarre behavior toward her of the night before to keep him comfortable for any great length of time. In all his mental perambulations, he could not account for why he had kissed her in the first place, save that she had practically

78

dared him to do it. And what of the pounding on her door and the professing of boundless love for her? What madness had seized him to have uttered such nonsense?

Damn and blast! Now that his thoughts had turned toward her, they ran rampant, and even more so when he considered her fine physical attributes.

Zeus, but Evanthea had beautiful, rich brown hair. It would have been considered her finest feature had she not worn it in the most absurd fashion for one with her clean, elegant lines and lovely features. He had never understood why, with an intriguing beauty and skin as delicate in appearance as the purest cream and ripest peach, she had chosen to wrap her hair up like an ancient matron, nor why she begowned herself as though she were a monk instead of a marriageable female. But then, there never was the least possibility of comprehending Evanthea Swanbourne and there never would be.

From the first, he had believed Evanthea born to spinsterhood . . . until now.

All seemed changed now, but why and in what way?

He laughed aloud. How odd life was at times, how curious! The moment he had placed someone in precisely the mold he believed proper for them, they set out to overturn his opinions. Shalford had done so, and now his worst adversary—Evanthea! And if he lived to be a hundred, he would never forget the feel of her in his arms as she responded so delightfully to his embrace, kissing him in return hard on the mouth. He would never have believed Evanthea, of all young ladies, to have held a passionate heart. She had even slid into his arms, wrapping hers about his neck as though completely caught up in the moment.

Not that he had pretended to have been indifferent to her. He had felt entirely swept away by her touch, by the way she had pressed herself fully against him and held nothing back.

What did it all mean? he wondered as he slowed his team to a walk, the manor looming large before him. If only he had not been in his cups and made such a cake of himself by approaching Evanthea's door last night, he would have enjoyed the prospect of greeting her this morning. He still could not credit that he had spoken such ridiculous words to her! What had prompted him to speak such lunacies? He had even professed a desire to marry her! The devil! There must have been something wrong with the brandy he had imbibed after all.

Thank God she had dumped water over his head before anything worse occurred!

When he had awakened this morning, he had been struck with how unreal the whole experience had seemed. For a moment, when caught in that peculiar time between waking and sleeping, he had been convinced he had only dreamed of having approached her door. But as sleep curled away from his reveries, he knew he had not been dreaming.

But what was he to say to her now? Only one possibility presented itself: He had to agree with her summation of his condition . . . that he had been completely foxed. This, however, was neither a compliment to himself nor to her, particularly since he was not willing to admit that the kiss they had shared had been enjoyed under the same intoxication.

What did any of it matter, anyway? he thought

with a frustrated thump of a booted foot against the floorboards. What was Evanthea to him but a proverbial thorn in his side, which she had been for years! He could not truly regret any of his behavior. Given her interference in his affairs and her persistence where the bust of Zeus was concerned, she deserved nothing less than to be overset by his indelicate advances, whether conducted with or without the benefit of wine.

He shook off the memories and set his mind to the near future. He had come to Flitwick for the sole purpose of persuading Lady Elle to accept his offer of ten thousand pounds for the bust of Zeus, in part to restore her fortunes, but also to please himself. From the first moment he had seen the carved marble statue, he had longed to own it. And once he concluded this matter of business with his aunt, he would then be free to leave Old Flitwick.

As he eased the horses to a stop and regained his seat in the curricle, he took in the vista of the old house. He felt toward the manor as he always did . . . that he had come to visit an old friend.

Flitwick Lodge was a charming mellowing of a pretty blue brick, a color peculiar to many Bedfordshire homes. Thick trails of dark green ivy rose in a sweeping arch over the front of the house and crept across the brick, draping in soft folds over the seven bay windows that fronted the manor.

He scrutinized the structure and the surrounding property with a keen eye. Everywhere signs of neglect and decay could be seen: in the chipped paint of the casements on nearly every window; in the overhang of the ivy across the lentel; in the unkempt appearance of the gravel where small pits had formed; in the weed-ridden, erratically scythed lawn; in the trees burdened with sagging, unpruned branches; in the absence of flowers in the beds, which were still packed with last autumn's abundance of dead leaves.

It would take a small fortune to restore the house, he thought, including the inside, which was already showing signs of mold and damp. Last night while sleeping, he had thrust his foot through the bed linen, awakening to a loud rip in the thinning cloth. Brandreth knew he was offering Lady Elle the restoration of her home and her former life in exchange for the bust of Zeus, and he had fully expected her to have simply thanked him for his generosity, taken the money, and given him the statue. When she hesitated, then deferred making her decision, and finally asked Brandreth to spend a few days with her that she might discuss the matter with him, he found himself taken aback.

Lady Elle was a woman who always knew her mind; he therefore had to ascribe some other reason for her indecision.

That was when he had discovered how mightily Evanthea was pressing Lady Elle to refuse his offer, on the basis that she was somehow entitled to inherit the bust. How selfish of her! How cruel she was being in preventing an aunt, whom she professed to adore, from regaining material security and comfort in this world.

No, there was no accounting for Evanthea. The last thing he would have expected of her was to stand in the path of her aunt's happiness. Perhaps he had simply never known this side of her. Regardless, he was not without hope that he could eventually persuade his great-aunt to avail herself of his generosity and perhaps even point out to Evanthea how unkind she was being in her persistence that Lady Elle should give her the bust instead of selling it to him.

When a female emerged through the front door of the lodge, a fierce jolt of excitement coursed through his heart — unexpected, unwanted. He realized, much to his dismay, that he had been wishing to see Evanthea again. What an absurd desire! Where the devil had it come from?

He knew both a sense of relief and of disappointment when the sun chose to glint off the lady's unbonneted golden hair.

"Hallo!" Annabelle called to him in her delightfully musical voice.

He responded in kind, but not without letting go first of a deep sigh. He enjoyed Annabelle and her schoolgirl flattery and flirtations, but as she drew near his equipage, the truly astonishing thought shot through his mind that if Annabelle had been Evanthea, he would have tried again to take her in his arms and kiss her just as he had last night.

Chapter Ten

Evanthea watched from the window of her bed-chamber as Annabelle again set about trying to win Brandreth's undying regard. He sat in his curricle with the reins in hand and one foot dangling off the floorboard, while Annabelle stood close to him, smiling up into his face. As she swung a flat-crowned straw bonnet from pink satin ribbons looped over her wrist he chatted gaily with her, returning her flattery with the ease of a man who has seen fifteen London Seasons. Evanthea was a little surprised that Annabelle could be so strongly attracted to a man who was thirteen years her senior, but then Brandreth was quite possibly every schoolgirl's dream.

They remained exchanging their pleasantries contentedly for some ten minutes, Annabelle's pretty trills of laughter frequently floating up to Evanthea's window. Finally, she supposed Brandreth had kept his horses standing long enough, and he set the beautiful pair in motion, heading to the back of the house where the stables were located.

When Annabelle disappeared from Evanthea's view, retracing her steps through the front door, Evanthea knew she needed to act quickly. She thought it would be unlikely she would find even a fraction of a second with which to speak privately with Brandreth once the day's round of activities commenced. She therefore decided she must seek him out at once, even while he was tending to his duties in the stable. Brandreth took excellent care of his horses and would undoubtedly make certain they were rubbed down before he returned to do the pretty with the ladies of the manor.

For that reason, she quickly dressed herself in an ill-fitting round gown of lilac sarsenet trimmed with bugle beads, coiled her plaited hair atop her head, threw a silk paisley shawl over her shoulders, and literally ran down the servants's stairs at the back of the house, all the while making certain Annabelle did not see her.

Once outside, she became acutely aware she had not properly tied her sandals, and the pea-gravel along the walk through the overgrown gardens alternately bit into her toes or became wedged between her feet and the sandals. She was reluctant to stop and repair her footwear, however, since she feared at any moment, until she was able to achieve the shrubbery at the far end of the garden, Annabelle would espy her. Annabelle was of such a nature that were she to see Evanthea running anywhere, she would quickly follow in pursuit, if only to satisfy her curiosity.

So she stumbled along, murmuring complaints of pain the entire way. When she had finally reached the ancient, tall holly and rosemary shrubs beyond the garden wall, Evanthea stopped and fell to the grass just beyond a tall oak in order to adjust her sandals. She had just finished retying them, when Brandreth gave her a severe start by saying, "You have the most delightful ankles, Evanthea — beautifully well-turned! I had no idea!

85

I don't know if it was your intention of displaying your limbs to me or not, but whatever the case, I am forever grateful."

Evanthea quickly pulled her lilac skirts about her ankles and felt a deep, hot blush suffuse her cheeks. Startled, she caught her breath and placed a hand tightly against her heart. "Good heavens, Brandreth, how you have overset me, and I didn't even hear you. I suppose you meant to frighten me out of my wits by stealing upon me like a highwayman!"

When she made as if to rise, he offered his hand and begged to assist her. She eyed him warily for a time, certain something evil was likely to befall her if she accepted his aid. But realizing if she did not quietly and demurely take his hand, she would undoubtedly again expose her limbs to his view, Evanthea acquiesced with a murmur of thanks.

"A highwayman," he said with a provoking nod of his head. "One of your cherished girlhood fantasies, I presume?"

Evanthea rolled her eyes and, recalling her purpose in running to the stables in the first place, responded hurriedly, "No, of course not. I was never such a missish creature! Never."

"No, I don't suppose you were," he returned quietly.

She wanted to ask him what he meant by the slight frown between his brows, but she was nervous about being discovered *tête-à-tête* with him. Dropping her voice, she whispered, "I particularly wished to speak with you this morning, Brandreth, privately as it were—"

"But not *in-the-house privately?*"

"No," she responded quickly. It had occurred to her in the early hours of the morning, as she was sorting through precisely how she ought to handle her delicate apology, that were she to be closeted with his lordship again, he might attempt to importune her a second time. Brandreth had such a reputation as an accomplished flirt that Evanthea had no doubt, no matter whether he actually liked the female or not, he would happily take advantage of her if he could.

"I apprehend you do not trust me?" he queried innocently, his voice also dropping to a whisper.

"Of course I don't," was her direct answer, which caused him to give a crack of laughter.

She placed her hand on his arm and bid him be quiet. "For I don't want Annabelle to come upon us like this."

"Like what?" he asked provokingly.

She released his arm and cried, "You can be the most infuriating man!"

"Yes, I know," he responded, shaking his head regretfully. "I'm afraid I am deeply flawed."

"You most certainly are," she agreed with a brisk nod of her head. "Now, pray do not interrupt me, for I have come in pursuit of you for a purpose and I don't mean to have you keep deterring me from my object."

"Oh, but you intrigue me," he breathed scandalously, drawing near her and just touching the fringe of her paisley shawl. "You have come in pursuit of me. Better and better. But why do you whisper? Why am I whispering? Have we done something we oughtn't to have?"

Evanthea found her temper mounting ominously. "Oh!" she breathed venomously. "How aggravating you are! You know we did something we oughtn't have. You know it was very wrong of you to have kissed me last night. Very wrong, indeed!"

"But you enjoyed it so very much," he responded innocently, placing his free hand against his chest and giving a tug on her shawl with his other. He appeared absurdly wounded.

Evanthea felt a second blush suffuse her cheeks. She could not look at him as she stammered, "It is to—to that quite humiliating point I wish to speak. I cannot possibly account for my strange and inexplicable response to your—your embraces. I had had a little wine with dinner. Perhaps I was affected more strongly than I thought. . . ." Here she could not keep from lifting her gaze to meet his, squarely, forthrightly. "I have been pondering the absurdity of it all night, for I don't hesitate to tell you I did not sleep very well. And if you comment upon my reddened, puffy eyes, I shall leave you this instant."

"I shouldn't permit you to walk away now if my life depended on it. I long to hear what you have to say."

Evanthea felt a tightness in her throat, which seemed very much like a bout of tears was pending such as she had endured after slamming the door upon his drenched countenance the evening before. She could not account for why, when Brandreth stood close to her, she felt nigh to swooning. As she gazed up at him, she felt just as she had not twelve hours earlier and knew a profound, reprehensible desire to fall into his arms all over again. She caught the scent of shaving soap mingled with the pungent aroma of horses, and the result was divine for one used to the rough existence with which her papa had provided her. He was dressed elegantly as always in country gear, sporting a blue coat, a plain waistcoat, and buckskin breeches fitted snugly into top boots. He was even more handsome than ever, if that were possible, especially with the glow of the morning's exercise still high on his complexion.

She was finding it difficult to speak, but after reminding herself for the third time that she would not be comfortable again until she had settled this dreadfully intimate matter with Brandreth, Evanthea finally said, "As I was saying, my lord, I cannot account for my behavior of last night, except to say that since I have not been in the general habit of kissing any man—"

He stopped her in mid-sentence and gave another tug on the shawl. "Are you telling me you've never been kissed?" he queried, his eyes narrowed. "For I'll tell you now I won't believe it. Your kisses were far too practiced for me to think otherwise of you."

"Well, I haven't!" she retorted, shocked that he would think such a thing of her. "You know very well indeed I have not. I have never enjoyed *beaux* as others have, Annabelle for instance. Not that I believe she has been kissed—at least not overly much."

He could not restrain a smile. "She will not like you revealing secrets."

"I hardly think the spectacle she made at Christmas beneath Lady Elle's *kissing bough* was a secret. There were at least five witnesses besides myself to the truly scandalous kiss she placed on your *willing* lips."

"It was scandalous, wasn't it?" he admitted, grinning. "To own the truth, I had forgotten all about it until you mentioned it just now."

"How can you speak so!" she cried, wrenching his hold on her shawl with a quick jerk. "For I assure you, she thinks of it often. Though I am not privy to her secret thoughts, I would not be in the least surprised if she does not reflect on the event once an hour. Brandreth, surely you know how deeply smitten she is with you, or are you so blind to her sentiments where you are concerned? She is very much in love with you!"

"She is suffering the throes of a calf love and will one day awaken to the true state of her heart."

"Not so long as you continue to encourage her. But I can see by the stubborn set to your jaw that you will remain unmoved in your opinions on this subject, and how we began speaking of Annabelle I cannot begin to imagine. . . ."

"You were remarking on your never having been kissed and Annabelle's previous experience."

"Yes, that's right," Evanthea said, giving her head a shake and feeling utterly bemused, "I can't explain what happened, Brandreth, to myself or to you. All I can say is that I am deeply chagrined, embarrassed, and repentant. Forgive me, I pray you, for leading you to believe . . . that is, for . . . for . . . Oh, heavens, I don't know what I am asking you. Only, I didn't want you to suppose that I ever wished you to accost me again, for I don't."

"Are you certain of that, Evanthea?" He was standing far too close for comfort as he lifted a gentle hand to touch her hair just at the temple.

Evanthea swallowed hard and felt strongly inclined to stroke his cheek with the soft back of her hand. She resisted the temptation and took a step backward. "Pray do not," she whispered. "I won't pretend with you, for I know you are an intelligent creature and would comprehend the truth, anyway. I think you already know I want nothing more than to tumble in your arms but I *will not,* for I know I am not in love with you, I could never love you, yet I feel the most wretched longing to have your arms about me again. That is why I must apologize for last night, for I was very wrong to encourage you. Very wrong."

He seemed utterly taken aback, his gray eyes

searching hers as if trying to discern the truth. "I have never known a female to speak so candidly as you do. But you are wrong to offer your apologies. It was I who importuned you. I seduced you with my practiced kisses, and later I absurdly professed a love I don't feel for you. I am the one who must beg your forgiveness, Evanthea. I can no more explain my behavior to you than you can to me. It is almost as though a madness has come over us, an inexplicable one. . . . Aren't we an odd pair? But we are not alone in our madness, are we, what with Lady Elle seeing visions of Olympus! At any rate, with regard to my horrendous visit at your door and my ridiculous speeches, I most humbly beg your pardon. I don't know what possessed me—"

"—or what possessed me to throw a basin of water all over you." She felt a giggle begin at the back of her throat. "Do you know how ridiculous you looked last night, standing in the hallway like a halfling not yet out of his salad days?" She started to laugh and watched an answering glimmer start in his eyes as he broke into laughter.

"I never expected to be drenched when I was making such pretty love to you," he said facetiously.

"You were positively howling, Brandreth! Was it a full moon? I have been given to understand that when the moon is full, madness can overtake even the most rational of persons." She continued giggling every now and again, especially when she would catch his eye. He was smiling now, too, appreciative of the absurdity of all that had transpired.

When silence fell between them, Evanthea grew uncomfortable in his presence. She was very happy that they could have settled with such amicability the distressing events of last night, and it occurred to her in what seemed like a brilliant inspiration that given his obvious good will toward her, he might be persuaded to relinquish his designs on the bust of Zeus.

She begged him to walk with her back to the house and he agreed readily, falling into stride beside her. She smiled up at him and, though feeling quite nervous of a sudden, began, "I have been thinking, Brandreth—to change the subject—that we might be able to end our brangling over the bust of Zeus if you would consider purchasing instead one of the other finds from my father's expeditions. I'm sure if you looked each of them over carefully, you would see that several are equally as . . . that is . . . oh, dear . . ."

She could tell from the expression on his face that she had erred. Gone was the teasing smile and his previous air of congeniality. "You needn't give me your answer," she said with a wry laugh, "for it is written clearly in your eyes. I should have known you would remain stubborn."

"If we are to speak of *stubbornness*, Miss Swanbourne, I don't know which of us would be accounted the worse offender. You have not precisely given me even the smallest ground, not even the compliment of believing I am capable of appreciating a truly magnificent work of art."

"You are wrong," Evanthea responded. "I have not known you these many years and more without being fully conversant in your abilities and your interests. I have only questioned your not having comprehended my sentiments in this situation. Well, I can see we are at *point-non-plus* and out of a wish not to further incur your wrath, I shall beg you to forget I even mentioned the subject to you again."

They had accomplished half the distance to the steps leading to the back entrance of the manor house when Brandreth suddenly took her arm and wrapped it gently about his own. "For the sake of the few kind words we have ever spoken to one another just a few minutes ago, I will do as you bid me. I will forget the matter entirely as though you had never spoken the words."

Evanthea looked up at him, startled by his chimeric shift in attitude. "You have surprised me," she said, searching his eyes. "I would have expected you to be angry for a fortnight." She smiled faintly, aware yet again of a strong tug of unwelcome attraction as she gazed into his gray eyes. "To see that you can actually be civil gives me some hope that you might one day become a tolerable acquaintance."

"Vixen!" he murmured beneath his breath. He appeared as though he wished to say more, but since in that moment Annabelle appeared in the doorway, the words were lost forever.

"There you are, Evan!" she cried, ogling suspiciously the sight of the marquis's arm wrapped tightly about Evanthea's. "Whatever are you doing out here with Brandreth? Do not tell me you have been flirting with my favorite beau?"

She seemed completely bowled over as she glanced from one to the other, and not in the least content in finding them *tête-à-tête*.

Chapter Eleven

Psyche, having left Olympus just after dawn in order to discover what work the night had wrought in the hearts of her protégés, leaned against the oak tree just beyond the holly and rosemary shrubberies and sighed deeply. The night had given her rest so that now, regardless of how desperate her own situation was becoming every moment she but turned around, Psyche could enjoy the results of her labors. She had listened intently to the entire recent exchange between Brandreth and Evanthea. She had watched their faces most particularly, because she had always believed that the expression on one's face was more telling than the words one might speak. She had also carefully judged every movement, however small, in order to discern just how the love affair was progressing.

She sighed again, closing her eyes dreamily. Brandreth had almost kissed Evanthea yet again, and she had shown every sign of wishing for his lips upon hers more than life itself!

Robins overhead chirped merrily under a canopy of oak leaves, cavorting among the twisted branches and chattering to one another unceasingly. Her heart felt as happy as the birds sounded. Her schemes were succeeding! And so well, she could hardly credit her eyes and ears. For one thing, Brandreth and Evanthea had actually conversed with and teased one another, feats at which they had both previously failed. And when Brandreth had tugged on Evanthea's shawl not once but twice, it was all Psyche could do to keep from giving a shout of triumph. In so restrictive a society as England during the Prince's Regency, when a man was not permitted to touch a woman in order to show his attachment, he frequently—whether consciously or not—touched her garments. To take Evanthea's shawl in hand, to tug upon it—these were wondrous signs of love, indeed!

"What are you thinking of, my love?"

Psyche's eyes flew open instantly at the sound of Cupid's voice. She was so startled by his sudden appearance that she did not at first respond. Ordinarily, she heard the fine flutter of his wings just before he arrived, but not this time. She stared at him unblinkingly, first wondering what he was doing here, then thinking how terribly beautiful he was with his white wings spread out to his full height behind him, his handsome face frowning slightly with an unexpressed concern, his figure as strong and virile as the first day she had met him. Love, pure and vibrant, flowed through her like a flood across a barren plain. She wanted to walk into his arms and feel his wings enfold her as they had a thousand times before. She wanted to hear him tell her how much he adored her, needed her, loved her, but she knew no such professions would pass his lips. No such happy words had flowed from his tongue since the turn of two centuries. No, she could not simply cast herself upon him. She no longer believed he truly wanted her to be his wife.

"Won't you tell me even what your thoughts are, Psyche?" he queried softly. "Have I become such a stranger to you that you cannot even tell me what you are thinking?"

"What I am thinking?" Psyche asked, not knowing what to say. How could she tell him the true, unhappy meanderings of her mind? What if she told him she believed he didn't love her anymore and then he admitted as much? It was one thing to have such thoughts; it was quite another to have them confirmed. No, she couldn't bring herself to tell him anything. Instead, she responded, "I was merely thinking of Lord Brandreth and his Evanthea. They are in love, you know, only they are just now discovering it."

Cupid frowned and cast his gaze anywhere but upon her face. He appeared to be considering what next he ought to say. When at last he spoke, he crossed his arms over his chest and regarded her intently. "You're not home as much as you used to be," he stated, lifting his chin to her. "I have been concerned over your absences for some time. Yesterday, when I found you here, among the mortals, I had my concerns justified." His words became more and more clipped. "That you are disobeying His Majesty, Zeus, is bad enough, but to learn as well that you stole from my mother . . . Psyche, I no longer know how to deal with you! You are almost a different person from the woman I married so long ago, and I don't hesitate to say that I—I miss the Psyche I once knew."

"You *miss* me?" she queried, her heart beginning to thump loudly in her ears. This was the closest he had come in so long to speaking his heart, and Psyche could hardly bear the wave of hope that washed over her. "I haven't changed, Cupid, truly I have not! It is just that I felt . . . I believed that you no longer had feelings for me."

"*I* no longer had feelings for you?" he asked, dumbfounded. "How can you say so? Of course I have feelings. My sentiments toward you have not changed one whit. It is you who have grown uncaring and disinterested."

"I?" Psyche retorted, shocked. "Every time I try to converse with you, you're simply not there! You nod at me, or *hmmm* at me from behind your daily scrolls, or completely ignore me, especially at night." She felt tears start to her eyes. "And I only stole from your mama because I knew she would not lend me her potions or her belt."

"Why should she lend you anything to do with the mortals? It is expressly forbidden!"

"Because at least I am interested in helping those unfortunate people who rarely know their left hand from their right in matters of love, while Venus only cares about whether or not Adonis will stand up with her at the next assembly and how she can next make Diana's life a misery! It is all so tedious to me! Why shouldn't I take her cestus if it will help Evanthea learn of love?"

"I can't believe you're trying to justify yourself in this manner! Stealing is a horrendous crime. Surely you are not such a simpleton as to believe otherwise?"

At the mere mention of the word *simpleton,* which was a favorite word Aphrodite employed to describe her daughter-in-law, Psyche bristled. "Simpleton?" she queried. "Why, whatever do you mean, Eros? I suppose next you will tell me that you have been speaking with your mother about me—again!"

Cupid appeared quite conscious as he responded, "As it happens, I was speaking with her only this morning, and she suggested that I command you not to return to Bedfordshire, or England, or any other earthly locality for a—a decade or two, just until we can sort out precisely what is wrong with you."

"What is wrong with *me!*" Psyche cried, outraged. "There is nothing at all *wrong with me,* Cupid, nothing! Nothing, that is, which a day full of rational conversation and a night in the arms of a loving man would not cure. You may tell that to your precious mama! She is a woman. She will know precisely what I mean. And as for your *commanding* me to do anything, I have but a brief message for you, one which these people have employed quite successfully since time out of mind"—she gestured to the lodge behind Cupid: "You may go to the devil, and your mother along with you!"

Cupid's cheeks turned a bright red in contrast to the white of his wings and the blond curls combed in a swirl about his head. He was clearly angered by Psyche's words and, clamping his lips firmly shut, turned toward the east, where he soared quickly into the air and disappeared into the mists of Olympus.

Psyche felt tears burn her eyes as she watched a blurred image of Cupid vanish from sight. There was nothing left for her any longer in her marriage to Cupid. He cared more for doing his mother's bidding than for trying to see her own point of view.

Turning away from the tree, she headed south, taking a path that led to a nearby grotto. She desperately needed a place of solitude where she could vent the breaking of her heart. With a sob, Psyche picked up her long white skirts and fled.

"Evan, I still don't understand," Annabelle said with a tight smile. "I had always supposed you hated Brandreth. And you never go out of doors to speak with him. Why won't you tell me what you have been discussing?"

For the past several minutes, Annabelle had been preventing either the marquis or Evanthea to pass into the house. She had been badgering them both, trying to determine the nature of their conversation and why they were alone.

Brandreth, who had gently tossed aside each impertinent question his cousin had posed, finally addressed her in a firm voice. "You are behaving missishly, cousin. But if the truth be known, we were trying to come to terms over the bust of Zeus but failed yet again."

"Oh, pooh!" Annabelle cried, her countenance relaxing at last, his answer appearing to satisfy her displeasure. "I am sick to death of hearing of that ugly little statue day and night. If it is not you or Evanthea, it is Mr. Shalford — who is here, by the way, with Mr. Allenby and waiting for us in the drawing room — exclaiming over the majestic slant to Zeus's nose or the elegant sweep of his hair. Really, I shall go mad if I hear another word about it!"

"No, pray do not do that!" Evanthea cried with a provocative glance toward Brandreth. "I am convinced there has been quite enough madness rampaging about of late. I promise I shan't utter another word on the subject of the bust in your presence. Only do promise me you will retain your faculties!"

The marquis bit his lip.

"Excellent!" Annabelle cried. "And what of you, Brandreth? Will you promise the same? Not a word of the bust of Zeus?"

Evanthea looked at the marquis, waiting for his reply. A glimmer of laughter shone in his gray eyes as he caught her gaze for a brief moment before directing his full attention upon Annabelle. "Anything to please you, little one!"

Annabelle seemed both content and discontent by Brandreth's choice of endearment. Clearly the sweet, flirtatious coo in his voice as he spoke the words *little one* were all that a young lady in love could desire. But the appellation could do nothing more than remind Annabelle she was both much younger than the marquis and of a petite stature compared to his own remarkable height. She straightened her shoulders and rose upon tiptoes. "I am not so very short," she said. "And I wish you would not call me little one!"

"Of course, you are not short," Brandreth responded smoothly. "And I was not referring to your stature."

"Oh, yes you were, wicked one," Annabelle retorted. With a pretty pout on her heart-shaped face, she took Brandreth by the arm, scolding him for using an appellation she vowed she had grown to detest and leading him toward the door.

Evanthea let them go, scrutinizing Brandreth's height. For a moment, her mind became completely caught up in the memory of how she had slid into his arms and how her own queenly stature seemed to mold so perfectly with his own. She felt a flush of remembered pleasure bring a tingly warmth to her cheeks. But this was nonsense to be thinking of Brandreth in such a truly reprehensible manner! Besides, he would never kiss her again, and for her part, she would never again permit him to do so.

Giving herself a shake, Evanthea followed in Annabelle and Brandreth's wake, overhearing Annabelle begin what would no doubt prove to be a stream of endless silly compliments. "How your boots do shine, cousin. Only tell me, does your valet employ his own receipt for blacking? Does he use champagne as some suggest?"

"And a touch of brandy as well," was Brandreth's teasing response as he winked at her.

"How absurd you are!" Annabelle replied happily, giving his arm a pinch as she drew him up the steps of the terrace.

Evanthea was used to being excluded from conversations in which Annabelle's object was flirtation, and she picked up her lilac skirts with the intention of following them both into the Lodge. She wondered what had brought the vicar, Mr. Shalford, out of his library so early in the day, but her thoughts went no further.

Something was wrong, but what?

She turned around, glancing in the direction of the ancient spreading oak tree, which bordered the meadow beyond the holly and rosemary shrubs. She did not at first know what had caught her attention, until she noticed the robins fluttering about the tree. "They're not singing," she murmured to herself, astonished.

Silence greeted her ears. The tree was alive with activity but heard nothing. She turned back to Brandreth and Annabelle, intending to remark on it, but the couple had already passed into the house, leaving her standing alone on the terrace.

Whatever was wrong? she wondered, setting her feet in the direction of the oak, her curiosity thoroughly aroused.

When Evanthea had taken but three steps, she heard what she believed to be the source of the birds' fright — the sound of a young woman sobbing.

Chapter Twelve

Evanthea followed the garden path through the break in the hedge. Near the ancient oak the path diverged, one trail leading to the stables and fairly well maintained with pea-gravel, the other, a plain dirt path ankle-high in weeds, angling toward the home wood and beyond.

She waited at the top of the path and listened intently. The birds were still silent except for the bizarre fluttering of their wings! For a moment, the strange sobbing sounds disappeared as a cool wind swept her skirts about her ankles. Had she only imagined hearing a young woman cry? Or had it been the wind, for she could not imagine who of her acquaintance could possibly be nearby, not to mention sobbing!

When the robins began to chatter again, Evanthea chuckled to herself, convinced she was merely imagining things. She turned back up the path, preparing to retrace her steps to the house, when a second, inexplicable hush fell over the fluttering creatures in the tree.

This time, she could not mistake the sad sobbing sound that came from the direction of the home wood and possibly the old grotto. Evanthea whirled around and set her feet flying down the dirt path, lifting her skirts high and ignoring the dust that crept between her silk stockings and her sandals.

Summer drenched the meadowland between the stables and the home wood. Bees abounded among the columbine, honeysuckle, and wild roses, which grew at great liberty on the untended property and filled the air with a sweet redolence. No free-roaming livestock rumbled about the land to keep the grasses short and the flowers in check. Every so often a stretch of brambleberry had crept among the thickets of weeds, grasses, and shrubs, once or twice catching at Evanthea's skirts and prickling the tender flesh of her ankles.

The home wood loomed before her, a tangled mass of oak trees, beeches, and limes, with an occasional fir tree brushing the trunks of the others with outstretched limbs. In former times, many of the trees had been pollarded and pruned regularly, but in the current sad state of affairs, even the forest, left to its own devices, had grown recklessly toward the sky, sending seedlings in every direction and propagating a mass of undergrowth that in turn sheltered a township of tiny animal folk. Evanthea was but a hundred yards from the wood and could hear the scampering and chattering of at least a dozen red squirrels as they raced up and down the trees, warning one another of her approach.

A bubbling sound greeted her ears — mingled with the sobs of the unfortunate woman — as Evanthea approached a small, steady-flowing stream. The rivulet, clear and rock-lined, formed a boundary separating the home wood from the meadowlands. A small, black wrought iron gate — a relic of Lady Elle's landscaping efforts of some twenty years earlier — guided the visitor toward a pond and a false grotto carved out of the gentle hills housing the wood.

Evanthea paused before the gate and lowered her head, turning it ever so slowly this way then that as she listened again for the sobbing sounds. They had grown quite faint, until only the smallest hushed sob was heard coming from the direction of the grotto.

Pushing the creaking gate open, Evanthea began moving down a leaf-littered path, the dirt giving way to gravel again, a reminder that this garden was once beloved of Lady Elle.

The path at this juncture was overgrown by majestic rhododendrons, which were beautifully in flower in thick patches of white and pink. Every now and then, Evanthea had to actually push branches of the woody shrub out of her way. Blossoms now clung to her gown of lilac sarsenet and to her hair. She pushed her spectacles up to the bridge of her nose, and as the rhododendrons gave way to the opening of the vista, the sight of a glossy pond, mirroring the trees and hill behind, came wondrously into view.

Evanthea paused at the sight, feeling as she always did when she visited her great-aunt's grotto, that some miracle had been at work for centuries to create such an exquisite sight. The only false part of the whole was the pretense of a cave where the hill had been slightly shorn away, exposing large patches of hard rock wall into which caches of mosses, ferns, and violets had been delicately tucked.

A stone bench, also home to a carpet of moss about its feet, sat in the semicircle of the cave. A breeze drifted over the pond, bringing with it a cool mist that enveloped Evanthea.

"How beautiful," she murmured, her original pursuit set aside momentarily in the enjoyment of the grotto. She had forgotten, or perhaps had never quite realized, how exquisite it was. She felt a shiver of delight travel all the way down her spine and had the completely irrational thought that she was viewing a scene of enchantment.

Ridiculous.

And where was the woman whose heart-wrenching sobs had called her to the grotto?

Faint, deep laughter danced toward her on another

breeze. Or had it? How dizzy she felt. She knew a sudden desire to leave the grotto, fear gripping her heart, when suddenly the sobbing sounds reappeared almost magically, emanating from the grotto itself. Evanthea began heading toward the cave, crossing a small footbridge that arched over the stream, when suddenly her vision seemed to play tricks on her. For there, with her knees on the moss beneath the bench and slumped in a truly pathetic manner over the stone seat, was the form of a young woman crying quietly, her shoulders shaking with sobs.

Evanthea blinked rapidly several times, trying to clear her vision, since upon arriving at the grotto she could have sworn no one was there. She shook her head in astonishment, unable to credit her eyes. Quickly removing her spectacles, she gave them a hasty swipe with the skirt of her lilac gown, hoping the glass alone was at fault. But when she set them back on her nose, the vision remained.

For there she was, a young woman begowned in a long white cambric gown trimmed with gold braid, her head buried in her arms, the condition of her heart evident in every unhappy rise and fall of her shoulders.

Whatever the reason for the initial invisibility of the young woman, Evanthea could scarcely bear the sight of so much misery. She covered the thirty feet that separated herself from the young lady, running lightly, and approached her with hands clasped nervously together. "What is wrong?" she queried. "Can I help you? Is it possible you have lost your way, for I don't remember having made your acquaintance? Pray do not cry! You tear my heart in two!"

The young woman spun about, her blue eyes round with astonishment.

As one, both women gasped at the sight of the other, each gaping in wonder.

"Goodness gracious!" Evanthea cried. "Your

beauty is so extraordinary that I vow you cannot be of earth! Who are you?"

Psyche had been so startled by the mortal's approach that she had whirled quickly about on her knees, sprawled awkwardly against the stone bench, and bruised her back on the immovable edges of the stone. "Zeus!" she cried aloud. "Good heavens! What a start you gave me." She then began wiping furiously at her cheeks, her forehead, her hair. The mountain of tears that finally burst forth—after so many years of pretending her heart was not truly breaking—was like a raging flood and had effectively covered her entire face. She stared at Evanthea, her mind only partially able to focus on her. She recalled her kind words and responded to them. "You cannot help me. No one can! You had best leave me in peace. I didn't mean to overset you, truly I did not, only, only . . ." Words escaped her as thoughts of Cupid strove for and won supremacy in her distressed mind. She had not known this much anguish in her entire existence, except perhaps during her first night in Olympus, when Aphrodite had commanded her to separate all the grains, one from another, in the first stage of that horrid test of worthiness! Her heart had been full of frustration then and was now, over two thousand years later, replete with devastation.

Cupid no longer loved her! She was convinced of it, else he would not have spoken so unkindly to her and he certainly would not have called her a—a simpleton!

The mere thought of this appellation, which had completely obliterated Evanthea's presence, brought a second wave of tears pouring from her eyes. Psyche covered her face with her hands and sobbed all over again, her heart in shreds.

"I am lost!" she wailed.

* * *

For a long moment, Evanthea could do little more than stare down at the young woman. In all her days, she had never encountered anyone as beautiful. The large blue eyes, dripping with tears, had been an exquisite oval in shape, fringed with thick dark lashes. Over the eyes, delicate feathered brows arched enchantingly. The nose was noble in line, both straight and slightly aquiline, almost patrician in appearance. High cheekbones rested in a face that could easily be a model for every Grecian statue she had ever seen. Gold ringlets, dancing over the lady's head, formed a gossamer delight and nearly prompted Evanthea to rudely touch the young woman's hair. She had caught her breath at the sight of her, stunned by so much beauty. Who was she?

One thing was certain: Brandreth must never know of her existence, else he most assuredly would be commenting on her beauty of person one minute out of two and inquiring of everyone where such a creature resided. And learning her direction, he would undoubtedly give up even his pursuit of the bust of Zeus in order to engage her in a prolonged bout of flirtation, the beast!

These last thoughts prompted Evanthea from her reverie and forced her to turn her attention to the lady's distress. She was suddenly overcome with emotion herself at the sight of the sorrowful young woman, tears stinging her own eyes. She was moved to great pity and dropped to her knees beside her, petting the silky curls with gentle strokes. "There, there," she murmured. "Don't cry. Even if you have lost your way, I am persuaded I can help you return to your family. Nothing could be simpler, for I have resided in Old Flitwick since time out of mind. I know every nearby lane, some that end at the base of ancient quarries and others that trail around the Chilterns to neighboring villages. Only pray stop crying or you will have me

107

joining you, and though I can see neither your eyes nor your nose are wont to turn red and swell when you shed tears, I promise you that my face begins to take on the appearance of a mummer's mask at Christmastide. I warn you, 'tis not a pretty sight!"

At these words, the Beauty lifted her face from her hands and offered a watery laugh as she again wiped away her tears. "You are very good and so very kind. I did not mean for you—or for anyone—to see my misery." She took in a ragged breath before continuing, "And I am not lost, not precisely. That is, I know where my home is, it is just that I don't wish to return there. You see, my husband—"

"Oh, you are married!" she cried, noting that the bride was not wearing a ring.

"Yes, to the most handsome man in all of Olym— that is, in all of *England*." Her visage took on an expression of complete and utter adoration. Evanthea wondered if she would ever feel so much for a man and at the same time could not imagine what had occurred to so disturb the Beauty that she would not wish to return to someone she obviously adored. "He—he is quite clever with his hands and is an amazing archer, you can have no notion! All the young girls where I live still fawn over him day and night even though he is given to me."

"He must be equally pleased to have such a beautiful wife," Evanthea proffered kindly.

The young woman shook her head and appeared ready to again burst into tears. "There you are out! I am nothing to most of the women of Olym—that is, of my hamlet."

"Then you must reside in a fairyland," Evanthea cried, much shocked, "because you are quite the most beautiful female I have ever witnessed . . . even prettier than Annabelle, who has won the heart of every buck within twenty miles of Old Flitwick, let me tell you! I believe you are a great deal too modest, and if your husband cannot appreciate your beauty, then I must confess he is quite addlepated, besides being positively *blind!*"

The most delightful trill of laughter escaped the young woman's lips, a sound that brought a sweet sense of peace to Evanthea's heart. Somehow it seemed of the utmost importance to her to make the young lady happy.

"Er . . . that is, Erwin would blanch at the mere thought of someone calling him addlepated. I fear he is become quite proud and — and even disagreeable of late."

"This, then, is the source of your unhappiness? I can readily understand as much. I am acquainted with a disagreeable, albeit extraordinarily handsome man, and he is a dreadful bore most every evening and can be the most provoking creature! Though of late, I must confess he seems *changed,* — inexplicably so — but I assure you, even at best he has to be far worse than your husband!"

"You refer to Lord Brandreth, of course," the lady said, sighing deeply.

"Yes!" Evanthea cried, astonished. "But how did you know? Are you acquainted with him?"

The young woman nodded. "Isn't — isn't everyone?" she queried innocently, a faint blush on her cheeks.

Evanthea realized this much was true. Whatever else Brandreth was, he was quite a famous character, particularly since he was a friend of Prinney's!

The young woman sighed again and reverted to the former subject. "I could easily tolerate my husband's ill humors if I *believed* I was loved, but you see" — and here she turned soulful eyes upon Evanthea before continuing — "he has tumbled out of love with me and there isn't a thing I can do about it!"

Evanthea blinked twice at her new friend and pushed her spectacles back up to the bridge of her nose, shaking her head in disbelief. "Impossible!" she cried. "Though I have known you but a few minutes, even I can see that you have a generous, tender disposition and could not fail to please even the most exacting of men. You must be mistaken. Either that, or he is unforgivably particular in his requirements."

"I am not mistaken. Cu—that is, Cuthbert . . . er . . . Erwin Cuthbert, as I call him—doesn't love me anymore," the young woman continued. "You see, he thinks I am stupid, besides meddling in affairs which are none of my concern. I suppose he is right, but then you cannot imagine how trying it is to be his—his mother's daughter-in-law. I am constantly being compared to the Divinity . . . I mean, the divine Mrs. . . . er . . . Lady"—for some reason she seemed confused and glanced hastily about her—" . . . er, Lady Lakeland. You would not credit, for instance, how beautiful she is. There is not a more exquisite woman than she in the entire universe, and if there were, I am convinced my mama-in-law would capture her and consign her immediately to Hades, merely to avoid losing her reign as the most beautiful female in all of—of the world!"

"Goodness!" Evanthea cried. "Your mama-in-law sounds like a veritable dragon." She then tilted her head at the strange creature next to her. She seemed gently bred yet spoke of Hades with an ease that surprised her. Rising to her feet, she suggested, "Why don't you return to Flitwick Lodge with me? I'm sure you could benefit immensely from a cup of tea and an apricot tartlet or two. Or if that is not to your taste, Cook has a marvelous receipt for macaroons."

"I would like that ever so much!" she exclaimed. "I vow I am famished! I know it must seem odd, but when I become a watering pot, I vow a tureen of ambrosia will not suffice!"

The young woman rose to her feet and brushed off the skirts of her soft cambric gown, prepared to join her newfound friend at once. Only then did Evanthea realize that instead of sporting the traditional empire style, the young lady's gown was crisscrossed in the front with a beautiful gold ribbon, enhancing a narrow waist.

"But how charming!" Evanthea exclaimed. "And how very Grecian. Do tell me that the fashion has changed and we are now to display our figures to greater advantage."

"I wish it were so," the young woman sighed. "For I don't hesitate to tell you that this style of concealing a woman's charms"—and here she gestured with an elegant sweep of her hand to the high waistline gathered beneath Evanthea's bosom—"can hardly succeed at charming your beaux."

Evanthea guided her toward the gate on the far side of the pond. "As to that I wouldn't know, for I haven't any beaux. To own the truth, I have never sought admirers as I know all my friends and acquaintances do. My papa raised me amongst the ruins of Greece, and my sole childhood playmate was a Greek boy who taught me how to climb trees and play at ducks and drakes." By way of displaying her acquired talent, she picked up a smooth, flat stone and sent it skipping five times across the pond.

"Well done!" her companion cried. "May I have a go at it?"

And with that, the fairylike creature, her feet arrayed in what Evanthea now observed were unique sandals of an iridescent gold she had never before witnessed, also picked up a stone and with a sideways, awkward thrust sent it plopping unhappily into the black waters.

"No, no!" Evanthea cried. "You must let it touch only the barest surface of the pond. Try again."

For several minutes she directed her friend, instructing her on the intricacies of making the stones skip. When the young woman was finally trilling her delicate laughter and enjoying some success, Evanthea queried, "But what is your name?"

As though startled by the question, the young woman again plunked her flat rock into the water and responded, "My name? Oh, to be sure I have not told you as much. Well, I think you ought to call me by my nickname, for I feel we have already become fast friends."

"And what is that?"

"Butterfly," she said with a shy smile. "I know it must sound odd to you, but that is what I am called at home. Butterfly."

Evanthea smiled. The name Butterfly seemed to suit the young woman uncommonly well. Her aunt had mentioned an acquaintance named Butterfly only recently, but of the moment she could not precisely recall what her connection to Lady Elle was.

"Butterfly," she repeated warmly. "May I suggest we return to the manor? I should delight in introducing you to my family."

"I would be ever so happy," she responded at once. "If you are sure you wish for it."

"Why ever would I not?" Evanthea asked, surprised.

"I don't know. Now that I think on it, it is just that I fear . . . that is, I am not certain that your family will—will approve of me."

"Don't be a silly," Evanthea cried cheerfully. "Not only will they approve of you, but they will take you most fondly to heart. Though I must warn you that one of the inmates of Flitwick is likely to tumble madly in love with you!"

"Oh, no, you are much mistaken. Brandreth will not find me amusing in the least. He prefers ladies of an intellectual turn—of which I am not—and enjoys brangling above all else—which I most certainly do not! My knees shake terribly whenever Ven—that is, whenever my mama-in-law rails at me!"

112

"But how did you know I was referring to the marquis?"

Butterfly blushed and bit her lip. "I don't know precisely. Perhaps because you mentioned him before, and he does possess a certain reputation for breaking hearts — even those belonging to married ladies."

Evanthea felt a strange rush of gooseflesh travel from her neck down her spine. She turned to stare at her companion and watched as for the barest moment Butterfly's body became almost opaque, then transparent! But that was impossible!

She pushed her spectacles up to the bridge of her nose and blinked several times, attempting to clear her vision yet again. The odd distortion disappeared almost as quickly as it had come, but not before what was now becoming a familiar and quite eerie low rumble of laughter traveled on the cool, moist wind from across the pond, striking her ears and causing her heart to skip a beat.

She began to wonder if Lady Elle's fantastic visions and conversations with her Olympian visitors had finally twisted her own mind. But since Butterfly began chatting about the lovely pink rhododendrons lining the path toward the manor and querying as to whether or not Lady Elle — whom she had heard of from one of her neighbors — meant to refurbish the grotto in the near future, her thoughts were diverted to a more *earthly* direction.

Chapter Thirteen

Annabelle sat in her most favorite place, upon a fine mahogany stool before the ivory keys of the pianoforte. In such a location, she could command the attention of several of her admirers at once. She was doing so now, surrounded as she was by the vicar on her left, a raucous Mr. Allenby on her right, and his lordship in front of her, who leaned charmingly upon the lid of the rosewood instrument and devoted himself to Annabelle. Lady Elle had initially begged the group to entertain her with music, but having settled herself cozily upon the sofa, she had since fallen into a gentle doze, her ear trumpet cradled in her arms.

Without Lady Elle's protests against her more outrageous conduct, Annabelle was wonderfully content, particularly since Evanthea was not in the drawing room and Brandreth, smiling broadly at her antics and winking at her in generous turns, filled her heart with hope and pleasure. She did not bother bestowing her best smiles on him, as she could plainly see he was fully attendant upon her. Instead, she gave her exclusive attention first to Mr. Allenby, batting her thickly fringed gold lashes at him one note out of seven — notes that plinked quite indifferently from modestly skilled fingers, since she positively hated to practice her pieces. And when Mr. Allenby obliged her efforts by sighing heavily or pressing an enamored hand against his dark green coat at the precise place where he vowed his heart beat only for her, or when he compared her eyes to the radiant sparkling of an exquisite emerald Lady Cowper had worn during the last ball of the season, only then would she turn her attention to the vicar, Mr. Gregory Shalford.

Here, much to the obvious amusement of Lord Brandreth, she met with little if any success. Mr. Shalford was clearly impervious to her charms, or at least pretended to be. She deduced that only from a sense of politeness had he agreed to join their quartet at the pianoforte, and from the first, when she had struck the opening chord of that most popular ballad "When the Bosom Heaves the Sigh," Mr. Shalford had remained standing in aloof disapproval at her elbow, his arms crossed over his chest. Twice he had requested she play a more decorous composition, but his suggestion had only brought down a rain of disapprobation from all three of his companions, effectively ending his attempts to curb her high spirits.

Not that he cared for anyone's disapprobation, Annabelle noted not without a little admiration as she stole a glance at him from beneath her lashes. For all of his most infuriating qualities — and he certainly had no less than a thousand by her current estimation, not the least of which was his steadfast refusal to be enslaved by a delicate gesture of her hand or by the appearance of her dimples — yes, for all of his extremely irritating faults, she would give him this much: He didn't give a fig for what anyone thought of him, not even the Marquis of Brandreth. And everyone, positively everyone, deferred to *him* — except Evanthea, of course.

When Mr. Allenby had most pleasingly begged to know if she had studied her exquisite execution at Apollo's knee, Annabelle knew she could safely turn her attention fully to the vicar once again and see if she could prompt a smile from his reluctant lips. Or if not a smile, then a provoked grunt of disapproval. If he refused to adore her, then she could be satisfied only if she knew she had irritated him sufficiently.

"Mr. Shalford," she began with false sweetness. Up went one of his eyebrows, his expression smug, as though he knew she meant to taunt him! What a wretched creature he was! She wondered how long it would be before he again expressed his *sincere* hope that time would soften her manners and that her talents might one day be better employed. "Mr. Shalford, do you truly expect to best Brandreth in your little race tomorrow?" At the same time, she struck an intentionally sour note and apologized to one and all for her clumsy fingers.

Mr. Shalford ignored Allenby's insistence that she played to perfection. "Clumsy?" he queried arrogantly. "Or merely well-timed? The latter, I think. Your dislike of me is not precisely a secret."

Annabelle was taken aback by his directness. She glanced at him nervously and was further undone by the fact that he was almost smiling at her. He was such an odd gentleman that she never knew what to expect of him. She countered defensively, *"Well-timed?* I should hope not, for then you could accuse me of unkindness."

"I don't think you could ever be willingly unkind, but I have already told you that I trust one day your manners will—"

"Oh, yes, I know, *improve* with my years like a good brandy."

His color was heightened as he chuckled softly, his brow furrowed in confusion. "Did I say like a good brandy? How very odd. I cannot imagine making such a comparison."

"No, of course you did not!" she cried, piqued in spite of her wish not to be. "How silly of me! *You* would never say anything so undignified!" She then turned her attention away from such an unsatisfying conversation and immediately engaged an enthusiastic Mr. Allenby in a discussion of which wines he preferred. She thought she had segued nicely from what was nearly a quarrel with Shalford to recommencing her flirtations with Allenby, but unfortunately, she could see from the corner of her eye that Brandreth was laughing at her. As Allenby again compared her eyes to the glitter of some jewel or other, she heard Brandreth in an aside, say to the vicar, "Don't pay anything she says the least heed. I never do and we get along famously!"

Gregory Shalford responded with but the smallest of bows to Brandreth's hint and found himself grateful that his arms were folded over his chest, so that he might clench and unclench his fists with no one the wiser. Lady Elle had requested him to call upon her beautiful great-niece and he had naturally acquiesced, since he considered it but one of the many duties he owed to his kind benefactress. But he had not cherished the notion of actually dragging himself away from his parish obligations in order to *do the pretty* with Miss Annabelle Staple. Far from it, for of all the creatures upon whom he might be required to bestow his attention, he could think of few less worthy than she. In his entire existence, he had never known such an aggravating, absurd, vain, useless female. Annabelle, in his opinion, epitomized her generation. Surely a more simpering, scatterbrained lot had never before been born and bred in England. Surely not!

What was worse, Annabelle had an excellent mind, one that he had tried to direct into more appropriate and more intellectual channels. But Jonathan Swift's essay *A Treatise on Good Manner and Good Breeding,* as well as the numerous works of Hannah More, which he had bestowed upon her during the celebration of her last birthday, she had treated with the utmost contempt. He was convinced she was a hopeless cause and would not have remained in the drawing room, except that it would not have been proper to have simply excused himself and departed. He had scarcely warmed the cushions of Lady Elle's frayed gold sofa when Annabelle had leapt from her queenly throne beside the fireplace and begged to know if any of the gentlemen present wished to hear her play. No man could offer any response, without offending every dictum of propriety, other than, "Indeed, yes, Bella!" as Brandreth had not hesitated to exclaim. Allenby's response had been considerably worse: "To hear your charming execution of the instrument would be akin to listening to the angels play upon their harps."

Doing it a bit too brown, Brandreth had thought with disgust. It was all he could do to keep his tongue from snapping a sarcastic retort at such an absurdity. But if Allenby was absurd, then Annabelle was nothing short of a ninnyhammer to encourage so ridiculous a form of address.

Brandreth glanced at Allenby now, who presently sang the lyrics to "When the Bosom Heaves the Sigh," in the manner of a dog howling at a full moon, and who could not keep from turning around to see how the marquis was enjoying his performance. Allenby was surprised to see that though there was a decided twinkle in his eye, his lordship endured the erratic rendition with tolerable composure and not one whit of censure.

Brandreth was something of a mystery to Shalford. He had known the marquis for several years, as long as he had held the living at Old Flitwick. He was not by any means on intimate terms with Brandreth, and if the truth be known, they rubbed against one another—chafed, more likely. He did not entirely approve of the marquis's habits, in the same manner in which Evanthea did not countenance the business of his lordship's pastimes. Ironically in turn, the vicar suspected Brandreth did not value the manner in which he conducted his own daily affairs. He had not

118

given a great deal of thought to what he supposed the marquis's opinions to be, but he intuited his lordship considered him to be quite a dull dog. Shalford had had his suspicions confirmed when after having accepted Brandreth's challenge to a race to Old Flitwick from Flitwick Lodge, the marquis had appeared stunned.

Theirs was certainly a disparate existence. Shalford hadn't a tuppence to his name beyond the small competence that the living at Old Flitwick provided him, while Brandreth was known to be nearly as rich as Croesus. He was himself the third son of seven and, not having been interested in a career in the legal profession and even less inclined to engage in trade, had chosen — as young men with adequate connections and no fortune were in the habit of doing — a career in the church.

Naturally, the church was not his first love, but he believed he performed his offices with a proper respect and an earnest application of his abilities — which was not always the case when a living was bestowed upon a gentleman.

His first love had always been the army. But without the funds to purchase a pair of colors, the opportunity of joining a regiment had long ago faded away into that dark place unfulfilled dreams were banished in the course of a man's life. He rarely spoke of his desires and only occasionally thought of them. Recently, however, he had revealed the truth of his sentiments to Evanthea, begging her to refrain from repeating his confidences, which he was convinced she would never do. She was unendingly trustworthy, and for this reason, he had been considering the prospect of requesting her hand in marriage. He was not precisely in love with her, but they were of such a similar mind and temperament — besides being accustomed to poverty — that he rather believed she would not only make him an excellent wife, but that she would herself be

119

grateful to have a home and the prospect of children, neither of which she stood the least chance of gaining, given her complete disinterest in matters of the heart and her utter want of fortune.

As for Allenby, the man was a buffleheaded clunch and deserved no particular notice. Brandreth therefore pulled his watch from the pocket of his waistcoat, snapped it open and, seeing that he had passed a full half hour in Lady Elle's drawing room, determined to take his leave the moment Allenby's screeching came to a halt.

His singing did end, quite abruptly, as Annabelle ceased playing and cried out, "Evanthea! Wherever did you disappear to? I had thought you were directly behind me, and when I turned to remark, 'Isn't it wonderful that Allenby and Shalford have come to call?' what must I do but find you had deserted us entirely. But why are you smiling?"

Shalford noted that Evanthea was wearing quite a winsome smile as she pushed her spectacles up to the bridge of her nose. She stood in the doorway, strangely to the side of it, and glanced several times, almost tenderly, at the opposite door. When she extended her arm toward the doorjamb, her smile grew quite warm and full of affection. "May I present my new friend, Miss . . . er . . . Butterfly? She has become lost, I fear, but I promised we would all help her find her way home again!"

Shalford's mouth fell agape, and at the same moment Annabelle murmured, "Oh, dear, she is become as addled as Lady Elle!"

The vicar could not imagine what Evanthea meant by her speech. *Miss Butterfly?* She must be playing off a joke. He watched her turn her head to speak several soft words of encouragement and heard her say, with a disbelieving laugh, "What do you mean they can't see you? I suppose next you mean to tell me you are invisible!"

Chapter Fourteen

"Precisely so," Butterfly responded as she set to nibbling nervously on her lip. "I ought to have told you who I was at the outset, but when you were able to see me, I suppose I wanted nothing more than to be *mortal* again and to forget all my cares. I also hoped I would be visible to everyone else as well. Don't be angry with me or think too unkindly of me. It is just that I have become so miserable — and you were so sweet to me!"

Evanthea turned to stare at the group about the pianoforte and felt the blood rush from her head. She was suddenly dizzy with embarrassment and shock. From the expressions of astonishment on everyone's faces she could easily discern that what Butterfly said was true: No one else could see her friend.

She looked down at Butterfly and placed a hand upon her own cheek, shaking her head dumbly as she scanned the beautiful young woman from head to toe. She did see her, she could not be mistaken in that, but how was it possible? Had she gone mad? Surely not!

Who, then, was the beautiful creature standing beside her yet unseen by everyone else? Evanthea tried to swallow but found her throat constricted in fright. She blinked but could scarcely focus. "Who are you?" she murmured. "No. Do not tell me. Do not say anything. Just leave at once, I pray. Go away! Go away!"

Upon these last words, Evanthea wheeled about and headed into the hallway.

Once out of range of Annabelle, Brandreth, the vicar, and Mr. Allenby, she pressed both hands upon her cheeks and exclaimed, in a terrified whisper, "I know I am not mad. I know I am not. Why, then, could no one see her? Have I imagined her as Lady Elle imagines her Olympian visitors?" She was walking quickly, hoping to escape the spectre whose sandals sounded relentlessly upon the wooden floors behind her.

"Evanthea," Butterfly cried. "Pray do not go! I will not hurt you. I am incapable of doing so. I have meant you no harm. I promise you! And I am real, I am!"

Evanthea, her knees now trembling, her heart racing, stopped in her tracks and spun around. "Who are you? What are you doing here? Why can I see you but no one else can? Are you a ghost come to torment me? Oh, dear! Surely I have gone mad! Mad!"

She again turned abruptly in the opposite direction and began walking quickly down the hallway toward the staircase. Somewhere in her mind she knew if she reached her bedchamber, she would be safe and the ghost would disappear.

Up the stairs she ran, lifting her lilac skirts in hand and breathing rapidly. Fear kept her plunging on until at last she reached the safety of her bedchamber. Once inside, with the door snugly shut against the apparition, Evanthea took deep breaths, staring at the door and wondering if Butterfly would insist upon entering. Her mouth was like cotton and perspiration had beaded upon her forehead as she watched the door handle.

Butterfly, however, did not open the door at all. Instead, she passed through the thick, carved oak, her expression apologetic as she clasped her hands beseechingly in front of her. "Pray do not be afraid. I—"

"Oh, dear," Evanthea murmured unsteadily. "You are a ghost!" She then promptly fell into a heap in the center of her room.

When Evanthea awoke, she was looking up at the ceiling of her bedchamber. The intricate plasterwork had fallen away in places, and the gilt on the once-delicate scrolls of the designs was now fragmented and worn. Two small cupids, with embroidered quivers and miniscule bows and arrows, posed gaily in fading paint, their cherubic smiles obscured by decay. Even so, she had always delighted in waking up to the sight of the young boys. Lady Elle had once told her one of the boys was Eros, also known as Cupid, and the other his jealous brother Anteros. She had never thought of them as characters from mythology, but rather as sweet children who kept her company during the day and guarded her at night.

Such silly ramblings, she thought as she turned her head to the side. She was cushioned on a soft pillow and felt wonderfully sleepy and comfortable, almost as if she had awakened from a beautiful dream and was now ready to slip back into sleep. She noticed, however, that beneath her bed were several tufts of dust, which she would mention to Mrs. Brown the next time she had occasion to speak with the housekeeper. The realization that she was lying on the floor instead of her bed brought her complete memory flooding back.

"Oh, no!" she cried, sitting up quickly, which only served to cause the blood to again rush from her head. Dizziness assailed her, and Evanthea dropped her head into her hands and groaned. "Do go away," she pleaded. "Please. I beg you!"

"If you wish for it, my child, but why? Wouldn't you be happier if I remained nearby? I have brought a little of my lavender water to place upon your temples."

Evanthea heard Lady Elle's voice and felt such profound relief that she gave a long sigh and returned her aching head — which she now realized had been situated upon a pillow held in her great-aunt's arms — to Lady Elle's care. "My dearest aunt!" she exclaimed. "Is she gone? Tell me she is gone!"

"You mean Butterfly?" she queried softly. "I'm afraid not. The truth is, I asked her to stay."

Evanthea lifted her head and stared at her aunt, her spectacles slightly askew. "You asked her to stay?" she asked, stunned as she put her lenses to rights. "Then you mean, you are able to *see* her?"

"Well, of course I am," Lady Elle returned, pressing a soft cambric handkerchief, soaked in lavender water, to Evanthea's forehead. "I have seen her quite often of late, as it happens."

"You have?" she asked weakly, then turned her head reluctantly and saw that Butterfly was standing beside the window, her long, delicate fingers pushing back the mended muslin draperies. She seemed distracted as she gazed down at the formal, unkempt gardens at the back of the house. Evanthea was again struck by how beautiful the young woman was. "But who is she? I expect she is one of your guests from Olympus, but which one? Is she Aphrodite?"

"Oh, no! And pray never speak such a heresy again, or Butterfly will likely never hear the end of it. Cannot you guess her real identity, though I did think it clever she told you her nickname was Butterfly. She is also thought to represent the very soul of man. Her real name is — "

" — Psyche, of course!" Evanthea exclaimed, remembering from her studies of mythology that Psyche was thought to be a butterfly. She then recalled all of Psyche's halting references to her mama-in-law, so exquisite and so beautiful. "And Venus is her mother and Cupid — Cuthbert, Eros . . . that is, Erwin — her husband! Oh, dear! I never supposed they

124

would endure difficulties in their marriage as we mortals do. Oh, Lady Elle, listen to how I speak, *as we mortals do!* I sound just like you, but I can't believe that she is here, that she exists, that she is real. I vow if *you* did not see her, I would suggest you commit me to Bedlam hospital without hesitation. But how is any of this possible? I had always supposed that you were — that your mind . . . er . . . that perhaps — "

"Perhaps what, my dear? Perhaps I had been sipping at the sherry more than I ought?"

"Oh, no, I would never believe anything so absurd, but I confess I had thought your mind had begun *wandering* a trifle, seeing visions that weren't really there and the like."

"I know," Lady Elle said with a chuckle catching in her throat. "And at my age, you cannot credit how vastly amused I have been to watch your various expressions of disbelief. Poor Brandreth is quite out of patience with me, you know. He has even stated that he is grown considerably worried for my health and that he would like me to remove to Staple Hall."

Completely diverted by the conversation, Evanthea sat up, stunned. "He never said so!" she stated, unable to believe Brandreth could be so generous.

Lady Elle handed the kerchief to her and bid her sniff it, "For it is quite restorative when you have swooned, and you will not be feeling at all the thing for an hour or more, let me tell you! As for Brandreth, you underrate him, Evanthea. You always have. Your opinions of him are not justified. Well, not entirely. I told him, however, that I had no wish to leave my home. He quite understood, and it was shortly afterward that he made his magnanimous offer to purchase the bust of Zeus."

"I don't understand him at all," Evanthea murmured. "But I do think it large-minded of him to have offered you his home. I shall tell him so the next time I chance to speak with him. Only, I wonder if he

125

will think I have taken complete leave of my senses."

"Why?" Lady Elle cried. "Because you would offer your approval of his conduct?"

Evanthea slumped her shoulders and threw herself back onto the pillow upon her great-aunt's lap. She encircled her aunt's waist with her arms and sniffed, "Because I stood at the doorway of the drawing room and tried to introduce *Butterfly* to him and to Annabelle and — and to the others."

Lady Elle began to laugh and could not stop. Her motions so jiggled Evanthea that the latter had to finally pull away from her cozy nest and bid her great-aunt to share her amusement with her. "For I don't know what I've said that can possibly have caused you to weep with mirth."

"It is all too perfect, too delightful! I am glad of it, glad, I tell you! You don't know how stuffy you are, Evanthea and now to have so seriously attempted to introduce Psyche to Brandreth! Oh, my dear, if he does not now think the better of you for it, then I will be amazed indeed! I only wish I had been . . . er . . . awake to have seen the expression on his face!"

"Had I done it for a joke, perhaps he would think more highly of me than he does, particularly since his entire existence is composed of nothing less than jostling from one *amusement* to the next. But as it is, I was so proper in my demeanor and afterwards so acutely embarrassed, he will know for a certainty that I actually believed Butterfly" — here she gestured to the phantom by the window — "was standing beside me."

"Even if he does, mark my words, he will insist upon discovering every aspect of the remarkable display. Psyche, wouldn't you agree that nothing could be better at this juncture?"

Psyche turned away from the window and crossed the chamber to kneel beside Evanthea. She did not immediately address the issue at hand, but instead began, "I do apologize if I frightened you and caused

126

you even the least bit of distress. I did not mean to, and for a moment there, I did *long* to be mortal again. Will you forgive me?"

Evanthea regarded the most soulful, appealing eyes she had ever seen. She felt a strong tug of affection upon her heart, a gentle, persistent pull that had the effect of completely dispelling her fears about the extraordinary fact that Psyche was both invisible and a fictitious character from a long-dead religion. She gently touched the young woman's arm and said, "Though I don't pretend to comprehend even in the slightest how it is you are actually sitting here before me, I wish you well and I extend my friendship to you."

"That's so much better," Lady Elle cried. Slipping her arm about Evanthea's shoulders, she kissed her hair and then addressed Psyche, "But what do you think of my great-niece? Isn't she a pretty one?"

"Indeed, yes!" Psyche exclaimed, much to Evanthea's astonishment.

"Don't be ridiculous!" Evanthea cried. "I am not in the least pretty. I am what one calls *passable,* and if one finds oneself reaching for a compliment, I have been told I have very *fine eyes.*"

"Nonsense," Psyche retorted. She then leaned forward, her eyes dancing with excitement. "You are merely backward in your attentions to your toilette, and if I can do nothing else while I remain under your aunt's roof, I can at least instruct you on how to dress your hair to better advantage and how to wear gowns more becoming to your lovely statuesque figure. I wasn't always in the condition you find me. Over the centuries, I have learned a great deal from my exquisite, albeit formidable, mama-in-law. You must trust me in this."

"But to what purpose?" Evanthea returned, her hands held palms up in a gesture of bewilderment. "I have no reason to *attend to my toilette,* as you have suggested. I have no fortune with which to enhance my wardrobe and no real interest in employing my efforts in a task which has matrimony as its only end."

"Not matrimony, not by half," Psyche retorted earnestly, her expression growing quite serious. "Love. The object must always be love and nothing less, else the stormy times which can afflict even the very best of relationships will virtually destroy the resulting marriage."

"But I have no interest in love," Evanthea stated.

"Oh, yes, you do," Psyche returned with a knowing nod of her head. "More than you know, though I can see by the quite stubborn expression on your face that you mean to argue with me. But I shan't permit you to do so. I will say only this: If you can tell me that you felt absolutely nothing when Lord Brandreth kissed you last night, then I shall depart from this house, right now, this very minute. I shall leave you entirely in peace and never return. So, what do you say? Were you completely unmoved by his lordship's embraces?"

"He kissed you?" Lady Elle interjected, awestruck. "But how wonderful! How wonderful! I knew he would, though! I knew it, the rogue!"

Evanthea felt her cheeks grow quite hot, both with the disconcerting nature of her aunt's remarks as well as with the warmth of a certain memory she had rather wished unremembered.

"Just as I thought," Psyche returned triumphantly.

Evanthea did not know what to say. She felt quite fuzzy as she returned Psyche's direct, smiling gaze. She wanted to speak, to refute Psyche's conjecture, but instead she found herself smiling in return and nodding dumbly. She had been moved by his embraces, by his kisses. Until this moment, however, she had not believed the event portended more. But what? Was she in love with him or could she love him? Could she love the Marquis of Brandreth? The *elusive marquis,* as he was known among the *beau monde.* It seemed too absurd to be believed, yet why did thoughts of him bring such a wondrous sensation of exhilaration to her heart?

"The first thing we must do," Psyche stated, bringing a halt to the quick train of her thoughts, "is rid you of these indifferent lilacs and whites and pinks. Your color, Evanthea, is meant only for the richest of blues and greens and reds. Yes, you may stare, but you will see, very soon you will see!"

Chapter Fifteen

Two hours later, following a nuncheon at which Annabelle was mysteriously absent, Evanthea felt a sensation of profound relief. She was flanked by Psyche and Lady Elle, both of whom were staring down into an ancient wooden trunk. The fabrics that Lady Elle had commanded her staff to unearth from the attics were moth-ridden and mildewed. The colors were still fresh since the fabrics had been protected from sunlight, but when Lady Elle attempted to lift one of the bolts of cloth, the top fabric, a peach-colored brocade, ripped apart where she had grasped it without support of the wood center spool. Even if the condition of the fabric had been acceptable, the bitter, musty smell of decay most certainly would have ended the possibility of making use of it.

"I suppose it was a hopeless notion, anyway," Lady Elle said, shaking her head. "Brocades simply aren't worn anymore, are they? More the pity. Such a fine, noble feel to it, but hardly compatible with muslins, cambrics, and silks."

So much the better, Evanthea thought. From the moment that both Lady Elle and Psyche had entered into plans for her transformation, Evanthea had felt overwhelmed and anxious. She had no real desire to change, to become that which she was convinced she was not, and wished that she had not agreed to submit herself to their ministrations.

They had moved from her bedchamber to the large morning room, in order to avail themselves of the wonderful light that two large, bayed windows at the back of the house permitted to soak the room. The chamber was tall-ceilinged and square, and it overlooked the west garden where former topiaries had been left to range at will, the shapes of teapots, rabbits, and chessmen having given way to a wild, erratic naturalness. Evanthea often spent her early morning hours in the room, sketching or reading, propped up by three comfortable pillows on a narrow settle by the fireplace.

In the center of the room was a fine old, heavily carved table upon which sat a silver epergne. When Lady Elle's husband had been alive, the three of them used to enjoy an elegant breakfast together in the chamber which, after seven years of impoverished neglect, was only a shadow of its former beauty. On the walls were several portraits, including one of Lady Elle, another of Henry Rawdon, her great-aunt's beloved spouse, and a third of a spaniel whom Uncle Henry, as he was known to Evanthea, had adored. Silver wall sconces sat uneasily tarnished upon what had once clearly been an exquisite dark blue damask. The ceiling was designed of beautifully scrolled white plaster and, for inexplicable reasons, had not suffered the chipping as other ceilings in the ancient manor had. A large crystal chandelier hung from the very center of the ceiling. Evanthea could remember the morning room in former enchanted times, with the wood floors gleaming, the chandelier sparkling, polished, and lit with three dozen candles, the table laden with refreshments for those attending a Christmas party, a roaring fire in the large, open hearth, the blue damask fresh and striking upon the walls, the windows hung with the same damask — a fabric that three years ago had served to fashion a redingote for Lady Elle, a cloak for Evanthea, and to reupholster all the chairs in the dining room.

And never had Evanthea heard a complaint from Lady Elle.

It was a marvel to her that her great-aunt, having for most of her life enjoyed every luxury, never cried out loudly and bitterly against her fate, as one would have expected, when these were removed from her. Instead, she had laughed and called her dead husband an adoring fool, but nothing more. She had buried him with love, honor, and respect, and she never permitted anyone to speak unkindly of him. When Evanthea had once asked Lady Elle how she bore her shift in fortune, her aunt had appeared thoughtful for a moment, then responded, "I have too many friends to consider myself impoverished."

What more could be said, and Evanthea tucked the lesson away in her heart.

Now, as she regarded the sweet, gray head, bent as it still was over the trunk of memories, Evanthea could only think she was grateful the fabric was unusable. "How truly unfortunate," she commented politely, turning away from the trunk and trying to appear disappointed. "And I was so hoping that we would be able to make use of it."

"What humbug!" Lady Elle cried, craning her neck to catch Evanthea's gaze. "For a droopier face I have not seen in ages. Whatever is wrong, child? Don't you wish to be as other girls? No, don't speak! For I can see you mean to tell me you are content with your lot, but I know better. I have seen your eyes when you watch the village children at play. And don't think for a moment that just because I haven't a groat with which to purchase a proper muslin for you, or because these fabrics are completely useless, I shall give up my mission. Never." Here, she dropped beside the trunk

132

and appeared to fall into a fit of reverie. "When Mama purchased these for me—goodness gracious, was it really over thirty years ago?—I had suffered my seventh miscarriage. She knew I was all but falling into a decline. I know I never said as much, Evanthea, but I did so wish for children. At any rate, my dear mama bought a dozen lengths of silks and brocades, just to cheer me up, of course. I made use of most of them, with the help of a talented dressmaker from Cardington, and these poor worm-ridden things, as they are, are all that is left." She sighed. "But I don't mean to make you sad, so you may dry your tears." She sat back on her heels and appeared thoughtful for a moment, "I haven't really wanted to, but if I must I suppose I will have to sell that silly bust of Zeus to Brandreth. . . ."

As one, Evanthea and Psyche cried out, "Oh no, you mustn't!"

Evanthea turned to stare at Psyche, wondering why on earth she would care who was in possession of her father's treasure. She saw, to her surprise, that Psyche appeared quite guilty as she chewed on her lower lip and glanced nervously from herself to Lady Elle. "That is," the pretty immortal said, "I don't believe you ought to. I know the bust means a great deal to Evanthea—"

"Yes, and even more to you," Lady Elle interjected.

Evanthea was about to ask Psyche what interest she had in the statue, when the door suddenly burst open and Annabelle entered the chamber triumphantly. "Hallo!" she cried out in her melodious voice. "Why so glum? Good grief! Don't tell me you intend to rig Evanthea out in *brocade*. Lady Elle, you cannot be serious!"

Evanthea thought that Annabelle's expression looked decidedly mischievous rather than horrified.

"Of course, I do not," Lady Elle responded impatiently. She lifted the torn fabric and continued, "Even

133

if I wanted to, my little ninnyhammer, do but look at it!"

"Most unfortunate," Annabelle responded with mock indifference. Evanthea could see that Bella was up to her tricks again, but the older woman did not immediately recognize the glint in her niece's eye.

"Yes, it is unfortunate," Lady Elle cried, regarding Annabelle with a great deal of hostility. "It is unfortunate that my poor, beloved Mr. Rawdon had to die beforetimes and in such a penurious state that all I could offer Evanthea—whom I hold in the strongest affection as though she were my daughter—is a moth-eaten brocade. And I hope you will never have to suffer such a reversal as I have, but in the meantime, my little heiress—"

"In the meantime, my darling great-aunt—before you bite off the rest of my nose—I have something to give to you, or rather, something to give Evanthea, if she will accept it from me."

There was just something in Annabelle's eye to cause Evanthea the first real fear of the afternoon. Lady Elle's response added to her concern, for she rose unsteadily upon her aging feet and crossed the room to embrace her great-niece. "Tell me you have been to the mantua-makers in the village! Tell me!"

"You know I have!" she returned, kissing Lady Elle's cheek, then releasing her to turn to the doorway and command loudly for Meppers to bring her booty in at once.

"Oh, you haven't," Evanthea cried, dismayed. "Not on my behalf! Say you haven't done anything so foolish!" She felt her heart constrict within her as Meppers and James entered the square chamber, their arms laden with packages of all shapes and sizes. The butler wore a curious smile as he laid his bundle upon the floor at her feet and instructed James to do the same. He bowed slightly to Evanthea and handed her the first unwieldly gift.

134

Evanthea felt positively panicked at the feel of the brown paper against her arms. It was one thing for Lady Elle to *wish* to begown Evanthea, but quite another for her to actually cull the resources to accomplish the deed. Until this moment, she had not truly believed the project would amount to more than the fashioning of a new gown out of the muslin perhaps in Brandreth's room. But Annabelle had changed all that.

"Do open it, before I succumb to a fit of the vapors!" Annabelle exclaimed.

Unwilling to slight Annabelle, Evanthea pushed back the protective wrappings and there, shimmering against the dull brown of the paper, lay an exquisite emerald-green silk. In spite of her wish not to be, she was enchanted by the mere sight of it. "It's so beautiful," she murmured. And as though spellbound by the fabric, Evanthea ran her fingers lightly down the length of it, the touch smooth beneath her fingertips. Did a miracle reside in the tight weave of the expensive fabric? Why did she suddenly wish for nothing more than a gown fashioned in this wondrous material? What would Brandreth think of her? Oh, foolish, foolish thoughts!

Psyche came up next to her and, slipping her arm about Evanthea's waist, whispered, "He will adore you in this color, I am convinced of it."

"Don't be ridiculous!" Evanthea countered, her cheeks warm from having her sentiments so easily discerned. Attempting to dissimulate, she added, "I don't give a fig what he thinks of this color. You make too much of it, surely."

"Make too much of what?" Annabelle queried. "What are you saying? I can't quite make you out. And what do you mean you don't give a fig what he thinks of the color! Well, I can tell you he will think it marvelous. He has always cared a great deal for you and for your opinions; it is merely that he is rather shy.

But he won't be for long when you are gowned in this extraordinary fabric!"

"Brandreth, shy?" Lady Elle cried, moving to stand beside Evanthea, where she began working the rest of the paper off the green silk. "Hardly!"

"Brandreth?" Annabelle responded, surprised. "Not my cousin. I was referring to Mr. Shalford, for in case no one has noticed, he is quite taken with our Evanthea. Oh, you may stare, Evan, but there it is! Now you will know how deeply I have your interests at heart. Wouldn't it be a grand thing to be settled in the parsonage so near Lady Elle? To be married! Just think of it! You will never be called a spinster again."

"I am very content in my spinsterish state," Evanthea responded, her cheeks darkening in hue. "And as for Mr. Shalford, what nonsense are you speaking? We are friends—quite excellent friends, I might add— but he surely does not look upon me with an amorous eye."

Annabelle dimpled, "Not yet! But when you parade before him in a walking dress of this elegant green silk—rigged out in style, as Brandreth would say—he most certainly will! And tomorrow, if you take my advice, you will give him a kerchief to carry in the race. I promise you, a gentleman sets a great deal of score by such attentions, and you will go a long way to winning his heart if you do so."

Evanthea was prepared to argue with Annabelle, but Lady Elle ordered Annabelle to stop putting nonsensical notions in Evanthea's brain, then changed the course of the discussion entirely by ordering Meppers to send Mrs. Brown to the morning room. When Annabelle was satisfied that all the packages had been brought to the morning room, Lady Elle dismissed both James and Meppers, with the admonition that none of the household's male staff were to come near the morning room again unless otherwise summoned.

Within a scant ten minutes, all of Annabelle's purchases had been scattered over the chamber to be intently reviewed by Lady Elle and Mrs. Brown, both of whom were accomplished needlewomen. Pattern cards were placed upon the various fabrics, along with pictures from *La Belle Assemblee, Le Beau Monde,* and *Ackermann's Repository.* The green silk would be used to create the walking dress Annabelle referred to, and a dazzling rose-colored silk would form a ball gown of three-quarter length over a delicate, sheer embroidered muslin, sewn in a modest double layer, which would reach to the tips of beautiful white satin slippers.

"And when would I ever make use of a ball gown?" Evanthea queried with a laugh. "I believe this fabric would be better served if it was fashioned into a valence for the window in our aunt's bedchamber."

Evanthea picked up the slippers and glanced at Annabelle, who was appearing much like a pleased peacock as she watched her friend. "There is something more," she said, her green eyes positively glowing. Annabelle glanced from Evanthea to her aunt, then exchanged a conspiratorial look with Mrs. Brown. "I have arranged for a ball—quite impromptu, I know— to take place tomorrow evening in honor of the winner of the race."

Evanthea and Lady Elle cried out in unison, "What?"

"But that's impossible!" Lady Elle exclaimed. "For a thousand reasons—the condition of the lodge, the time involved in merely dusting the furniture, and what of an orchestra . . . Good heavens, Annabelle, what were you thinking? I hope you haven't irresponsibly begun inviting anyone who happened to be at the village today."

"That is precisely what I have done. Besides, I don't think you realize what is going forward! Both inns were crowded with sporting men, their wives and sisters—many of the *beau monde,* you've no idea! . . .

137

All have come to see the race between Shalford and Brandreth. I don't know how it is, but the entire county seems to have been alerted, and you know what men are! They can't resist a good mill or a shooting match or, in this case, a race. And would you believe it! It would seem, much to my utter astonishment, that Shalford has as fine a reputation as my cousin in matters of sport! I could not credit my ears when I learned that nearly half the bets were on the vicar of Old Flitwick, that he should take the day! Could anything be more absurd?"

Lady Elle slumped into a chair at the table. "Annabelle, I have never known you to be more foolish. What of food and the state of my house? I am humiliated just thinking about it!"

Annabelle rushed to her side and leaned over to kiss her cheek. "Don't be such a goose. Do you think for a moment I would let such a thing happen? Never. In fact, at this very moment, a veritable army of servants and laborers are headed in the direction of the lodge. I know the noise will be difficult to bear, but you shall have your home restored to you — at least in part — by tomorrow night."

"Annabelle, you shouldn't have! Whatever will your mother say when she learns how you have squandered your fortune on me?"

"For once, she might even approve. She was ever so angry when I purchased that silver gauze ball gown May last for seven hundred pounds."

"Seven hundred pounds!" the ladies called out in unison.

Annabelle had the good grace to color up, and she laughed out of sheer embarrassment. "We quarreled severely over it, I assure you, but I have since begged her forgiveness and promised to do better. And now I am."

"But not by hiring servants to repair my home."

"And to what better use could I employ my for-

138

tune?" she queried. "I have a great fondness for you and wish to do you a little service, which will cost me far less than that stupid gown did, I assure you. Besides, I know Mama would be pleased, Papa, too, for they both felt it unconscionable that you were made to suffer for poor Uncle Henry's difficulties."

"But —" Lady Elle began, trying to remonstrate.

Annabelle drew back from her and said, "I shall hear nothing more on this subject. I hired the schoolteacher to pen all the necessary invitations, half of which have already been extended to my acquaintances at both inns. Sufficient servants have been engaged to do the work, including laborers to tidy the gardens and trim the hedges and the topiaries. . . ." Annabelle broke off, tears suddenly starting to her eyes. "Do you know until today I did not realize how many unfortunate families there are. When it was learned that a day's wage could be earned at Flitwick Lodge and I had hired two dozen laborers, my carriage was besieged as I was leaving the village by many of the workers, all thanking me profusely. Lady Elle, is it really so bad in this day for so many?"

"I'm afraid so. The Corn Laws have done a great deal of mischief, driving up the price of bread, and the harvests have been so poor of late."

"Then I shan't permit you to argue further with me about squandering my fortune on repairs to your home," Annabelle said, her demeanor solemn.

Evanthea watched her curiously. She could not remember a time when Annabelle had shown either such remarkable selflessness or a sweeter heart in her evident concern for the plight of the poor in Old Flitwick.

With an odd laugh, Annabelle wiped a tear from her eye and said, "Well, I hope Shalford will be pleased with me for once! He is forever lecturing me on my frivolous nature! But enough of this. I also hired three needlewomen to fashion Evanthea's walking dress and her ball gown. They will be here around four o'clock. Now we must decide which of the trims will best suit each fabric. I chose several, unable to make a decision when I was at the shop. Evanthea, do but look at this pretty Brussels lace." She unrolled a small packet and now presented the contents for Evanthea's inspection.

"I don't know what to say," Evanthea began uneasily as she regarded first the lace, then Annabelle's face. She shook her head at Annabelle and continued, "I only wish I could have stopped you. It is too much, Annabelle, far too generous. I can well comprehend your wish to help Lady Elle, but as for me, I fear your efforts—"

"I won't insult you by telling you that I am sorry for your circumstances," Annabelle said, refusing to let Evanthea finish. "I know well enough not to do so, for your pride is so great that I daresay you would give my head a severe washing! But I will say this: For one of the first times in my life, I have actually thought of someone other than myself. So I believe you would be doing my character a great service to simply *thank me* for this gesture. I somehow doubt it will ever happen again."

She then moved to stand by the table and began examining the ribbons, lace, beads, and embroidered bands that she had selected at random to adorn the fabrics she had purchased.

"What nonsense," Evanthea returned with a smile. "You are one of the most openhearted creatures I have ever known. Yes, yes, it is true that you very rarely give gifts, but you have such an ebulliency of spirit that cannot help but enliven even the dullest of surroundings. What greater gift can a woman give than this?"

"I suggest you praise me as much as you can since, I promise you, if any of my beaus become enchanted with you in any of the gowns fashioned of my fabrics, I shall take it none too kindly."

Evanthea wondered what Annabelle would think if she knew Lady Elle's object was nothing less than Brandreth, the man Annabelle had been determined to wed since she was a child. The heiress had never known a serious disappointment in her life, and one day she would have to realize that her cousin, the marquis, was not and probably never would be in love with her.

Lady Elle commmanded Evanthea to join her by the tall looking glass brought down from her own bedchamber. Here she positioned Evanthea directly in front of the glass for the purpose of laying each length of colorful fabric over her shoulder and fitting at least one gown to her figure.

"But you must remove this exceedingly hideous lilac muslin," she insisted with a disgusted frown between her brows. "However have you been able to bear wearing such a ridiculous morning dress all these years? Mrs. Brown, will you help me? I fear my poor fingers are becoming useless."

Evanthea, who submitted to Mrs. Brown's agile fingers as she unbuttoned the round gown, smiled mischievously at her aunt and said, "But what better garment in which to climb the orchard trees and retrieve succulent peaches in late summer? If you remember, Aunt, you always tell me that I bring you the most savory fruits of all. How do you imagine I achieve such a feat?" She pulled mockingly at the skirts of her worn gown and dropped a small curtsy.

Mrs. Brown, of course, protested that Evanthea's movements made it impossible to unbutton the gown, and Lady Elle merely rolled her eyes. "Well!" she cried in response. "I certainly hope you don't mean to climb trees in these silks or jaconets or, heaven forbid, the tulle!"

"What an interesting picture that would present, dearest aunt!" Evanthea cried as Mrs. Brown slipped the gown from her shoulders, the garment dropping into a neat circle about her feet. "The tulle would undoubtedly be torn to shreds and form a kind of moss hanging all over the branches."

"You are very nonsensical today."

Psyche's voice intruded. "Aphrodite was right," she murmured, sounding stunned.

"About what?" Evanthea and Lady Elle queried at the same moment.

Psyche, who had remained standing quietly aside during the course of the proceedings, directed her response to Evanthea. "She said that you *mocked* her in the manner in which you treated your beauty and your figure with such indifference. And I now comprehend why she said such a thing." She glanced over the lithe, tall, well-proportioned frame of her new friend and shook her head. "I vow you compete even with *her* in how exquisitely you are formed. Evanthea, if I had but half your charms, I daresay Cupid would never have strayed in his affections."

Evanthea felt her cheeks burn. "I have never heard such absurdities in my entire existence," she cried, pressing her hands to her face.

"Who are the pair of you speaking to?" Annabelle cried. "And what do you mean, *absurdities?*"

Psyche ignored the interruption, as did both Lady Elle and Evanthea. She drew close to her friend, who stood in front of the looking glass wearing a simple muslin shift trimmed in a frail, faded pink ribbon. She placed her hands about Evanthea's waist and opened her eyes quite wide. "I have never witnessed so narrow a waist before. It is a pity the current fashions do not enhance what must be your most perfect attribute."

Evanthea was decidedly uncomfortable. She glanced at her reflection in the mirror and tilted her head slightly. She pushed her spectacles up to the bridge of her nose and looked at herself critically. She saw shoulders that sloped from a long, elegant neck, arms that curved gracefully — probably from having been in the habit of climbing trees, she thought rue-fully — full and well-formed breasts, a waist that was indeed quite narrow, moderate hips, and long legs, ta-pering to a pair of pretty ankles. She remembered sud-denly that Brandreth had admired her ankles but a few hours ago.

But what would he think if he saw her now? she wondered.

Giving herself a shake, she then wondered how it was her thoughts had become so obsessed with Bran-dreth of late!

Chapter Sixteen

Lord Brandreth slapped his riding crop hard against his buckskin breeches. The afternoon summer sun was hot on his back as he made his way from the stables, past the large oak, through the shrub gateway, and into the formal garden behind the lodge. Once in the middle of the garden, he paused in his frustrated stride and turned around in a slow circle to look at the unhappy state of what he remembered as one of the prettiest mid-seventeenth century formal arrangements he had ever seen. The entire pattern was in a series of unique diamonds set on their points perpendicular to the house. The pattern remained, but the beds were wild and weed-ridden, the roses in particular having sent out thick, flowerless suckers, robbing the productive limbs of their fruit.

In a moment of paralyzing insight, he realized he was distressed because the state of his heart felt just like this garden, yet why he could not comprehend. After all, there wasn't a single aspect of his life, his well-being, that he had neglected, not one that could be construed as weed-strewn. He was always groomed to perfection, his estates were managed with a firm, consistent hand, he performed his winter and spring duties in the House of Lords with great care and deliberation on every matter, whether significant or otherwise, he attended to his social obligations and showed every respect to his family. Why, then, did he feel as distorted as the garden about him, revealing only a shadow of what he was convinced his life ought to? Somewhere within the dark reaches of his mind, however, he suspected his discontent had something to do with Evanthea. But why?

Shrugging his shoulders and deciding that he would be best served to leave Flitwick Lodge soon after his meet with Mr. Shalford, Brandreth turned his feet toward the back doors of the manor house. Of late, his thoughts where Evanthea was concerned seemed particularly disturbing. Earlier, for instance, when he had been flirting with Annabelle on the drive, he had known an irrational desire for Evanthea to open the door of the lodge, walk out into the sunshine, and join them. Strange longings seemed to beset him nearly every waking hour—longings to see her, to brangle with her again about anything or nothing, to watch her push her loose spectacles, for the hundredth time, back up to the bridge of her nose, or to return that secret smile of hers, which she always reserved for the precise moment when she knew he would be amused by something that few others could laugh at.

Lord, what was happening to him? It was almost as though he had come to value her company, her presence, in a manner as surprising as it was absurd. Evanthea, for God's sake! Evanthea who tried his patience sorely one minute out of two. The woman who had effectually ended his one chance for happiness some eight years earlier when she had spoken against him to the lady he had loved and hoped to make his wife.

His heart contorted in his chest as he thought of Susan Lawrence, now Lady Felmersham. He had loved her as he had loved no woman before or since. He had been on the brink of offering for her when Evanthea had spoken words regarding his character, which had obliterated his chances of wedding the beautiful, lively, charming Miss Lawrence. That Evanthea could

145

not recall her misdeed seemed outrageous in the extreme. But for him, to be harboring even the smallest grain of affection for or interest in her seemed not only impossible, but faithless — a betrayal of his love for Susan.

With these thoughts jumbling unhappily about in his head, Brandreth quickly mounted the terrace steps, pushing away all thoughts of Evanthea save a need to be gone from her and from Flitwick Lodge. He had only the race to run and Lady Elle's commitment to sell him the bust of Zeus, and then he could leave.

He had spent the last two hours practicing for his race with Shalford, which would take place on the following day. He was reasonably assured of success, particularly since he had mastered the ability of maintaining his balance while setting his horses to a spanking pace. Of the moment, he found himself famished and set his booted feet in the direction of the kitchens, where he meant to badger Cook into preparing him a nuncheon that he might carry away to the billiard room and enjoy in solitude.

He had been given to understand by the head groom, when he had been rubbing down his horses, that the ladies were closeted in the library and were not to be disturbed. The billiard room was next door to the morning room, both of which were situated in the west wing of the lodge. The east wing housed the library, which was next to what was once Mr. Rawdon's office and private refuge from his wife's domestic concerns. He would have preferred the library, since the smell of the leather-bound books and the generally warm, masculine feel of the chamber always tended to soothe him. When Rawdon was alive, Brandreth used to challenge the old man to as many games of chess, cribbage, or backgammon as an entire decanter of brandy would permit.

He had loved Rawdon just as he had loved his own

father. Had he known how badly dipped his great-aunt's husband had been before his demise, he most certainly would have taken steps to help the old boy. As it was, only the horrific settling of affairs following the funeral had revealed the dreadful tidings that Rawdon had fallen into the hands of the moneylenders. To his credit, however, this bizarre twist to what had for years been the steadiest of characters had occurred only in the six months prior to his death. The last ruinous months were similar to Beau Brummell's experience, who, though not perishing in the end of his compulsive run of gambling, had been forced to flee a mountain of debts in order to avoid prison. He had crossed the channel to France, where he was currently residing in what friends of his had described as hideous poverty.

Whether or not Brummell would be able to restore his fortunes, time alone would tell. But Rawdon had died before he could repair his estates or make safe the future of his beloved wife. Brandreth had only now to convince Lady Elle to sell him the bust, and he was convinced all would be well.

Soon after complimenting Cook on the supper of the night before, he found his arms laden with her munificence — a tankard of ale in one hand and a platter of fresh bread, cold chicken, and three raspberry tarts in the other. Mounting the stairs, he headed for the billiard room.

His thoughts were still full of Rawdon and Lady Elle's pile of debts, when he heard a traditional giggling that, in his opinion, always heralded the gathering of women. He enjoyed the sound. There was something about a woman's laughter that could sweeten the sourest and dullest of days.

He turned around slightly to stare down the hallway in the direction of the library, wondering who he heard laughing in the morning room if the ladies were supposedly in the library.

The door to the morning room opened quite suddenly and the housekeeper, Mrs. Brown, burst through carrying a bundle of clothing. He recognized the lilac fabric that constituted the round gown Evanthea had worn only that morning and could not imagine why Mrs. Brown held it in her arms.

She seemed flustered as she entered the hallway, her head bowed as she caught up a trailing ribbon, and did not perceive the marquis until she had bumped into him. A splash of ale spilled onto the lavender muslin.

"Oh, sir!" she cried in a hushed whisper, jumping backward and swallowing hard. "I mean, my lord! I do beg your pardon, but you oughtn't to be here. That is . . ." She fell suddenly silent, apparently bereft of words or explanation, her cheeks aflame.

Brandreth knew well enough that the tall, quite homely housekeeper was humiliated by the encounter, and he responded with a kind, "There, there, my good woman. No harm done. Only tell me what is going forward. I was told the ladies would be in the library, but I can hear Annabelle's voice as well as Lady Elle's. I suppose Evanthea is with them?"

Encouraged by his tone, the woman nodded and replied, "I don't know who told you they would be in the library, m'lord. Whoever it was was quite mistaken. All of the ladies are in the morning room, and even another person, at least I thought I saw—" Here she halted and an even hotter wave of embarrassment flooded her thin cheeks, "I mean, Miss Annabelle brought Miss Evanthea a—a gift of sorts and they are all exclaiming over it." She dropped a sudden curtsy and appealed to him, "But if you don't mind, my lord, I must fetch her ladyship's workbox immediately. They are all in something of a state and will wonder if I am not returned within a very few minutes."

"I see," he said slowly, wondering what the devil the ladies were up to. He was filled with curiosity but had no desire to prevent the housekeeper from completing her task. "I shan't detain you, then." He opened his arms wide, careful with both the tankard of ale and the full plate of food, and permitted her to pass.

Brandreth watched Mrs. Brown move quickly down the hall and turn the corner, waiting for her footsteps to disappear before he looked back toward the door, which was provocatively ajar. He approached it on a soundless tread, light from the cheerful morning room spilling into the dark, wainscoted hallway.

The ladies were not grouped together and the first one he saw was Annabelle, who was seated at the table organizing ribbons of various colors. Lady Elle came into view next, backing away from some object or another that she was scrutinizing intently from narrowed eyes.

"I feel quite naked, Lady Elle," he heard Evanthea exclaim. The next moment she appeared in front of the tall looking glass, also clearly within his view, and stood before it biting her lip. She seemed worried, as well she might, since she was standing with only her fragile shift on.

He was dumbstruck, first by the realization that she was scarcely clothed and second by the difference in her appearance in silk-stockinged feet, her ankles uncovered, her figure only slightly disguised by the thin fabric, the creamy whiteness of her arms fully exposed. He watched in mute fascination as she reached up to the coil of hair atop her head and slowly unpinned, then unbraided it, as though she, too, were in a misty state of disbelief.

"How was it you wished my hair cut?" she queried, as she pulled apart the braid and her hair fell in a rippled wave to her waist.

There was no immediate response, but when Lady Elle spoke her answer was a trifle enigmatic. "I can't agree with you there, Butterfly. To leave it long would not enhance the shape of Evanthea's face. I should

149

think a short cut, like Caro Lamb's, might be just the thing."

Butterfly? Who the devil was *Butterfly?* Now he remembered. That was the name Evanthea had employed earlier when she had stood in the doorway of the drawing room and attempted to introduce a ghost to them all. How her cheeks had flamed in acute embarrassment. Brandreth had not known what to make of her in that moment, and he remembered how oddly pleased Lady Elle had been when Annabelle had awakened her from her slumbers and explained Evanthea's peculiar behavior.

"I quite agree with . . . er . . . Butterfly," Evanthea said, turning to scowl a warning at Lady Elle. "Perhaps I ought to have it trimmed and curled, but I wouldn't want it cut short."

"Who is *Butterfly?*" Annabelle cried from her post at the table. She was untangling a knot of cherry-red ribbons.

"Only one of our aunt's . . . er . . . Olympian guests," Evanthea said.

"She's here?" Annabelle asked, glancing briefly about her, then returning to her ribbons. "I don't recall who she is, though. I don't remember a goddess called Butterfly."

"Butterfly was not a goddess. She was—is—the mortal Psyche, who married Cupid."

"Oh," Annabelle returned, completely uninterested. She resumed picking at the knot of silk ribbons and said, "Well, whoever she is, I quite agree with her. Only Caroline Lamb can sport such a short cut, but what of Emily Cowper's fashion? It is a trifle longer, and quite pretty, I think."

Lady Elle interjected, "You forget. Lady Cowper's hair is rather wispy and her style would not do for Evanthea at all. Her hair is too thick. Now that I think on it, I believe Psyche has the right of it. We should keep your hair long enough to wear as she wears her own, in a beautiful cascade of curls. But what I wish to know is have you ever used curl-papers?"

Evanthea shook her head. "Of course not," she responded with perfect candor.

Brandreth was listening to the conversation only in part. He was too mesmerized by the sight of Evanthea's thick hair to give a fig whether she ought to have it dressed like Caroline Lamb's or like Emily Cowper's. He only knew that it was quite magnificent. He had never realized how long her hair was, nor how thick or how rich in texture. He had always thought her mane was a pretty color, but until this moment, perhaps because it was displayed against the smallness of her waist and the thin white of her shift, he had never before experienced the quite remarkable desire to catch up her locks in both hands and bury his face in them. Lord, had he gone mad? Where had such feelings come from?

He wanted to speak, to command Evanthea not to cut her hair, but he was at least sensible enough to know he would humiliate her if he revealed his presence. He knew he ought to move on, to make his way to the billiard room, or better yet, to retrace his steps to the entrance hall and from there march in the opposite direction of the morning room to seclude himself in the library. But his top boots seemed pinned to the wood floor. He could not move. He was immobilized by the sight of Evanthea. His eyes were again drawn to her waist. He wondered if he could fit his hands around it. He believed he could, and Brandreth realized he would give a fortune for the opportunity to try.

With this last thought came the realization that something had changed. There was now a tension in Evanthea's body that had not been there before. He glanced quickly at the looking glass, where her face was completely visible, and saw that she had become aware of his presence. Her eyes were opened wide, her thoughts inscrutable behind her spectacles. Any other female, he realized, would have shrieked at the knowledge she was being observed in a state of undress by a man. But not Evanthea, and he found his interest in her increasing mightily the longer she simply held his gaze.

And then she smiled, that faint smile of hers, so typical of her when she knew he would be amused as others would not. He could not keep from smiling broadly in response, grinning, in fact, like a schoolboy. Had she been alone, he would have entered the room boldly and probably kissed her all over again just as he had . . . good Lord, was it only last night?

His wrists had begun to ache from holding the tankard and the laden plate for so many minutes. He was preparing to offer Evanthea a bow of approval and leave her to the ministrations of his cousin and his great-aunt, but to his surprise she turned suddenly and walked straight for him, saying, "Oh, dear. Mrs. Brown must have left the door ajar. I'll close it lest someone accidentally see me in my undergarments!"

He was so surprised she would actually move closer to him that his mouth dropped open and he nearly let go of both the tankard and the plate. She held her head high as she approached the door and stared at him in what was most certainly a challenging manner, yet she said nothing. Completely incapable of doing aught else than scan her from head to foot as any quite normal, warm-blooded male would do, Brandreth swallowed hard. Would she come into the hallway and speak with him? Perhaps he could persuade her to close the door behind her. He would be ever so happy to set his food and drink on the floor and and take her in his arms! He swallowed again, a familiar hunger overcoming him the closer she got.

Once at the door, however, Evanthea stopped a foot short of it and quite out of his reach. She shook her head at him and said, in a provoking yet amused whisper, "Libertine," then closed the door upon him with a snap.

His head jerked at the sound of the closing door and at the same moment he seemed to awaken as from a reverie, as though the sight of her had cast a strange spell over his sensibilities and now at last he could think again.

Slowly, he turned and headed back toward the entrance hall. Each booted foot, which overtook the next, was lethargic in movement. After five steps he took a deep breath, another five and he let out the breath in a long, slow sigh.

Evanthea, he murmured, ignoring Mrs. Brown as she came running down the stairs in front of him, stopping herself just in time to prevent colliding with him again. On he went, blinking only occasionally. He had the odd feeling that he was being followed, and not more so than when a low, masculine chuckle sounded near a tarnished suit of armor. He turned and glanced all about the area where he believed the laugh originated, but saw nothing.

Brandreth gave himself a shake. What the devil was happening to him? First he finds himself unreasonably drawn to a female he had set down as an ape-leader all these years, and then he starts hearing voices, or at least laughter.

Perhaps the same bizarre occurrences were afflicting Evanthea as well. He recalled the moment earlier when she had spoken of Psyche as though she saw her just as Lady Elle professed to.

Ghosts perhaps?

When he finally achieved the library door, he gave it a gentle shove with the toe of his boot and entered Mr. Rawdon's sanctuary with a relieved sigh. Here, at least, he would be spared company, certainly any of the lady's visits and hopefully those of any wandering spirits who seemed to be taking a hearty interest in the affairs of the inmates of Flitwick Lodge.

As he took a long draught of the fresh, home-brewed ale, he decided he ought to take greater care with Evanthea. He suddenly feared, if he continued to take advantage of her innocence, she might construe his attentions to be something far more than what they were.

But if he continued to experience so strong a desire to take her in his arms, he wondered if even he would know what he meant by flirting with her so outrageously.

Chapter Seventeen

Psyche glanced from Lady Elle to Annabelle, wondering if either of them were aware that Brandreth, his hands occupied with meat and drink, had actually seen Evanthea unclothed! She swallowed, feeling enormously guilty since she knew she ought to have at least warned Lady Elle of his presence. But she could see that both ladies had been so preoccupied, Evanthea's great-aunt in determining which fabrics should serve which patterns and Annabelle in organizing the various ribbons and trimmings, that neither had noticed his lordship's quite scandalous conduct just outside the morning room.

She chewed on her lip and clasped her hands nervously together. She ought to have alerted Lady Elle the moment she caught sight of him through the thick wall of the morning room. But as each second passed, particularly from the time Evanthea realized she was being observed by the marquis until she finally shut the door in his face, she found herself compelled to remain silent. Something wondrous had occurred, not especially in Evanthea, for she saw that her new friend held the remarkable attribute of being comfortable within the confines of her physical body, but rather in Brandreth. He had seen a new facet of Evanthea, one that would never have had occasion to arise in ordinary earthly circumstances! Never! It was the most brilliant stroke of good fortune that that silly house-keeper, Mrs. Brown—who was nearly as forgetful as she was platter-faced—had left the door ajar. Really, she could not have concocted a more helpful scheme herself and indeed wouldn't have, for she had assumed until this moment that all mortal women of gentle birth were deeply mortified by the state of undress, just as she had been.

Not Evanthea, Psyche thought as she tilted her head in curiosity to watch her friend pull her hair to the top of her head, then let it fall to the sides as she stood before the looking glass. She doubted, however, that her reaction would have been the same had either Mr. Shalford or Mr. Allenby been ogling her instead. Evanthea would probably not have failed to inform her great-aunt if either of these gentlemen was staring scandalously at her. Nor would she have crossed the room and shut the door to further expose her limbs to them as she had to Brandreth.

All in all, therefore, Psyche was pleased with what had transpired. Approaching Evanthea, she whispered that she found it necessary to return to Olympus for a brief time but that she would most definitely be present at the race on the morrow.

How saddened Evanthea appeared as she listened to her leave-taking, an expression that touched Psyche's heart. Impulsively, she embraced her friend and thanked her for listening so kindly to her tales of woe where Cupid was concerned.

"I fear I have been of little use to you," Evanthea said. "But how could I possibly comprehend what it is like to be married for several thousand years, nonetheless to Cupid! I only wish I could visit your home, Olympus! I vow I am intrigued beyond words."

"If only it were possible, but I fear if Zeus saw you, he would have both our heads, literally, and probably serve them up to the Cyclops!" She pretended to give a horrified shudder, then laughed all over again, since

Zeus had not done anything so truly despicable in centuries.

"Pray don't make me laugh," Evanthea whispered. "Annabelle would never understand and would probably think I've gone as mad as Bedlam. Only tell me, is Cupid truly so angry at your involvement here that he will not forgive you?"

"Much I care whether he does or not," Psyche said with a spirited pout. "I only wish . . . oh, never mind! If I don't leave now, I never shall!" After giving Evanthea another quick hug, she disappeared through the wall of the morning room, into the formal garden where she hurried toward the east and Olympus.

An hour later, Psyche sat mute with her heart dipping lower and lower into her stomach with every word Eros spoke to her. She was seated sideways on an elegant chaise longue of the purest, whitest silk damask, twisting the gold ribbons of her gown about her fingers. Her sandaled feet hung several inches off the amethyst and marble floor, and she thought if anyone observed her now they would think her a mischievous child rather than a grown woman.

"And for another thing, my wife, why is it you must continue to disobey Jupiter himself and involve yourself in the affairs of these absurd mortals? I don't understand your fascination with them. They are all hopeless creatures, as you very well know. . . ."

"I was a mortal once," she interjected quietly, staring at the weblike patterns of the amethyst as it swirled among the hard marble stone.

He appeared not to hear her. "And I don't need to tell you that a great deal of gossip is beginning to circulate about your activities, even among the lesser beings. The Eumenides have been laughing at your antics for some time. One of them, her snakes twisting wildly about in her hair, taunted me with her whip. *Where is your Psyche, oh, beloved one? If she does not take care, she will join us in the pit of hell. Zeus*

157

himself will send her there! You may imagine how I felt to learn that you, and therefore I — I — was being made sport of even from Erebus! Don't you care for my feelings anymore, Psyche? Do you think only of yourself?"

Psyche was not moved by this plea, which seemed to her to be centered entirely on Cupid's greater concern with the opinions of others than with the happiness of his wife. "I have done nothing with the intention of hurting you, Eros, only with finding amusement" — here she lifted her chin to him and held his gaze squarely — "that I might fill the lonely hours and days of my life."

"An entirely unsatisfactory response," he countered. "Whatever your feelings toward me — though I can only guess you think me a monster — I beg you to stop your involvement with the mortals. Should Zeus discover you have broken one of his most sacred commandments, I cannot protect you from his wrath. Besides, what are these mortals to you? They do not pay heed to the lessons Fate attempts patiently to teach them, nor do they honor us as is their duty. They have forgotten us entirely."

"Well, is there any wonder?" Psyche could not keep from crying. "For all the gods ever used to do was steal maidens from their families and their homes and deliver them up to other lascivious gods. And *Olympus forbid* if anyone crossed the wrong goddess at the wrong moment, for then you could be turned into a tree or a deer and cut down or slaughtered as pleased the offended deity. I only wonder that worship continued as long as it did. Too long, in my opinion!"

"You are speaking sacrilege," Cupid whispered. He had been pacing their bedchamber in great strides, his enormous wings causing all the thin muslins draped about their postered gilt bed to flutter like linens on a clothesline when a gust whirls through. But when she had spoken so heinous an opinion, he had stopped

158

abruptly, an expression of fear and deep hurt marring his face. Taking a single step toward her, he said, "I am afraid I will lose you to your erratic conduct. Don't you love me even a whit? Do you wish now I had never fallen in love with you, never taken you from your home and family?"

Psyche felt tears constrict her throat as she met his gaze, for he was clearly cut to the quick.

He added, "Is this what you have been attempting to tell me all these decades, that you never wished to become my wife, that you resent my having swept you away from your papa and your village, from all who have been dead for so many thousand years? Did I err so greatly, my love?"

Psyche nearly leapt from her unhappy seat as she regarded her heart's desire. She wanted to smooth away the pained ruffles in his brow and silence the words upon his lips by kissing him. But she had done so three times in the past century, and each time, only a sennight later, her spouse had reverted to his coldness and distance.

So she remained where she was and replied, "You oughtn't to have married me. Your mother was right. And of the moment, I do wish I had been buried with my family."

Once the words were spoken, it seemed as though a veritable dam of unrealized feelings again broke over her tender soul. Tears poured from her eyes, and she ran from the vaulted chamber to seek solace in the little painting room off the grand dining hall. There, she fell to her knees before a settee of the purest gold fabric and gave full expression to the unhappiness that had been dwelling in her heart for what seemed an eternity.

It was several hours later, when night had fallen, that Psyche finally arose from her aching knees. She was grateful Eros had not tried to follow her into what was her own little world. She no longer trusted him to

159

speak the words, nor to follow up his words with appropriate deeds, which would restore her affections for him completely. Her heart was closing up and the sensation of it was sheer pain. She began thinking of Evanthea, reviewing every recent significant turn of events with great care, finding yet again that her own pain dimmed in stages to almost nothing. She wanted to tell Cupid that she helped the mortals because in offering her assistance, especially where matters of the heart were concerned, she could find a measure of peace for herself, just as she did now. But how could he possibly understand?

Feeling much better, she glanced about the chamber, delighting in its varied designs and colors, the whole scheme as different from most of Olympus as night was from day. Using bright greens, blues, and violets, she had painted butterflies all over one wall, the delicate creatures fluttering above a meadow of tall grasses. She had woven fabrics herself, since none like the ones she had wanted to have in her private chamber existed in the shops abounding throughout the kingdom. The fabrics were of deep reds and purples, out of which she had fabricated pillows that now littered her settee. On the walls next to and opposite the butterfly wall hung her paintings, amounting to nearly twenty in all, half of which were portraits, the other half landscapes. The latter were of earth, several of the village she came from, and several more of England, which was her most favorite place to visit in this century.

Eros disliked the chamber immensely and two decades ago had set it down as vulgar, afterward refusing ever to enter it again.

For that she had been grateful, since she could always rely upon being left completely alone while closeted in her painting room.

Psyche checked the clock on a table near the door and saw that it was eight minutes after eleven. She listened to the traffic of the night and heard only the silence of sleep. Everyone seemed to retire early on Olympus — unless, of course, Bacchus was giving one of his notorious *fetes* — and she found it a simple matter to travel through the streets completely unnoticed, which was precisely what she needed to do now. She had not mentioned the matter to Evanthea but her purpose in returning to Olympus when she did had not been to see her husband, but rather to transgress her mama-in-law's apartments again and to steal both the cestus she had returned to Venus as well as the bottles of love potions. It was time to bring Brandreth and Evanthea together at last.

Chapter Eighteen

Psyche slipped from her palace into the soft, misty night, her sandaled feet silent against the mother-of-pearl streets as she moved with butterfly quickness toward Aphrodite's abode. She wore a gossamer cloak of thin gauze over her shoulders, which floated behind her like a billowing sail. The long, winding avenues that connected palace to palace, grove to grove, shop to shop, were lit in sparkling intervals with oil lamps. A sense of exhilaration had already begun to flow in her veins, quickening her steps and lightening her heart. She breathed deeply of the moist night air, each breath causing her to feel giddy with excitement.

Whenever she appropriated articles of the gods and goddesses—for the strict benefit of those mortals in whose lives she was involved, of course—she always felt beyond content. She sighed happily, racing through the streets as though she had wings on her feet like the messenger Mars.

Everywhere, wildlife and herbage proliferated, the mild scent of lilies, the blossoms of the pomegranate tree, and the cry of peacocks heralding Juno's palace. Psyche was particularly frightened of the vengeful goddess who was married to Zeus and she hurried past.

Athena's owls, which were the warrior goddess's favorite animal, hooted at her as she passed by her home. Her gardens were landscaped in terrace after terrace of beautifully pruned and shaped olive trees.

The tall silhouette of young, green cornstalks, which could be seen waving above the walls of Demeter's palace, greeted her eyes next. Of all the goddesses, Psyche was most partial to this wife of Zeus, whom all the other deities taunted by calling her Corn Goddess — an affectionate nickname the people of earth had given her. Much Demeter cared, Psyche thought with pride. Demeter loved the earth and the mortals, and whenever she could she blessed those who labored in the fields and produced food for the cities of the world. The avenue leading to her palace was a sea of beautiful orange poppies and yellow daffodils, which surrounded several ponds in which cranes walked about on long, stately legs.

When the heavy fragrance of roses and the murmur of hundreds of doves assailed her senses, Psyche slowed her pace.

Roses were her mama-in-law's favorite flower, and the doves drew Aphrodite's chariot through the skies.

Psyche stopped beneath an oil lamp, its faint, dewy light casting a glimmering shadow on the mother-of-pearl beneath her sandals. She clutched her light cloak tightly about her shoulders, some of her excitement dissolving into terror at the thought of what she meant to do — yet again. Treachery was the only word for the crime she was about to commit. How could she even think of stealing from her mama-in-law? Of course, she had but to consider how much mother and son seemed aligned in both their ill opinion of her as well as their desire to see her conform to their joint perceptions of just how she ought to behave, and her initial resistance to stealing the cestus and the vials of love potion dwindled to a small gnat of fear in her stomach — a gnat that was soon squashed by the excitement the mere thought of thievery brought to her heart.

Onward, she set her feet.

At the distance of one hundred yards, Psyche could see Aphrodite's palace clearly. There were no doors on the majestic palace and the window apertures were without glass. Crime was unheard of in Olympus, only retribution and vengeance ruled the land. As for a protection against the elements, the weather was wondrously temperate. Olympus knew rain only as the gentlest of mists and the sun's rays were welcome as a soothing balm on the skin.

When Psyche's initial fright began to subside, all former excitement became sharp and pleasurable. Using the alley on the east side of the palace, a breezy lane that separated Aphrodite's home from Artemis's, Psyche quickly gained the back door of the formidable mansion. The proportions of Venus's abode were lofty, the ceilings rising to nearly thirty feet, the walls supported by Corinthian columns and decorated with both intricate latticework, sheets of marble, and sometimes lengths of exquisite white- and rose-colored fabrics. These latter were laced with gold filaments, and when a wind would rise, rushing through the house, the lengths of cloth would shimmer like waves on the sea at sunset.

Everywhere, roses, enhanced by maidenhair ferns, filled heavy crystal vases. The fragrance was nearly overpowering to Psyche, an accurate reflection, she mused, of her mama-in-law's temperament — *overpowering.*

Venus's bedchamber was located in the center of the house, and as Psyche stole into the lavish apartments, she noted again with awe that in a marvel of architectural technique the roof had been set at an angle and left open to the sky, in order to allow the stars to shine in upon Aphrodite's bed at night. She glanced at the bed and saw that Venus was there, asleep. She was quite startled, for this was the first time in so many thousand years she had actually seen her mama-in-law asleep. Her earlier thefts had been during the day when she knew Venus was absent. When she saw her now, she thought the deity had never looked more kind nor more vulnerable. She slept, childlike, with one hand beneath her cheek.

Psyche drew closer still to better look at her, thinking that only in sleep could Aphrodite appear so harmless and sweet. Once her wrath was aroused, Olympus help everyone! She had heard enough tales of Venus's exploits in centuries past to last her an eternity.

As she stared down at her husband's mother, she suddenly knew a longing for the comfort of her own mama, a thought that brought harsh tears to her eyes. If only Venus had welcomed her as a real daughter, how much she would have enjoyed her new home. With Cupid's love, her life had been tolerably happy, but without it, particularly in the face of Aphrodite's continual harangue, Olympus had been a prison she could not escape.

On these thoughts, her resolve to continue her involvements in Bedfordshire sharpened and she returned quickly to her former purpose. She crossed the chamber to Venus's wardrobe, where the deity kept all of her jewels, robes, adornments, secret potions, and other weapons of love, chiefly the cestus.

Since Psyche had been there once before when she had first taken possession of the gold velvet belt, she knew precisely where her booty was located. Knowing that Venus was of a structured mind, she was not surprised that her mama-in-law had returned the cestus to the exact place it had been before. She could have laughed at her mama-in-law's stupidity. Did Venus really think she would never attempt to steal it again? She smiled to herself, thinking that Aphrodite was as trapped by her own obsessive qualities as Psyche was bound to displease her husband by her unfailingly mortal ways.

Just as she slipped both the vial for the love potion

and the vial for its antidote into the pocket of her gown, she heard a noise that originated not from the bed, but from somewhere near the entrance to the bedchamber. Her heart immediately picked up its cadence and threatened to pound through her ribs. Was someone else in the palace with her? Or perhaps one of the doves had gotten trapped in the lofty ceilings of the palace and could not find its way out?

This latter thought caused her to breathe a sigh of relief. Surely it was just one of the doves.

Rolling up the cestus, she tucked the thick velvet belt beneath her arm and left the wardrobe. Silently, she picked her way across the cool marble floor and disappeared into the dark hallway beyond, not once hearing Aphrodite stir upon her bed.

Swiftly, Psyche hurried through the palace, heading for the same back entrance she had first used to steal into Venus's mansion. A darkened doorway, leading to the bedchamber in which the goddess's maid, Penny, slept, was the final obstacle to the completion of her crime. Only when she had successfully left the palace could it actually be determined she had stolen anything from Venus.

She held her breath, slowing her pace to a tiptoe march, her gaze fixed on the shadowed aperture. Psyche was nearly beyond it, when a hand reached out, grabbed her roughly, closed another hand about her mouth, and dragged her backward several steps.

She was so frightened by the sudden attack, and so surprised by the violence of it as well as by the obvious strength of her assailant — surely poor little Penny could not have captured her so easily! — that her first instinct was to struggle mightily.

A voice, familiar and irritating, rang in her ear. "Do stop kicking up such a dust, Psy, or you will awaken Mama's maid."

"Anteros!" Psyche whispered viciously as he removed his hand from her mouth. Anger flooded her,

166

serving to replace the fear she had previously felt. "What in Hades do you mean by accosting me like this?"

"And what are you doing in Mama's apartments?"

The hallway was dark and all that was visible of Anteros, Cupid's younger brother, was a dim outline of the hateful sibling's black wings. He was as different from Cupid as water was from ice. His skin was olive in complexion, compared to Cupid's fair tones, and his eyes were a hard, steely gray, always cold and arrogant, while Eros had an open, confident look that emanated from his rich, brown eyes. But in greatest contrast was Anteros's silver hair, so shocking next to Cupid's blond curls, which seemed to glow in the night and presented a strange beacon even in the hallway.

What lie could she manufacture for the cunning god of rejected love? "I — I —" Psyche had no answer for him as she drew away from his grasp and felt for the vials tucked into her pocket. Mercifully, they were still in place and unbroken, but somewhere on the floor lay the cestus. "I merely came to see if — if your mother was sleeping well. She complained to me the other day of having some difficulty —"

"What a rapper!" Anteros interjected with a snort. "And since when have you become concerned for the sleeping habits of the dragon queen?"

"I have always felt compassion for your mama. I know she and I seem to rub one another, but does that mean I cannot show her affection?"

"If she had ever shown even the smallest mite of concern for you or anything bordering on one of the warmer sentiments, I could agree with you. As it is, I find your conduct quite suspect and I begin to wonder if the rumors about you — about your unfortunate habit of *stealing* — are not true after all."

"Rumors you undoubtedly started or confirmed, beast!" Anteros had already witnessed her steal one of

167

Artemis's bows and even a sword from Vulcan's workshop. He was merely taunting her with his words. Psyche had only one objective now: to find the cestus and to escape Anteros's piercing scrutiny before he awakened the household.

"You wound me," he responded, still whispering as he placed a hand against his heart. "I would never reveal anything of your exploits or *ours!*"

"*Ours?*" Psyche queried, startled.

He chuckled. "Our previous affair—"

"We had no affair, Anteros," she countered readily. "It was all in your mind! Just because I permitted you, in a moment of great stupidity, to kiss me does not mean we were ever in the least . . . er . . . *entangled.*"

Stepping backward, she felt her heel sink into the soft fabric of the cestus. She dropped quickly to retrieve it, ending her conversation with, "I suggest you let your imagination run in more profitable channels and leave me to live my own life." Then Psyche turned on her heel and headed back to the main hall.

Once there, however, with the flutter of wings growing louder behind her with each step she took, she was not surprised to find that Anteros leaped to place himself between her and the door.

"Had I found you first," he began, impassioned, "you would have loved me and not my weakling brother! Admit you were—are—fascinated by me. How else can you explain your willingness to submit to the kiss we shared, a kiss I don't hesitate to remind you left you quite weak-willed. Had I but carried you away to my palace, which I most certainly could have—"

"Had you done so, a war would have erupted, and I've little doubt that either you or your brother or even the pair of you would have been killed or banished forever to tote barges on the River Styx."

"I wouldn't have cared," he responded in a throaty whisper. "I am willing to die for you. What of Eros? Has he even come near you in the past decade?"

Psyche wished more than immortality itself that he was not so observant. Feeling her throat constrict yet again with the pain of her current estrangement from Cupid, she cried, "What does it matter whether he has or not? I am not such a simpleton as to think I could ever be happy with you!"

"I could make you happy. I could! And I want to."

"You only want to best your brother. That is all you have ever really wanted, Anteros. I am not as clever as most of the residents of Olympus, but even I know at least that much."

"You are wrong," he responded. Suddenly, his arms and wings had enveloped her, holding her captive in their tight circle.

Psyche had not been kissed in a very long time, and the mere closeness and warmth of Anteros's passionate, intense embrace affected her deeply. Desire to remain with him, to submit to his obvious lust for her, rose to an almost uncontrollable pitch. She found herself responding, despicably so, to his lips, which importuned her fiercely. "No," she murmured as he kissed her cheeks, her eyes, her lips, ever so gently. "You mustn't."

"You love me," he commanded, kissing her again briefly. "You love me. You have ever since we danced together at Zeus's masquerade two hundred years ago . . . the same night I kissed you."

"I had imbibed too much of Bacchus's new wine, you know I had."

"Then tell me why you cling to me now?" he cried, holding her roughly and tilting her head back with his hand to permit the starlight from the back doorway to flood her face.

"What more could you expect from a neglected housewife?" she responded quietly, feeling broken and alone.

He held her only for a moment, until he came to a sharp awareness of what her words meant. He then released her with an expression of hurt passing across his handsome features. "You still love him, don't you, Butterfly?"

Psyche nodded. She watched him blink and thought that in one way at least the brothers were nearly identical—in their features. Perhaps that was why Psyche found herself drawn to the dark brother, since the handsome shape of his nose, the arch of his brows, the cleft of his chin, were the same as Cupid's.

Anteros backed away from her to stand mute beside the doorway. "Go," he murmured. "I will not stop you."

Psyche swallowed hard as she again rolled the cestus up between fingers that now shook. She again tucked it beneath her arm, and as she passed by Anteros, she said, "I am sorry that my heart cannot be given. I beg however, that you will not tell Venus I was here."

"Of course I will not," was his quiet, gentlemanly reply.

As Psyche stepped into the moonlight, she heard Aphrodite's doves flutter their wings as they rose in a quick rush up into the misty night air. Higher they swirled to a height of nearly fifty feet, before finally dropping back to their dovecote to rest. Vaguely, she wondered what had startled them into flight, but then dismissed her concern in face of her pressing need to place as much distance between herself and Aphrodite's palace as soon as possible.

Shutting her recent encounter with Anteros completely out of her mind, as though it had not even happened, she set her feet toward Cupid's palace, where she would remain until the following morning, until eleven o'clock, when the race between Shalford and Brandreth would begin.

Eros rose higher and higher into the sky, the sounds of his beating wings having been disguised by the flight of the doves. He was spiraling upward toward the brightest star, his heart near to bursting. Pain seemed to explode in his chest, throat, and head, a blinding pain he had experienced only once before when he had first seen Psyche in the arms of his brother. Anger spilled through the pain, turning into hatred as quickly as fireworks might burst onto a night sky. He hated his wife, he hated his brother. Somehow he would find a way to take revenge upon them both.

Upward he soared, until the air grew thin and he found it increasingly difficult to breathe. Only then did he stop his wings and set them back toward Olympus, spreading them to a twelve-foot span and riding the gentle currents of the night air.

He had followed Psyche to his mother's palace and was only waiting for her to return the way she had come before approaching her about her misdeeds. Mostly, he wanted to see for himself that her purpose had been to steal something from his mother yet again before he confronted her. But when he had heard the ensuing conversation between his wife and his brother, he had waited only until he had seen Psyche give herself so thoroughly to Anteros's embraces, before leaving the faithless pair. He had heard Psyche deny her affections for Anteros, but he was not fool enough to believe she had no sentiments whatsoever, when she all but cast herself upon his chest.

So it was true, he thought, crushed. Psyche loved Anteros and, for all her silly protests, had done so for nearly two hundred years.

His only interest now was in discovering the very best form of retribution possible. As he gently glided toward his palace, his thoughts flew quickly, one after the next, until — as though inspired by Zeus himself — he knew precisely what he ought to do.

Chapter Nineteen

On the following morning, Evanthea was gazing into the looking glass in her bedchamber and could not credit her eyes. She was certain that some bizarre apparition had taken her place in the mirror, for she did not recognize her own image. How was it possible that the cut of one's hair could go so far in changing one's appearance?

But it wasn't just her hair that had caused the miracle. For though the full chignon caught up to the crown of her head and further adorned with a delicate fringe of curls upon her forehead complemented the shape of her face to perfection, Evanthea realized it was the sum of her toilette that had so effected the startling change.

As she touched the pretty pearl and diamond drops upon each earlobe, she could see that it was the combination of jewels, hair fashion, bonnet, new silk stockings, pretty embroidered slipperlike shoes, and her delightful walking gown that served to complete the task.

She was not wearing her spectacles — which all three ladies, Annabelle, Psyche, and Lady Elle, had insisted she dispense with for today's race — and could only clearly see herself when she was but a foot away from the looking glass. She simply did not recognize the Evanthea she knew as she touched her fingers to the cool glass and smoothed her tips over the reflection of her green silk bonnet trimmed with white ruffles, the tall, but flat crown decorated with a single bunch of glossy cherries. Past the bonnet, she touched the curls upon her forehead and downward to her pretty, arched brows. Here she paused in the tracing of her finger, for she realized that even though she appeared so different, her features could not have changed. Her brown eyes were still brown; her nose was still straight and, as Psyche had told her, patrician in form; her face was yet as oval as it had always been. How could she appear to such advantage with only a change of *decor?*

Her gown was finer than any she had ever yet worn, though the very sort Annabelle had been accustomed to wearing nearly from birth. The tight, high bodice and puffed, long sleeves had been constructed of Annabelle's green silk and matched the bonnet. At the shoulders, a stand of elegant Brussels lace gave the appearance of soft, elegant epaulettes. The collar rose to a high stand at the back of her neck, trimmed in white lace and descending at an angle to her breastbone, opening slightly at the throat and revealing the smallest pearl broach pinned to a thin ribbon of green silk. Her fingertip touched the glass at precisely the spot where the broach was reflected in the mirror. She felt awed by the experience.

Her gaze drifted to where her bodice joined the waist of her skirt. How clever the ladies had been, wishing to accent the smallness of her waist. They had done so by shaping the sides to slightly follow her figure, letting the remaining fabric gather high in the back as was the fashion. The two layers of soft cambric that comprised the skirt and so neatly held to her figure draped to a charming double tier, both of which were trimmed in points of ribbon that faced upward and were balanced with points of lace that led the eye to her pretty embroidered green slippers.

How hard all the needlewomen had labored, sewing

until all hours of the morning to achieve such an extraordinary result. She had but to slip on her gloves of white silk and her costume was complete.

As she turned, almost in a stupor, to retrieve her gloves from her dressing table, Evanthea was startled by a quick rap on the door and Annabelle's subsequent abrupt, enthusiastic entrance.

"There you are!" she cried, with a bright smile in her green eyes and upon her pink, bowed lips. "Everyone is waiting! Why ever do you dawdle, or is it . . . oh, Evanthea! . . ." She broke off suddenly, her entrance into the room coming to a complete halt as the change in Evanthea suddenly struck her. She blinked twice and shook her head in disbelief. "I had imagined that you would suffer an improvement but not a *transformation!* Evan, you have become quite beautiful! I vow, you will break every heart today. I am sure of it."

These last words were spoken in an almost disbelieving hush and Evanthea found herself very uncomfortable. She ought to have been pleased with the younger woman's dumbfounded response to her appearance, but because she was intuitive, Evanthea realized it wasn't only surprise that had been reflected in Annabelle's eyes, but fear as well, an anxiety that she knew was often the foundation for nothing short of jealousy. She experienced the most absurd desire to reassure Annabelle but suppressed the impulse as absurd. After all, nothing had really changed and the younger woman's court was well-established. Thoughts of jealousy, however, caused her to wonder if much of Aphrodite's unkindness toward Psyche emanated from something as simple as her jealousy of the younger woman's exquisite face, hair, and figure. Somehow, she knew it was true.

Stepping forward and ignoring Annabelle's now-worried expression, Evanthea took the younger woman's hand in her own and expressed yet again her

174

gratitude for Annabelle's unselfishness. "I only hope you are pleased with the results."

Annabelle appeared to swallow very hard, smiling what Evanthea could only term a decidedly brittle smile, and responded, "Of course I am, Evan! How could you doubt it? I am certain Mr. Shalford will be utterly enchanted!"

Evanthea took her by the arm and guided her toward the door. She immediately begged to know where Annabelle had gotten her own charming gown of light blue silk adorned with gold braid. "From your London modiste, I've little doubt?" she queried.

Annabelle murmured that it was indeed the case, but had Lady Elle not joined them in the hallway before descending the stairs, Evanthea was certain their conversation would have languished. Having reigned for so long, Annabelle was destined to suffer from being usurped by Evanthea, even if it was only for the brief space of time required for everyone to adjust to her transformed appearance.

Lady Elle, however, hugged Evanthea so hard when she first laid eyes on her that the girl could scarcely breathe. Her whisper of encouragement, which landed in Evanthea's ear and could not be heard by Annabelle, caused her heart to quiver, *"He will be astounded, my dear, and then we shall see . . . oh, yes, indeed! We shall see!"*

Evanthea wanted to tell her she was speaking absurdly, but odd tears clogged her throat as Lady Elle leaned slightly away from her and released her, only to take each of her hands within her gentle grasp and give her fingers a tight squeeze. This last gesture was nearly her undoing as tears now brimmed in her eyes. She had always known that her great-aunt loved her as a daughter, but in this moment she sensed that she had been her own special mission for a long, long time.

"I don't know if I told either of you," Lady Elle said, releasing Evanthea and changing the subject entirely, "but I hired the parlor at the George Inn for a celebration in honor of the winner of the race. Naturally, I've invited all those families with whom Annabelle spoke yesterday concerning the ball tonight to join us." With a gleam in her eye as the ladies began descending the stairs, she addressed Evanthea, "Besides, I thought it might help our cause if you were presented to all of the unattached gentlemen at once. It will do no harm at all for *him* to see you as an object of general interest! The more hearts you enslave, the more *he* will desire you."

"I wish you would not speak so," Evanthea whispered. "I have no such designs nor do I wish to enslave anyone." She believed what she said completely, except that for some very disturbing reason, when her thoughts turned to Brandreth, she wondered again and again if he could be enslaved, if his affections could be affected by a new bonnet, a dazzling gown, and pretty eardrops.

Ever since Brandreth had kissed her and gentled in his manners toward her, Evanthea had experienced profound sentiments where he was concerned. Chief among them this morning was a terrible hope that he, above all others, would be pleased with her new walking gown. She suspected she had begun to form an attachment to the marquis and it frightened her, since she was convinced he could never really return her regard. How had it all happened, and so quickly? she wondered, glancing down at her smooth white gloves, hoping her thoughts were indiscernible. How had it happened that a seed of love for Brandreth had begun growing so rapidly and so fiercely in her heart that when Lady Elle had said *He will be astounded,* Evanthea's heart had nearly cried out with joy.

"It's not true, anyway," Annabelle said with a pout, interrupting the unsettling train of Evanthea's thoughts. She was standing slightly apart from Lady Elle and Evanthea as they waited in the entrance hall for their carriage to be brought round. "Brandreth has never been moved by the sight of me surrounded by beaus. Indeed, I have always had the impression he was laughing at me. As for Shalford, he is even worse than Brandreth and thinks my flirtations are wicked! If you hope to *enslave* Shalford, I suggest you remain aloof from all the other gentlemen."

Evanthea stared in surprise at Annabelle, whose gaze shifted guiltily away from her.

Lady Elle only responded quietly, "Well, to be sure, Shalford would not value such conduct—or at least insist he does not—but I have yet to meet a man who does not attach more value to a horse that is exclaimed over by a half-dozen Melton men than one that is not!"

Evanthea could not resist giving her great-aunt a teasing, gentle pinch on her arm. "Do you compare me, then, to a horse? You are as bad as Papa, and twice as hopeless."

Lady Elle lifted her chin, her eyes sparkling, "No one will dare say anything like that of you today!" She sighed with great satisfaction and bid Meppers to throw open the front doors. "We are going to the village, Meppers, and into the future!"

Chapter Twenty

Gregory Shalford stood on the gravel drive with his back to the house and shook his head, his fists planted firmly on his hips, his whip, secured in one clenched fist, jutting out behind him. He was facing the avenue of lime trees, where his scarred gig drifted slightly with each movement of his restless horses. When Shalford had passed Brandreth just before turning down Lady Elle's drive, the vicar felt a bolt of jealousy afflict him with such strength that he swore if he had not been seated, he would have toppled from his light Stanhope gig.

Brandreth's gleaming black curricle with its new wheels and tight springs made his own ancient vehicle appear like a dung cart by comparison. Ordinarily, he was able to dismiss disparity of fortune, but today— especially given the extraordinary turnout for the race all along the highway into town—he found himself irritated with envy.

He felt a sudden desire to kick the gig in front of him. The old, faithful Stanhope had seen its prime over twelve years earlier and since then had known intimately every type of weather imaginable. The wood of the wheels had swollen in the heat of summer, traveling on macadamized roads, and constricted in the harsh freeze of winter as it carried him from cottage to cottage and back in the usual rounds of parish duties.

And his horses! Lord bless them, he thought unhappily. They were a sturdy, quick pair—one brown, the other black with a white star on its forehead—but hardly a match for Brandreth's chestnuts.

With a grunt of frustration, he slapped his buckskin breeches with the handle of his whip.

"But I thought you were supposed to use that on the horses, Mr. Shalford," a voice called to him from the direction of the lodge.

He recognized Evanthea's voice and, after composing his spirits, turned around to greet her. Shalford felt a wave of confusion assail him, for before him were three ladies, two of whom he recognized—Annabelle and Lady Elle. He frowned slightly at the third and glanced to his right and left, first wondering where Evanthea was, then wondering who this stunning creature was standing to the right of the other ladies. He had heard no gossip about the arrival of an unexpected visitor at the manor and felt his cheeks grow warm with consternation.

"How odd!" he cried as the ladies smiled mischievously at him. "I thought I heard Evan . . ." He broke off. The smile on the third female was deucedly familiar.

"Good God!" he cried, taking two halting steps forward and peering at Evanthea in what he was sure was a rude manner. "Is that you? Impossible!"

Annabelle, pert and lively in her blue silk, blond curls peeping from beneath a white muslin bonnet trimmed with white satin ribbons, stepped forward. "Isn't it incredible!" she cried, playfully taking his arm and drawing him near to Evanthea. "I do not wonder that you stare, even though I must say, you show a great want of character and manners in doing so. And yes, it is *our* Evanthea!"

Shalford approached Evanthea with his heart in his throat. He would never have believed it possible she could appear to such advantage. He extended his hand to her as one in a stupor. When she gave him her own, instead of merely shaking it as was his custom with her, he lifted her fingers to his lips and kissed them softly.

"Shalford!" she cried, evidently surprised.

"I—I beg your pardon for not at first recognizing you, but I hope you will forgive me."

"Of course I will. I only hope you don't mean to fuss over me, or I'll tell you now we shan't be friends any longer." She then glanced meaningfully at her hand, which was still held in his firm grasp.

"Oh, I say!" he cried with a laugh, his cheeks again becoming heated and uncomfortable. He gently released her fingers and continued to smile stupidly at her.

Eros sat in the branches of the foremost lime tree and removed a single arrow from the quiver strapped to his back. He had but barely recognized Evanthea himself from his last visit to earth, remembering only a rather tall, unimpressive female with little knowledge of fashion. But here, in an exquisite gown and bonnet and transformed with the help of his wife's hand, no doubt, she could rival even his mother—oh, what a blasphemous thought! He knew Psyche was most concerned for Evanthea's happiness, and most especially that she intended for Evanthea to become leg-shackled to the Marquis of Brandreth. To this point, he was directing his efforts not to help her cause, but to hinder it!

He slipped the arrow into the strong filament of his bow and, with the strength and control acquired from centuries of practice, drew the arrow backward, steadily and firmly. He sighted his target, the swell of Evanthea's bosom beneath the green silk, and took a deep breath. Perhaps he couldn't change the fact that his wife was in love with his own brother, perhaps he

180

couldn't make her love him anymore, perhaps he couldn't forgive her for her infidelity, but he could make her as unhappy as he was by causing Evanthea to fall in love with Mr. Shalford! Psyche delighted so much in orchestrating the love lives of others that he knew well the pain and unhappiness she would suffer if her schemes were destroyed.

He took another deep breath, closed one eye, leaned his cheek near to the soft feathers of the arrow. One second more . . .

"Cupid! Whatever are you doing?"

With a sharp jerk and a twang, the arrow of love flew erratically through the air and struck, not Evanthea's heart but — good God! — Annabelle's posterior.

"Oh, my," Annabelle murmured, placing a discreet hand upon her hip. She felt as though she had just been stung by a wasp in the center of her buttock and wondered how it was possible a large flying insect had been able to climb up the inside of her skirts. She thought an accompanying pain would follow the attack, but instead, her flesh grew warm where the sting had occurred and she felt the gentlest of heat begin spreading over her skin in outward, continuous circles, until it felt as though her entire body was aglow. She looked up at Shalford and felt curiously nauseous, yet exhilarated all at once.

Goodness! What was happening to her?

Annabelle regarded his profile as though seeing him for the first time. He was quite handsome, she realized, and wondered why she had not noticed it before. That he had kissed Evanthea's fingers had nothing to do with it, of course. At least, not precisely. Come to think of it, she didn't like it at all, the way he was fawning over Evanthea.

Annabelle watched the blush on his cheeks and felt quite strange suddenly, as well as completely distressed. She perpetually brangled with Shalford, to be sure, and she disliked nearly everything about him, from the stuffy manner in which he was always picking at her, to his clothes that weren't in the least fashionably cut like Brandreth's, but that didn't mean she had *no* attachment to him. As a matter of fact, it dawned on her, as one awaking from a dream, that she was deeply attached to the man.

The realization so startled Annabelle that for a moment she simply stopped breathing. When had Gregory Shalford become so important to her happiness? She did not know, but the more she considered the true state of her heart, the more she understood that she had been in love with him for a very long time, perhaps from the first when he made it clear that her silly flirtations were of no interest to him. How often had she been pursued by fortune hunters so willing to pander to her vanity? Yet here was Gregory Shalford, a proud gentleman, living in relative poverty in her great-aunt's quite obscure village and completely uninterested in one of England's wealthiest heiresses. He had always been unamused by her cajoling and wheedling, but once, not long ago, they had engaged in serious conversation and the good vicar had actually hinted to her of his love for the army. He denied, of course, having ever wished for anything other than his career in the church, but his guard had been sufficiently lowered in that moment for her to see the longings of the impoverished man beneath his discreet heart.

He is such an excellent gentleman, Annabelle thought as she continued to watch him. How was it she had been so prejudiced against him that she could not fully value his character until now?

She looked over his bottle-green coat, buckskin waistcoat and breeches, and dusty top boots, thinking that with her fortune, she could rig him out in real style. As it was, he couldn't afford a master like Weston or Stultz. And with her fortune, he could even purchase a pair of colors if he so desired it.

He remained chatting with Evanthea, and the longer he attended to her, the more she experienced a profound fear that either he would tumble in love with Evanthea or that her own wretched manners of the past two years had effectually put herself beyond the pale where his affections were concerned.

She watched Shalford smile down upon Evanthea with just such a mooncalf expression as caused her heart to flip over. Shalford couldn't fall in love with Evanthea just yet! Not when she had just come to realize how very much she loved him!

"What do you mean, you did not intend to hit Annabelle?" Psyche cried, standing on the ground near the lime tree and staring up at her husband. She saw mostly his knees, shins and sandals, which were visible from beneath his short toga of white cambric.

"You heard me," Cupid responded coldly. "You startled me and my aim went awry. Annabelle was not my target."

"Then Shalford?" Psyche pressed, confused as much by his presence in Bedfordshire as by his objective.

"No."

"Evanthea?" Psyche cried, horrified. "But Brandreth is not here. If you had struck her she could have—could have—Not Shalford! Not when you know how I particularly mean for her to marry the marquis. Do you tell me you meant for her to tumble in love with Shalford? But why?"

Cupid leaned over the branch and tumbled forward, stopping himself from falling to the ground by one hard beat of his wings. Standing before her, he responded, "Because I am sick to death of your machinations on behalf of these ridiculous mortals. And I thought to have a little fun! Something you are quite proficient at. Last night, it occurred to me that you are always dashing off, hither and yon, while I wait for you to return. . . . And you rarely do, or if you do, it is in the small hours of the morning—" Here he paused and narrowed his eyes at her. Psyche realized he must have known at what hour she returned from her *visit* to Aphrodite's mansion, and she felt the blood drain from her face. He seemed satisfied with the expression on her face and continued, "—and I am left to while away the years of my life reading the latest scrolls from Jupiter's palace and not enjoying myself one whit."

"Not enjoying yourself! What about the time I found you transformed into a mortal shape and flirting with that truly wretched female in Gloucestershire? Not enjoying yourself! What humbug! After all, it was you who . . ."

Evanthea knew that Shalford was paying her a string of outrageous compliments but of the moment she was entirely distracted by the sight of Psyche, whom she could see just to the right of the vicar's shoulder, arguing heatedly with the most magnificent man she had ever set eyes on. Beyond the fact that he had a pair of enormous white wings that gave off the faintest hum every time even the smallest breeze crossed the avenue, he was simply gorgeous. His golden hair was curled in a delightful halo about his head, *à la Cherubim,* his nose was straight and pinched just below the bridge in a ghastly attractive manner, and his jawline was marked, rugged, and led in a firm line to a cleft chin. *Kissed by angels,* she thought with a smile. His lips were full and sensuous, and his eyes were large and piercing as he watched Psyche.

This must be Cupid, she thought. Except for Brandreth, she had never before seen such a wondrous face and figure, and such a remarkable *leg,* as her aunt would surely agree. When gentlemen used to wear satin knee breeches and silk stockings, it was an absolute requirement of fashion that a man's leg appear shapely and attractive. But nothing was as pleasing as the sight of Cupid's leg, strapped with the golden leather ribbons of his sandals from the ankle to the knee. In addition, his draped short tunic, belted at the waist, exposed muscular thighs. He was clearly a powerful man, however much modern poetry presented him as a baby with a silly miniature bow and arrows and wings the size of a butterfly's. She could easily see why Psyche was madly and hopelessly in love with her husband. But whatever was Cupid doing here? Psyche had already told her that Cupid wanted nothing to do with her schemes in Bedfordshire.

Whatever his purpose in coming to Flitwick Lodge, Evanthea was sorry to see that the god of love had begun arguing immediately with his wife, instead of simply taking her in his arms and kissing her as she knew Psyche so longed for him to do.

"Do you see that?" Lady Elle whispered to her. "I wonder what is wrong."

Both ladies by now had leaned at an angle to peer around Mr. Shalford's arm.

"I cannot imagine, but from what I understand, the problems are of a long-standing nature," Evanthea returned quietly, forgetting for a moment that Shalford was speaking to her. The last few words she had heard from him were something about being allowed to carry her kerchief into battle. But she could not seem to drag her attention away from husband and wife long enough to give him an answer.

"He appears to be very angry," she added. "I only wish I could hear what he is saying."

"Who?" Shalford queried. "Who is angry?"

As one, both ladies drew to attention in front of the vicar and gasped in turn. "No one!" Evanthea re-

sponded, startled to have been so caught up in the unfolding scene before her that she had actually risked
exposing herself to Shalford. "That is, I thought I saw
Brandreth at — at the end of the avenue! He seemed
rather piqued."

Shalford and Annabelle both turned around. Lady
Elle exchanged a glance with Evanthea and added, in
support of her halting whisker, "I thought I saw him,
too, but now he is gone. Didn't you say you passed
him along the lane coming toward the manor, Mr.
Shalford?"

The vicar turned back, a confused furrow between
his brows. "I did pass him, but I don't recall having
said as much."

Lady Elle nodded. "Well, I am not at all surprised,"
she returned enigmatically, "since you know I can't
hear very well. My great-nephew informed me earlier
that he meant to take his chestnuts out before the race
to warm them up, but I didn't see him. I wonder what
is keeping Sidlow with our carriage. Oh, dear, where is
that man? The race will begin in but a few minutes,
and I had so wished to be at the village by now. We intend to watch you cross the finish line, Mr. Shalford,
indeed we do! I have wagered a guinea on you. I trust
you mean to best Lord Brandreth?"

Evanthea had been acquainted with Gregory
Shalford for several years and comprehended his character as well as did Lady Elle. The question was meant
to tease the vicar since, for all his efforts to curtail his
competitive nature in light of the decorous requirements of his position as a clergyman of the Church of
England, he entered into every challenge determined
to win.

He bowed slightly to Lady Elle and, with a lift of his
brow, responded politely, "I hope I do not disappoint
you, ma'am, but I do wish you had not wagered on
me." He cast a disparaging glance toward his gig and
pair.

"I'm sure you will acquit yourself with honor, Mr. Shalford," Lady Elle said, patting him on the shoulder.

He smiled and thanked her for her confidence in him, then turned to Evanthea and said, "But you have not told me whether you will bestow your kerchief on me. I would be deeply grateful if you would."

"Of course, I shall," Evanthea responded. Without hesitation, she drew a colorful embroidered handkerchief from her reticule and handed it to him. In taking the kerchief from her, he permitted his fingers to touch hers, and for the first time in the entire interchange, Evanthea realized that Shalford was flirting with her. When she placed her attention fully upon him, she could not help but notice the warm glint in his eye.

He continued, "I would also take this moment to beg your hand for the first dance this evening. I suspect that once you appear among what I understand will be a considerable throng of sporting men this afternoon, you will no doubt be besieged with requests in preparation for the ball this evening. What say you, Evanthea? Will you trust me to lead you down the first two sets?"

Evanthea nodded her acceptance, not knowing what else to say or do. She was, in fact, quite unused to such attentions from any man, even Shalford, and though she had been hoping that Brandreth might request the first dance from her, she simply did not know how to refuse the vicar. The fact that Shalford, who was by nature of a serious turn, seemed determined to garner the first set for himself disturbed her greatly. Was this the manner of conduct she was to expect from all the gentlemen she met this afternoon, or was the vicar intent upon a more permanent course.

Marriage? she wondered, a little stunned by the possibility that Shalford was attempting to fix his interest with her. When he returned to his gig, doffed his hat to the ladies, and set his team in motion, Evanthea would have immediately broached the subject with Lady Elle, but the expression on Annabelle's face stopped her fast. The young beauty was watching the vicar depart, her features adorned with an expression of longing so profound that she nearly glowed with love. This sudden switch in affections was even more pronounced when not once did Annabelle's gaze waver from Shalford's back even though Brandreth was seen passing the vicar and heading toward the stables.

Though she wanted to alert Lady Elle to this unusual occurrence Evanthea did not have time since, at that moment, she heard Psyche cry out, "Oh, do go away, Eros! You've quite done enough!"

Shifting her gaze toward the avenue of lime trees, Evanthea's attention became riveted to the unhappy couple caught in the midst of yet another quarrel. Psyche continued, "You clearly don't give a fig for me, so I don't see why you can't simply leave me in peace to amuse myself however I might!"

"You may amuse yourself however you wish," Cupid returned facetiously, "and with my blessing. But if I also choose to involve myself with your earthly friends, I don't see why you should object."

"Because you haven't their interests at heart."

"And exactly who are you, Psyche, to know what their interests are or ought to be? If I shoot Evanthea or Annabelle, who is to say that my choices for them won't be better than yours?"

"Because you fire off your arrows at random, without consideration for any of their feelings!"

Evanthea now suspected that Cupid had shot Annabelle with one of his arrows. How else could her obvious love for Shalford be explained?

"Do you see him?" Evanthea whispered to Lady Elle.

"Indeed, I do. Magnificent, isn't he? It is no wonder

Psyche is driven to distraction. Who wouldn't be in trying to keep such a man content?"

"He seems a trifle petulant, doesn't he?" Evanthea said. "As though there is still a bit too much of the little boy in him to make an entirely agreeable husband."

At that moment, Cupid looked directly at Evanthea. Whether or not her words had traveled to his ear, she could not say. But he seemed to realize she could see him, for his expression took on a startled appearance after which he simply vanished, the sound of beating wings the only indication he was near, as the god of love rose in the air and flew toward the east.

Chapter Twenty-one

Brandreth held a rein in each hand, the thin leather straps looped between fourth finger, middle finger, and thumb, and drawn up tight to keep his mettlesome pair well in hand. His eyes were focused on the road in front of him, on a spot exactly dead center between the horses' heads.

The race needed only the firing of a pistol by good old Meppers himself in order to commence. To the marquis's astonishment, the King's highway was lined with every manner of familiar and unfamiliar vehicle arrived for the sole purpose of witnessing the spectacle of two gentlemen engaged in an unusual competition. When Annabelle had informed him of the forthcoming ball, she had mentioned that quite a few sporting bloods were in the village, but he had not been prepared for how many there actually were.

Glossy rigs of all sorts—Stanhopes, like Shalford's, curricles, whiskies, high-perch phaetons, landaulets—were in abundance along with their owners and guests, all sporting high-crowned beaver hats, stiff shirtpoints, belcher neckcloths, fashionable coats, breeches, and top boots. He suspected that the small village of Old Flitwick and its two inns would be overflowing with the complement of these gentlemen—a bevy of frilled and chattering damsels, dressed to the nines and giddy with the delight of an unusual summer morning's entertainment.

The highway itself was proving an unfortunate choice for the race, for the simple reason that at least five coaches had been delayed by the closing of the road.

Of the moment, however, all he cared about was winning the race. His body responded with tense anticipation to the fine duel ahead. As his hands kept his horses firmly in check against the riotous cheers and cries abounding from the spectators, Brandreth's blood flowed with the wondrous exhilaration attached to rivalry.

He was ready. He had practiced the art of standing and driving, and he had not foolishly underestimated his rival. His only real concern was that some mishap would occur to throw either himself or Shalford onto the road. But he was a careful man and so was the vicar. There was nothing for it, then, but to begin.

"All ready?" Meppers called out.

Silence ensued, of the deafening sort. The sort that caused the sound of a nearby robin to seem as loud as the screeching of a night owl.

A pistol shot rent the air.

Brandreth gave his horses a slap of the reins, not too hard since he had to gain his feet at the same moment the wheels began to spin. Upward he rose as the curricle started forward, his knees carefully bent, his feet planted wide apart, his thighs taut with needful strength. He achieved the weighted balance he sought, ignoring the fact that Shalford in his gig had already pulled slightly ahead. He began speaking to his horses, just as he had practiced a hundred times, coaxing them firmly and just loud enough to be heard over the din of cheers that marked the beginning of the race. His horses responded, knowing

191

his voice and obeying it as he expected them to.

All seemed forgotten—the blue of the sky; the green of the surrounding hills, trees, and shrubs; the bright, restless colors of the summer flowers; the cheering spectators; the crunching of the roadbed beneath his wheels. Sights, sounds, and smells faded away, leaving only the reins, his voice, and the twitching ears of his horses within the recognition of his senses. He would not have even noticed the wind on his face, except that it picked up his hat and tumbled it from his head. After that, nothing marred the intensity of his concentration.

Reins, *that's it, Jupiter,* ears.

Reins, *easy now, Zeus,* ears.

The course was a brief two miles long on well-laid gravel, the highway wending slightly at an incline through gentle hills and bordered by hedgerows. Shalford had achieved an early lead, but every few yards saw Brandreth closing the distance between them. He knew he would pass the vicar in plenty of time to win the race but took no chances as he encouraged his horses along.

A moment later, and he was driving neck and neck with Shalford, the carriages fitting easily onto the highway, both men standing in bent submission to the difficulty of the race. He did not glance once at the vicar, and from his peripheral vision Brandreth knew that Shalford paid him not the smallest heed, either.

Perspiration dripped form his forehead, seeping into the corners of his eyes and irritating him. There was nothing he could do, however, since his hands held the reins firmly.

As they rounded the final bend in the road and the charming thatched village came into view, with a hundred spectators raising their voices into the air in a mighty roar, Brandreth felt a jolt of excitement course through him. Only then did he look at Shalford, and both exchanged a wild expression of competitive force. Each slapped the reins hard upon the backs of their horses and the race seemed to rise to a final level of ferocity.

All four animals snorted and pushed on, seeming to enjoy the heat of the moment as much as did their masters. Brandreth's superior team began proving itself, inching into the lead with every stride. Time smoothed to a blur of slowness for the marquis as he stood recklessly master of the moment, of his carriage, his horses, and the road.

To the right, beneath a spreading, fully-leafed and ancient oak, a familiar carriage rested in sedate pleasure. Three ladies sat within, not cheering, he noticed, as were the wilder sort nearer the finish line. His lead was assured, he knew he would win, and perhaps for that reason Brandreth permitted himself to nod to Annabelle, who for some odd reason was looking beyond him with an expression of extreme anguish toward Shalford.

He found himself amused. Poor Annabelle, he thought, always seeking beaus.

Next he saw Lady Elle, who smiled at him in her fond way, bobbing her head slightly and appearing to encourage him on.

Finally, his gaze stopped dead on the third female, whom he did not at first recognize and who did not seem to recognize him. His instantaneous impression, however, was of an exquisite young woman dressed in green and white. He wondered briefly, in the misty exhilaration of winning a race, who she was. But just as his curiosity piqued, he realized he was looking at Evanthea, who returned his gaze at last, in part unseeing because she was not wearing her spectacles, with a sweet smile.

He was so startled by the sight of her transformed

almost beyond recognition that he relaxed the hold on his reins in a spasm of disbelief. His horses lost their sure stride, he nearly tumbled forward at the unexpected change in pace, and in the process of regaining his balance and bringing his horses back to order, Shalford flew past, winning the race. The roar of triumph that followed the vicar's victory seemed to literally shake the air.

Brandreth was in a state of shock immediately following the race. The astonishment of the moment, of actually losing the race because he had looked at Evanthea, did not at first make sense to him. He was breathing hard and sweating so furiously at his recent effort that all he could think about were simple things, like wiping his face and seeing that his horses were properly attended to. For this last reason he did not draw his horses to a stop among the squealing multitude, nor did Shalford to his credit, until both teams reached the end of the village and the Swan Inn, where their respective horses would be attended to by the inn's exceptional hostler and grooms.

Brandreth released his team into the care of the hostler. A strong measure of confusion still held rein over his mind and he was experiencing considerable difficulty putting his thoughts in order. Having lost momentary control of his horses, his legs shook badly from the knowledge that he could have endured a severe fall. These feelings, however, were all wrapped up in a chaotic way with the vision of Evanthea in her new bonnet and green silk gown. She was so deucedly pretty! Add to this the fact that the sight of her had cost him the race, and he didn't know which to feel first — anger, astonishment, fear, or a rather simplistic gratitude that he was still alive.

Shalford, who had led the way into the inn yard, approached him, slapping his hat against his thigh, dust from the road puffing about him like miniature clouds. He wore a concerned frown between his brows. "What the devil! I mean, what on earth happened, man? You were winning the race, then seemed to drop your reins! I feared for a second you were going to fall right under the wheels of my gig!"

Brandreth could only stare at him for a moment, quite stupidly, he was certain. And as the crowd neared the inn and turned the corner of the stable yard, he could only respond, "I saw Evanthea and lost my head!"

Shalford opened his mouth and lifted his eyes to the heavens. "Good God!" he cried. "Of course! I, at least, had had the opportunity to see her before the race. It is no wonder. . . . She is a new creature, isn't she? It has certainly changed my intentions toward her—or at least strengthened them. I am not surprised that—" He got no further.

The vicar, who was a favorite of the townspeople, was swiftly descended upon by an enormous crowd and lifted high into the air, to sit upon the shoulders of the smithy and one of the strong local thatchers. He was carried off to the George Inn, where Lady Elle's celebration would take place.

Brandreth watched him go, his spirits plummeting in that awful place of loss where the blood in his veins could find no release in celebration and the adulation of the crowds. He remained, hatless and alone, standing in the yard amidst the noise of the horses still blowing and uncomfortable after their ordeal.

Evanthea descended from the carriage, along with Lady Elle and Annabelle. There was much confusion in the small village and in the street. Those spectators who had watched the beginning of the race were just now reaching the village, along with

195

several conveyances that had been halted from progressing through the King's highway because of the race. A great deal of dust had been kicked up into the air, and with the press of the crowd and everyone coughing and sneezing, it was not long before Evanthea became separated from her great-aunt and Annabelle.

It was just as well, she thought as she forced her way to the opposite side of the street, avoiding the George Inn. She had put on her spectacles so that she might clearly see all that was going forward. What a din there was near the center of the village! She could see Shalford being carried on the shoulders of at least two of the villagers and transported to the George, where he would be accounted a hero since he had won for many of his loyal parishioners their wagers. Nowhere, however, could she see Brandreth, and it was to him she meant to go immediately.

She wasn't certain why, but her conscience smote her heavily. She knew she had cost him the race and nearly his life. Not that it had occurred to her that he would be so startled by her appearance that he would actually weaken his hold on the reins, but so it had been. Evanthea could not entirely disclaim responsibility, and if she could do it all over again, heaven knew she would have acquainted him with the change in her costume before the race. As it was, she wanted to find him and apologize.

As she worked her way past the crowd jostling elbows outside the door of the George, the street thinned of people considerably. Only a few diligent shopkeepers, both afraid of the many strangers who littered the High Street as well as hoping to take advantage of their fat purses while they were in Old Flitwick, remained at their doors watching the festivities from afar.

Evanthea knew that both Brandreth and Shalford would make certain their rigs were cared for immediately following the race, and so it was she headed for the Swan, which she knew Brandreth preferred over the George.

As she turned the corner of the far side of the inn, which led to the cobbled inn yard, Evanthea was caught short by the sight of the marquis sitting on an old stump near the stables. His face was turned into the sunshine as he watched his horses being rubbed down and occasionally directed one of the grooms to perform some office or other. At the same time, he mopped his face with his kerchief. A tankard of ale sat lopsided on the cobble near his dusty top boots. Except for a telling slump in his shoulders, he seemed to her as he ever was — confident, concerned for his horses, and terribly handsome.

She approached him slowly, experiencing a peculiar fear that caused her heart to beat fast in her breast. Her intent had been only to apologize, but now that she saw him, she wondered if her motives were quite so pure. So many strange things had occurred in the past two days, including the devastating kiss they had shared, that she knew a familiar yearning to simply be with Brandreth and, in this case, to comfort him if that was what he needed.

When she was about twenty yards from him, Evanthea heard the faintest humming sound, like the beating of wings. She looked about to see if a bird or perhaps an owl was passing by, but she saw nothing and the sound seemed to fade away. Cupid? she wondered. She hoped so. She hoped he would ply them both full of his arrows.

She took another step and suddenly, at the base of her neck, just as it had happened the night Brandreth had first kissed her, Evanthea felt an infinitesimal burning sensation. She wondered if she had been stung by a bee, but then the most languid warmth began to flow over her, followed by a delicious spattering of gooseflesh all down her neck and side. It must Cupid's mischief. But how wonderful!

She touched her neck, her gaze returning to Brandreth, who was in the process of taking a deep pull of ale from his heavy pewter tankard. She felt breathless and strange, her eyes blotting out every sight and sound of the stable save Brandreth's face. She removed her spectacles, remembering Lady Elle and Annabelle's advice, slipping them into the hidden pocket of her gown.

Brandreth did not notice her presence until she was but ten feet from him. When he saw her, over the rim of his tankard, he blinked twice, then slowly lowered the vessel as though stunned, all over again, by the sight of her. What he was thinking or feeling she could not guess, and somehow, to her oddly befuddled senses, it did not even matter. He did not smile at her as he set the tankard again on the cobbles and rose to his feet, scrutinizing her from the ruffled brim of her silk bonnet to the tips of her silk shoes.

Behind the marquis, she could see that the hostler and his grooms were leading the four horses into the stables. When they had disappeared within the timber-framed building, she drew close to him and finally spoke. "I came to apologize," she said in a whisper, staring up at him as one mesmerized. "I ought to have shown you my gown and my new bonnet beforehand. It never occurred to me that you would be so dumbfounded that you would lose your grasp on your reins. Brandreth, you could've been hurt!"

"It wasn't your fault," he returned, his voice low. "I behaved like a perfect gapeseed, and for that you

198

have nothing to apologize for. But, by Jupiter, I've never seen anything so extraordinary in my life as how pretty you've become. How is it possible?" He drew off one of his gloves and touched the white ruffle edging the brim of her bonnet, then gently stroked the curls about her face and fingered her eardrops, which were nearly obscured by the hat.

"Damme," he whispered enigmatically, and gave a strong tug on the bow of her bonnet. Afterward, he pushed the bonnet away from her chestnut curls and her face, then placed a light kiss on her forehead and a gentle one on her lips. "Why is it whenever we are alone—or relatively so—I experience the most overwhelming desire to take you in my arms?"

"I don't know," she murmured, searching his eyes and feeling warm with deep affection for him. Somewhere in the back of her mind she knew she ought to draw away from him, even a little, lest he assault her in earnest as he had before. Thus far, an innocent kiss upon the lips was truly nothing, but if he were to grab her and hold her . . . well then, she would have to begin wondering whether or not the manner in which they had begun conducting themselves in recent days was not leading to something as serious as *love*.

However, when he touched her neck ever so lightly, she felt a second wave of shivers creep from just below her ear all the way to her ankle. Her senses again became quite useless. She could not move if she wanted to and perhaps for that reason, or merely because Brandreth was so wondrously close to her and smelled of horses, leather, and soap, she instead slipped her arm about his neck and cried, "Oh, my darling Brandreth!" She then kissed him very hard and very much in earnest.

Apparently unwilling to offend her by spurning her amorous assault, the marquis drew her close to him in a tight embrace and returned her kiss with a mighty fervor. Evanthea again felt herself disappear into him, as though in the simple act of being held by Brandreth and kissed by him, she had joined herself to him. Her mind seemed like a misty white sheet of nothingness save her affection for Brandreth and the joy she received by being held in his arms. She permitted herself, as she never had before, to taste of the sweet bitterness of his lips, the ale still lingering on his breath . . . to feel the strength of his arms around her, to delight in the sensation of her fingertips touching the hair at the nape of his neck.

"Evanthea," he whispered, his breath on her ear sending a shiver down her neck, just as before. "My darling girl. I believe I have fallen —"

He could not complete his thought, however, for at that moment, a feminine voice, only but vaguely familiar to Evanthea, intruded. "Well, I must say I consider this odd conduct, and yet how charming! My dear Brandreth, are you receiving *consolation?*"

Chapter Twenty-two

The tenor of the lady's voice was so bold that the spell between Brandreth and Evanthea shattered like delicate glass on a hardwood floor. Evanthea found herself recoiling from the marquis as one who has been caught in a terrible crime. She immediately pulled her bonnet close about her face and retied the white silk ribbon beneath her ear.

As she regarded the lady before her, a woman whom she believed was a few years her senior, Evanthea knew an intense dislike of the particular smirk the woman wore, an expression of arrogance and cunning that she instinctively mistrusted.

"Susan!" Brandreth cried. "I mean, *Lady Felmersham!* By all that's wonderful! Whatever are you doing here? How . . . I mean, I don't understand."

"Are you acquainted with Mr. Sawley?" the lady returned sweetly. "He is a particular friend of Felmersham's. He has a lodge not ten miles from Old Flitwick. Once he heard of the race, nothing could keep Sawley or my husband from dashing off. Naturally, I insisted upon joining them. I do not tolerate being left to kick my heels at Sawley's house, particularly when the housekeeper has taken a most unwarranted dislike of me."

"Dislike of you?" Brandreth returned warmly. "Impossible!"

Lady Felmersham tilted her head and smiled honeylike upon the marquis. "Isn't it just like you to compliment me when you know very well I make a terrible guest. The poor woman has been driven to distraction by my many requests. She deserves to be pitied."

Evanthea had the strong impression that however much Lady Felmersham wished to appear innocent, she suspected Sawley's housekeeper would be grateful to see the viscountess depart.

"Again, I tell you it's impossible," Brandreth cried. "You may disclaim your goodness till you are fatigued by your protestations, but I know better. Far better."

Susan. Lady Felmersham. Evanthea pondered both names and tried to remember who this lady was and, more precisely, what her previous connection to Brandreth had been. She scrutinized her carefully, from her exquisite gown of embroidered pink muslin, to the cut of her light brown hair wisped delicately over her forehead, to the intricate jewels upon several of her fingers. She could see that Susan was a highly fashionable woman of impeccable taste. Her features seemed familiar, yet unremembered. Evanthea must have met her during her first Season, but who was she? She strained to recall her identity, for she had a clear prescience that her own future happiness somehow rested upon this lady's good graces, or rather the lack of them.

She glanced at Brandreth, whose expression was one of wonder. Perhaps because of the light in his eyes she suddenly knew who the viscountess was—Susan Lawrence of Wiltshire, an heiress, accounted a considerable beauty in her day, high-in-the-instep, hypocritical, uncompassionate. Evanthea had never cared for her above half and remembered avoiding her insinuating conversation and cutting remarks whenever she could. For some reason, it seemed to her that Miss Lawrence had wished for her friendship, though why she had never comprehended. Unless, of course, it was her vague connection through Lady Elle to Brandreth.

And it was this woman Brandreth had once loved yet failed in his timing to make his wife. It had been generally known he was trying to fix his interest with her.

"Well, I won't argue with you further," Lady Felmersham responded brightly to Brandreth. "And I hereby place all my finer qualities within your care. I command you to remind me of them at every turn." She laughed lightly, a musical trill that Evanthea suspected had been cultivated for the strict purpose of charming men. "But I am all agog, as you must very well know. Am I to wish you joy, for you cannot imagine how astonished I was to find this lady in your arms — and no hint of a betrothal?" She lifted pretty, arched brows and inquired of Evanthea, "But I don't believe I am acquainted with you, am I, my dear?"

Evanthea disliked the condescending manner in which the viscountess called her *my dear,* as though she were speaking to a chit just out of the schoolroom instead of a woman quite near her in age.

Brandreth rose to the duty of performing the hinted-for introduction. He turned slightly toward Evanthea and said, "I suppose it has been many years since my *cousin* was once in London, but I believe you were acquainted with her during her first Season. If not, may I present Evanthea Swanbourne?"

"Evanthea Swanbourne! Never say it is so?" To Evanthea's critical ear, this seemed to her to be the first genuine remark the viscountess had yet made. "But you are so changed!" Lady Felmersham added, appearing not entirely pleased. "You are not at all the creature I remember from so many years ago."

Even Brandreth seemed surprised by the uncharitable nature of this remark and an awkward silence ensued. Evanthea would have posed a polite question in an attempt to smooth over the breach in conversation, but at the very same moment, she heard Psyche's voice issuing a single sharp command from somewhere behind Brandreth. "No!" she cried as a harsh whistling noise sounded very close to Evanthea's ear.

Evanthea turned to seek out the origin of Psyche's cry. She saw nothing yet feared that Cupid, with his quiver full of arrows, had decided to do some mischief. She could not have mistaken the distinct sound of one of Cupid's arrows and touched the spot on her own neck where she now knew she had once been struck by his careful aim. She quickly turned her gaze to Brandreth, wondering if her surmise was correct, that Eros had chosen the marquis as his next target.

She could see that Brandreth was considerably dazed as he weaved on his feet. When he set about rubbing the back of his neck as though it pained him, Evanthea new Cupid had succeeded in his deviltry.

"What was it you asked earlier, about wishing us joy?" Brandreth queried, his words halting and strange, his eyes shut.

"What is the matter?" Lady Felmersham asked, stepping close to Brandreth. "You do not seem well. The race must have been a difficult trial. The sun is too much for you. Only tell me how many miles you covered standing up so bravely as you did?"

"A little more than two," he responded, out of breath. "Damme, but my senses are reeling."

Lady Felmersham needed no greater invitation and was at his side at once, taking his arm and wrapping it tightly about her own. "I am not as weak as I appear. You may lean on my arm. I promise you, I will not tumble over. Perhaps you ought to sit down for a moment."

"No, no, it is nothing, truly," he murmured unsteadily, taking her arm nevertheless.

Evanthea felt a sense of panic begin rising in her. She called his name softly, hoping to attract his attention, but he did not respond. She knew precisely what had happened. Cupid had shot the marquis, intending for him to look at the viscountess. If he did, he would be lost to her, possibly forever. "Brandreth," she called again a little louder, but he seemed not to hear her. There was still time, she realized. He had not yet gazed into Lady Felmersham's eyes. Only somehow she must make him look at her!

Lady Felmersham, whose back was to Evanthea, glanced over her shoulder and said, "Be a good girl and fetch his lordship a brandy. I am persuaded the race has taxed him dreadfully."

Evanthea felt an arm slip about her waist and knew Psyche had come to support her. Her friend whispered intently, "Forget what that wicked woman is saying. She means to distract you. Brandreth has not looked at her! Pray run, Evanthea, catch his gaze! It is not too late!"

Psyche gave her a shove and Evanthea rounded Brandreth on his far side. *"Cousin!"* she cried, hoping to distract him by employing the connection over which they always brangled.

"What was that?" he queried. He blinked twice, and for some reason followed not the direction of Evanthea's voice but turned toward Lady Felmersham. Only then did Evanthea notice that the more experienced woman was pinching the marquis's arm.

In horror, Evanthea watched as Brandreth's gaze connected with Lady Felmersham's, the expression on his face changing from one of confusion to one of complete adoration. "As for wishing me joy," he said in a bedazzled voice, responding to her earlier question, "why, it is no such thing. Though I must say your sudden appearance has come closest of all to bringing happiness to my poor existence."

With Lady Felmersham on his arm, Brandreth began drawing her toward the High Street, where the sounds of an exhilarated crowd could still be heard in the occasional shout that rose into the air. Brandreth passed by Evanthea, ignoring her entirely. His attention was all for the viscountess as he lifted her hand and pressed a kiss upon the smooth silk of Lady Felmersham's gloved hand. "How do you go on, Susan?" he whispered softly. "I have not seen you in far too many years. I trust your husband is very good to you, for if he isn't, I may just have to call him out."

She leaned into him, looking up into his face as though he were Zeus himself. "What nonsense you speak," she chided him with arch tenderness. "For though I am given to understand you excel at the art of firing pistols and shooting at targets, I must tell you that Felmersham has no equal, at least not in Hampshire, where he is quite master of his world. Therefore, for your own sake, I will tell you that my husband positively dotes on me and is as adoring a father as one could wish for. I want for absolutely nothing. Yet for all this, when you ask how I go on, I would be telling a whisker if I did not confess that I have been utterly miserable, disconsolate, cast upon my couch day and night, ever since I can remember. I have not known a moment's happiness since . . . well, since the day you decided I was unworthy of you."

"When I decided? Now who is speaking nonsense?" he responded forcefully. "Though I must say I have for a long time believed the fault of our misunderstanding lay elsewhere." He chose this moment to look back at Evanthea, a clear message glittering in his gray eyes. When he returned his attention to Lady Felmersham, he continued, "You must remember, however, that it was you who accepted Felmersham's hand without having given me the opportunity to speak."

"It was no such thing!" the viscountess exclaimed in mock horror. "But pray, let us not quarrel over whose fault this terrible breach was. Rather come with me, and I shall see that you are well entertained this afternoon. I am sure Felmersham is quite anxious to reacquaint himself with you."

"I should be more than delighted," Brandreth responded.

They progressed five languid steps, when Lady Felmersham pretended surprise and turned back slightly to address Evanthea. "I nearly forgot," she cried. "I hereby relieve you of the task of procuring the brandy, Miss Swanbourne, and if you wish for it, do come with us. Your great-aunt was kind enough to invite our party to her celebration."

The invitation was polite enough, but the expression on the viscountess's face was akin to a wish that Evanthea would simply drop off the face of the earth.

"Thank you for your kind attentions to me," Evanthea responded. "But I think not." She then curtsied facetiously and bid her good day. Within a minute, the enchanted couple had passed into the street and disappeared around the corner.

Evanthea watched them go, feeling as though her heart had been punctured with a shoe nail and left to bleed. A pain as she had never known seemed to be all that held her together, squeezing her chest so tightly she was finding it difficult to breathe. She had learned one important item from Brandreth's exchange with Lady Felmersham: He blamed her for his rupture with Susan Lawrence. This, then, was the source of his rancor toward her, the heretofore unspoken crime she had committed against him. But why did he blame her for Miss Lawrence having married Felmersham? She could not think in what way she had been responsible for it.

"Evanthea!" Psyche called to her.

Evanthea had nearly forgotten about Psyche and Cupid in the intense discomfort of the moment. She whirled about and saw that Psyche was beckoning to her from the hedge behind the stables, but Eros was nowhere in sight.

Evanthea hurried toward her friend, who quickly drew her behind the hedge of hawthorn and cried, "Do you know what has happened?"

Evanthea bit her lip. The mere thought of expressing to Psyche that it was clear to her now that Brandreth had been in love with Lady Felmersham for a very long time brought stinging tears to her eyes. "He — he is in love with her."

"Of course he is not!" Psyche cried. "Cupid shot him, that is all. You know he did, or you seemed to."

Evanthea shook her head. "You don't understand. However powerful your husband's arrows are, Eros only enhanced what was years ago a blossoming love. I am convinced of it."

"You are speaking like a bird-witted ninnyhammer! Brandreth could never love such a creature. Yes, perhaps at one time he fancied that he did, but of the moment he is merely suffering the effects of Cupid's arrow, that is all! And he shot you as well! You know that, don't you?"

"Yes," she breathed, frowning slightly. "The odd thing is, it only lasted for a moment, but now I feel as I always have . . . toward Brandreth, I mean. I don't feel burdened with passion as I did the very moment Cupid's arrow struck me. I just . . . well, I guess I just *love* him. I think, in my very quirky way, I always have!" Tears again stung Evanthea's eyes.

"Oh, I knew it!" Psyche cried, grasping one of Evanthea's gloved hands and pressing it fondly to her cheek. "I knew it, I just knew it!"

"But he doesn't return my regard, does he? Though I can hardly fault him when I have been such a monster, always reviling his character and pinching at him as though he were the worst gamester and libertine that ever lived."

"You did no harm by your remarks. Can't you see that he respects you mightily?"

"I don't know. What I do know is that he blames me for having lost Lady Felmersham and she is so very pretty, isn't she?"

"What does that matter? I tell you, he wouldn't have cast a single eye upon her had not that stupid poison entered his neck!"

"Why is Cupid even here?" Evanthea queried, her attention finally diverted from her concern about Brandreth's interest in Lady Felmersham. "I saw you arguing with him earlier, beneath the lime trees at Flitwick Lodge. He seemed very upset, and oh, Psyche, he is quite the handsomest man I have ever seen . . . And those wings!"

209

Psyche's shoulders slumped ever so slightly. "He is, isn't he?" she said, smiling hopelessly upon her friend, releasing her hand at last and turning toward the vegetable plot behind the hedge. "I was always struck absolutely dumb by the mere sight of him. I suppose that's what makes our troubles even the more difficult to bear. If he were ugly, maybe my heart wouldn't be breaking as it is!"

Evanthea could not help but laugh at the silly nature of Psyche's remark as she followed her down a row of beans. "Did he mean for Brandreth to look at me when he shot him with the arrow?"

Psyche cocked her head. "What do you think?"

"I daresay he had no such intention. He's here to make mischief, isn't he?"

"Precisely!" Psyche returned. "Everything went just as he hoped it would. You see, my wretched husband has come to Old Flitwick to wreak havoc with all my schemes. First, he meant to shoot you with an arrow much earlier, hoping you would fall in love with Shalford and just now—oh, dear, it is too horrid to be believed!—he intended for Brandreth to tumble head over heels in love with Lady Felmersham!"

"He must be very angry with you, then, but why?" Evanthea queried. "I know he is distressed over your visits to Old Flitwick, but is this the only reason he has to take a sort of vengeance on you?"

Psyche cocked her head, a frown furrowing her brow. "I don't know," she said slowly. "Sometimes I wonder if . . . well, let us not discuss my difficulties at present. Right now, I am deeply concerned for you and for what we must do next. I don't trust Lady Felmersham."

"Nor do I. But what I can't determine is in what

way I am responsible for Susan Lawrence's decision to marry Felmersham instead of Brandreth."

Psyche seemed taken aback. "Merciful Olympus!" she cried. "Evanthea, don't you remember what you said to Miss Lawrence one rainy and disagreeable London night, during the Season of 1806?"

"Of course I don't. I daresay I never exchanged more than a dozen words with her. We never did get on, as you must see for yourself."

"Then I shall remind you. The month was April, late April after the Easter holidays. You were enjoying your first Season—and your last, silly girl—and Lord Brandreth, by request of Lady Elle, had just finished waltzing with you."

At that, Evanthea could not repress a smile. "I bruised his feet a hundred times during that unfortunate waltz. I took lessons from a dancing master afterward, but he never approached me again. Besides, by the end of the set I was grateful I had hurt him, for never had a man so wounded me as he did."

"I know very well what happened," Psyche responded, drawing Evanthea across a row of tomato bushes clustered with ripe, red fruit. "I remember it as though it were yesterday."

"Why do I get the impression that you have been privy to my comings and goings for a very long time?"

"Haven't you come to realize that I have been with you for years now? I have been trying ever so hard to bring you and Brandreth together. But never mind that. I do remember it as though it were yesterday. He quite bruised your tender, open heart . . . no, do not disclaim it! You had just begun telling him of your hopes to return to Greece and to continue your papa's excavations, and he dashed your ambitions by saying curtly that there was considerable civil con-

211

flict in the country and that you would be little more than a fool to go there. What an idiot he was to have spoken to you so harshly. And what was worse, he expounded upon that theme until even I was ready to plant him a facer."

The reference to how hurt she had been by the marquis's complete disapproval of her desire to return to Greece seemed to open a floodgate, releasing a memory she had shut away forever. "I remember now. Susan Lawrence approached me immediately after the disastrous waltz, in her sneering way, of course. And I was so overset by Brandreth's high-handed and unkind remarks, besides being irritated by Miss Lawrence's demeanor, that I did not censor my speech to her. I fear I spoke unkindly of Brandreth to her."

Psyche let out a crack of laughter. "And here we are, all of us, so many years later, confronted by the same, quite unresolved conflicts which afflicted us then." She paused for a moment in her steps and grew thoughtful. "Do you know, I am suddenly come to believe that Nemesis is about, busy in her desire to torture the pair of us. Otherwise, how is it possible Miss Lawrence should come to Old Flitwick, like a spectre from a bad dream?" Resuming her progress, she let her hands drift over a tall stand of broccoli leaves. "Though I don't hesitate to tell you that Nemesis is usually a great deal more strident in her efforts—cruel even, certainly more cruel than to merely bring a pretty female around to tease Brandreth." She shook her head. "Really, I am quite confused. I sense that something is afoot, but what? Oh, never mind. I have a secret to tell you. That same night in which you spoke disparagingly of Brandreth to Miss Lawrence, I had *borrowed* a little of my mama-in-law's love oil and placed it upon the

212

tip of Felmersham's nose. Do you not think it clever of me to have chosen his nose, since it is his most prominent feature? Why, I think it is as big as that pickling cucumber!" She gestured to a cucumber that was bulbous at one end. "Well, after that, Felmersham but laid eyes upon Miss Lawrence, just as I wished him to, and I needn't tell you that he offered for her not fifteen minutes later."

Evanthea blinked at her friend and began to recall certain other long-forgotten details of that night. "Miss Lawrence had asked me for my opinion of Brandreth. You see, I never held her in esteem. She was always such an unkind female, clawing at the reputation of other young ladies and speaking unhandsomely of her friends when they were not present, not to mention making it known that her sole object in coming to London was to get a handle to her name! At any rate, I simply could not restrain my opinions. My speech was meant entirely facetiously, but now that I think on it, I would guess she believed the whole of it—given her general character."

As though having a veil lifted miraculously from her memory, Evanthea found herself able to recall the incident as though it happened yesterday. She was at Almack's, sipping at a glass of lemonade, when Miss Lawrence, her pretty pink complexion adorned with a false smile, approached her. "What a delightful gown, Miss Swanbourne," she had begun sweetly.

Evanthea remembered straightening her spine and responding, "It was altered from one I made up when I was just out of the schoolroom not a year ago. It is hardly suitable to the occasion nor to the use of the term *delightful*. I had much rather you speak frankly to me, Miss Lawrence. I cannot possibly think how you might gain by attempting to flatter me."

Miss Lawrence had unfurled her fan and wafted it over her features. "You always speak the most charming nonsense, and I again tell you that your gown is delightful. Such clever banter! It is no wonder your cousin hangs upon each word you speak!"

"You refer to Brandreth, I apprehend."

"You know I do," she replied demurely.

"Then I must tell you that you have been grossly misinformed. He is not my cousin. We share a favorite great-aunt in Lady Elizabeth, but otherwise there is no connection. And he does not hang upon my every word. If anything, he takes great pleasure in contradicting whatever I might say."

Susan stared at her in astonishment. "Whether or not that is the case I cannot say. I have merely noticed that unlike the rest of us mere mortals, you seem able to hold his attention forever. What an odd creature you are. And as for not calling Brandreth cousin, as he is wont to address you, I can only tell you that every other lady present would beg to be addressed as such, whether it were the truth or not. You would do well to follow suit. You cannot but benefit by his patronage, particularly since he is the head of your family."

Evanthea remembered wanting to inform her that Brandreth was not in the least the head of the Swanbourne family, but she held her tongue. Miss Lawrence evidently chose to see events and people in the manner that best suited her own interests, truth being entirely irrelevant.

Evanthea smiled ruefully at the memory as she related the particulars to Psyche. "When Miss Lawrence begged to know what my opinion of Brandreth was, I told her that he was one of the most arrogant, high-handed gentlemen I had ever known, valuing his own opinion so mightily that he could not give an ear to anyone else's. For good measure, I added that he was so smitten with his own reflection in the mirror that it was unlikely he could ever love anyone, save himself. I suggested, quite sarcastically, that if she was hoping to bring him up to scratch she was likely to fail in her ambitions, and wouldn't it be wiser of her to accept another man — Felmersham, for instance, since he was in possession of a title — and be done with it."

"You know she took your advice, unaware that Brandreth meant to offer for her the very next day."

"Did he?" she queried, frowning. "Then it is little wonder he is still angry with me. But how did he know I had said anything to her?"

"He overheard you. I have never seen a man so crushed in my entire existence. But I believe your words had a beneficial effect, since from that time he seemed to have tempered his manners considerably — toward everyone."

Evanthea was silent for a pace. She bent down and tore a sprig of mint from its thick carpet near the peas. Rubbing one of the leaves between her fingers, she lifted it to her nose and said, "I find it very strange for Miss Lawrence to have so little trusted her own discernment. Did she truly not know that she had won Brandreth's heart?"

Psyche shook her head. "Her inability to recognize Brandreth's intentions cost her the one man she desired above all others."

"Is she happy in her choice?" Evanthea queried, feeling to a degree responsible for the incident.

"At times. But I believe her general unhappiness stems from her own selfishness and willingness to sacrifice her contentment to her worldly ambitions.

If the path she has chosen with a man who spends nearly every waking hour on the hunting field has not brought her happiness, she has only herself to blame."

"Or me."

"If she blames you, then she truly is a fool, though I've little doubt she will ingratiate herself with Brandreth at your expense to further alienate him from your affections. She may have made her own bed, but I believe she would do anything to keep you from lying down in the one she had originally wanted for herself!"

"What do we do now?" Evanthea queried.

Psyche smiled mischievously at her friend. From her reticule, she withdrew a small glass bottle. "Aphrodite created this potion, which is supposed to end love. I mean to use it on Brandreth as soon as I can."

Evanthea regarded the vial dubiously. If her sentiments, though enhanced by Cupid's arrow, remained essentially unchanged, perhaps no magical potion could end what she believed was Brandreth's real love for Lady Felmersham.

Chapter Twenty-three

Annabelle stood in the parlor of the George Inn near the diamond-paned windows, crushed in the crowded chamber between Lady Elle and Lord Felmersham. She did not particularly notice that his lordship's elbow bruised her arm every time he lifted his tankard of ale to his lips, nor did she feel overly warm, as did her great-aunt, from the pressing of the crowds. Her attention and her gaze was fully fixed instead upon the sight of an exhilarated Mr. Shalford.

He sat in a handsome carved chair, which was perched on a dais in front of the hearth. Visible to everyone, the winner of the race reigned over the festivities, drinking liberally from his own tankard and appearing more like a hero from the Peninsular Wars than a humble cleric. The parlor, small as it was, smelled ripe with celebration, the home-brewed ale of the George Inn having been spilled upon lapels, shirtfronts, chins, and neckcloths. Laughter, chatter, and a constant flow of congratulations swirled about the air. Through the thick atmosphere of adulation, Annabelle watched the man she loved and could not keep from trembling.

"You were born for the army, Shalford, damme if you weren't!" a voice called out.

"Here! Here!" others chimed in, followed by a familiar bellowing of, "Huzza! Huzza!"

Annabelle watched a faint, brief expression of forgotten disappointment pass across the vicar's handsome brow. *He wished for a career in the army,* she thought, her heart quivering at the knowledge of his misplaced dreams.

Her thoughts drifted back to a time, six months earlier during Christmastide, when he had spoken to her of many serious things. It had all begun when she had been so incensed that he had not responded to her flirtations. She had boldly begged to know why he was so high in the instep that he could not answer her clever banter with good humor, as did all the other gentlemen of her acquaintance.

She remembered how fiercely he had regarded her—quite unlike any clergyman she had ever known—and how he had said, "Because, Miss Staple, I am not like all the other gentlemen of your acquaintance. If you wish for rational conversation, I would delight in knowing what your thoughts truly are, what activities you enjoy most on a winter or a summer's evening, and whether or not, if a man were to ask you to follow the drum, you would. Beyond these unexceptional subjects, I will not pander to your vanity by *answering your banter with good humor.*"

Whether it was because she had been intrigued or provoked by the dark, forceful expression in his eye, she would never know, but she had submitted to his notion of conversation and had actually enjoyed a *tête-à-tête* with him. They had exchanged confidences, hers that she was frequently bored with London life, however exciting it was to most young women, and his that he had been one of so many sons, seven in all, that it had not been possible to

218

follow every interest that had intrigued him. He had only hinted at the army, of course, but when she had carefully questioned him about events at Salamanca and Vitoria, his considerable knowledge, along with the fire in his eye as he spoke of Wellington and the Peninsula, confirmed her suspicion. In her opinion, he was a man fit for soldiering, daring yet calm — how easily he had driven his Stanhope while standing — and England had certainly lost one of its best officers to the Church.

With a shudder, she remembered her unhappy behavior on the following day. She had felt inexplicably vulnerable because of the intimate nature of their conversation. When he had approached her the next morning, with a smile and a warm light in his eye, she had repulsed him with a flirtatious sally, which had set a rigidity to his jaw that had never again relaxed toward her. How could she explain to him that in her young mind, she had not been mature enough to accept his very real friendship or the probability that love could easily grow from such a warm, kind, honest beginning?

She wondered if it was too late now to redress such a wrong and earnestly hoped for the chance to redeem herself and to begin again.

A stir in the doorway caused her to glance the direction of what proved to be a growing hum of well-wishing. She saw at once that Evanthea had arrived. How her heart collapsed within her as she saw how pretty she was, how changed, and how *admired* as the guests complimented and petted her.

Annabelle's gaze flew quickly back to Shalford, and she saw mirrored in his expression the admiration buzzing all about Evanthea's head as he watched her enter the parlor. His dark brown eyes shone with appreciation and something more, some-

219

thing Annabelle recognized as determination. A terrible fear rose in her already-anxious heart. Did Shalford love Evanthea? she wondered. He couldn't! Dear lord, he simply couldn't. Not now! Not when she had finally discovered her own heart!

For a moment, Evanthea was stunned by the murmured accolades she received as she began passing through the crowds. She had forgotten all about her new bonnet, her new gown, and the fluff of curls on her forehead. Gentlemen who had heretofore paid her but the smallest of smiles and compliments now seized her hand, kissed her fingers, and ushered her to the next gentleman, as she was sent onward toward her aunt and Annabelle. She felt her cheeks warm with embarrassment, but not more so than when she passed by Brandreth, whose arm was still tightly adorned by Lady Felmersham. She wondered if Lord Felmersham knew of his wife's interest in the marquis, but when she caught sight of the viscount, she saw at least one reason why Lady Felmersham flirted so heartily as she did. His lordship was leaning against the diamond-paned window, his arms folded across his chest, his chin sunk into the folds of his white neckcloth. He had fallen into a doze — no doubt from having imbibed too many tankards since his arrival in Old Flitwick.

A table laden with food prevented further progress, and Evanthea found herself trapped too near Brandreth for comfort. For one thing, even above the din of those still exclaiming over the race, she could hear Lady Felmersham's voice. She tried to shut it out, but when the word *divorce* rang through to her ears, it seemed all other noises disappeared entirely.

"I know it isn't done, my darling," her ladyship

cooed. "But what else are we to do? I can't bear losing you a second time, knowing that your sentiments have not changed in all these years. How difficult could it be?"

Brandreth, his brow furrowed, his expression miserable, responded, "We are speaking of an act of Parliament, Susan, nothing less!"

"I don't care," she murmured into his ear. "Only say you will do this for me."

"Susan," he breathed in return, "I vow I would do anything for you. Anything."

Evanthea heard the manner in which he whispered to Lady Felmersham, the impassioned tone in his voice, the earnestness of his vow, and she felt her heart sink clear to the tips of her pretty embroidered slippers.

Could Psyche truly deny that Brandreth loved this woman? Her denial would be only a wishful thought.

She felt dizzy with unhappiness suddenly, the heat emanating from the press about her causing her stomach to weave about unsteadily. She sought a way to leave but found herself blocked by Brandreth, by the table, by the crowds and, in front of her, by Shalford. She glanced at him and realized for the first time that he was not only speaking but was addressing her. She lifted her face to him and saw that he was asking her something.

His words came to her as through a long tunnel. "Will you?" he queried.

She felt a blush creep up her cheeks. *Will she what?* Evanthea wondered frantically, searching for some fragment of his speech that might have caught her hearing. But none came forward in her brain to rescue her from her inattention. When he rose to his feet and extended his hand to her, she became aware

221

that a solemn hush had fallen over the crowd. Because her thoughts were so full of Lady Felmersham and her intention to seek a divorce from her husband, Evanthea could not imagine what his proffered hand meant save that he wished to help her escape the heat of the crowd. Surely he had seen her discomfort!

Feeling that she could no longer bear standing next to Brandreth and Lady Felmersham, she lifted her hand toward Shalford and said, "Oh, yes. Indeed, yes, if you please!"

The ladies and gentlemen in front of her gave her way immediately, but a crushing moment later, the entire chamber was filled with an unexpected roar of applause and congratulations.

For three heartbeats, Evanthea thought she might faint from the mere shock of the clamor in the parlor, but when she saw the look of joy on Shalford's face, she realized something terrible had gone awry, that she had entirely misjudged the vicar's innocent query *"Will you?"* The purport of his words was made known to her in full when, having reached his side, he planted a bold kiss full upon her lips. Only then did she deduce the truly horrible conclusion that she had accepted the vicar's hand in marriage!

She glanced quickly toward Lady Elle, hoping that somehow her great-aunt would comprehend her mistake, but the older woman was occupied with Annabelle, who it appeared had fainted.

All the while, she noted with a bizarre sense of the absurd, Lord Felmersham snored gently on, his bulbous nose pink with evidence of his enjoyment of the celebration.

Chapter Twenty-four

Psyche pressed her nose to the diamond-paned windows of the George Inn. She was standing in a bed of pansies, carefully straddling the delicate velvet petals as she looked in upon Shalford's victory celebration. Horror kept her transfixed to the window as she gazed first at Evanthea, then Shalford, then Brandreth, and finally Annabelle.

"Good heavens!" she murmured. "What a coil!"

She felt for the two vials secreted in the hidden pocket of her gown and withdrew both. She tore her gaze from the sight of Evanthea's eyes dilated with shock and examined the vials carefully, replacing only the love potion in her pocket. The antidote to love she cradled in her hands, anticipation of the work she had to do warming her heart.

Just as she was preparing to step backward, however, a soft mewing sound rose to her ears. Looking down, she gazed into the sweetest eyes of the prettiest yellow striped cat she had ever seen. "Oh, what a love!" she cried.

The cat began purring and rubbed against the smooth cambric of her white gown, pressing against her leg. She leaned down and began to pet the cat, cooing to the affectionate creature and generally forgetting all about her mission. She set the vial down on the mulched earth beside her gold sandal and became engrossed in the charming feline.

And then, without warning, the cat darted away, slipping into a nearby rose garden and seeming to vanish. In its wake, a deep masculine chuckle rang through her ears. She glanced about her yet saw no one.

Psyche, in her fright at the strange chuckle and the disappearance of the cat, caught her breath and tumbled backward, landing on the grassy border next to the bed of pansies, her feet sticking up through the flowers like two gravestones. She felt scared and dizzy, yet unable to move. She was certain an Olympian deity had taken the shape of the cat, but which one and why?

And then she watched, horrified, as the flowers beside her feet began to wilt and shrivel, disappearing into the ground and leaving the flower bed bare. Stunned, she scurried to her knees to examine the now-empty bed and saw to her dismay that the vial had somehow shattered and the contents had spilled over the ground, killing the flowers.

She was immobilized, afraid that her own life was in jeopardy. No insignificant deity was at work here, she thought, wondering what she ought next to do. Whoever it was didn't want her to use the vial, but worse, would the deity tell Zeus of her mischief? Would she then be consigned to work the barges on the River Styx?

She shuddered, not more so when the wind carried a voice to her, an unrecognizable masculine voice. She did not at first discern the words, but after the third repetition of his message, she understood what he was saying.

Ask your husband why he is so angry with you.

224

Psyche shook her head. She knew why: because she involved herself with the mortals. Whatever could come of raising that hackneyed subject again?

Ask your husband the real reason why he is so angry with you.

"The real reason?" she queried, glancing all about her but still seeing no one.

The wind and its voice drifted away, apparently satisfied that she had finally understood what she needed to do.

Psyche sat mute, staring at the barren earth. In two centuries it had not occurred to her that Cupid might have some unspoken reason for being angry with her, and if that were true, it would explain so much of his distant, uncaring behavior, not to mention his heated outbursts.

As she lifted herself out of the flower bed, she looked down at the broken vial and felt heartsick. When it was possible, she would confront Cupid, but of the moment she was more concerned with her present difficulty. How was she to reverse the effects of Cupid's arrow with Aphrodite's antidote to love seeping uselessly into the flower bed? Brandreth would no doubt follow Lady Felmersham's lead. He would forget about Evanthea entirely and pursue the truly horrendous course of forcing the viscount to petition for a divorce in the House of Lords.

After considering the dilemma for a hard moment, she realized there was only one hope—the cestus. If Evanthea wore the cestus at the ball tonight, she could possibly break Cupid's spell on Brandreth's sensibilities.

With that, Psyche headed east to retrieve the cestus from where she had secreted it in her painting room.

The roar of congratulations that flowed toward
the dais caused Brandreth to at last drag his gaze
from Lady Felmersham, if for no other reason than
to seek the origin of the din. When he saw Evanthea standing next to Mr. Shalford, her arm fixed
within the circle of his and the reason for the com-
motion evident in the vicar's broad, triumphant
grin, a peculiar, unexpected pain twisted through
his heart as quickly and as sharply as the crack of
a whip. He pressed a hand against his chest, his
breath catching in his throat.

When had she become betrothed to Shalford and
why? Only a few minutes ago, he had held her in
his arms and kissed her so thoroughly that he
would not have been surprised if their feet had
sprouted wings and they had flown heavenward.
When, therefore, had Evanthea determined she
loved Shalford and wished to become his wife?

But then, what did it matter? He had no real interest in Evanthea. He was in love with Susan Lawrence and always had been. He turned to gaze at
her and saw that she was looking in the direction
of her husband, whose mouth had fallen unattractively agape as he snored, ale-laden, through the
tumult around him.

Brandreth squeezed her hand, needing the comfort and reassurance, not so much that she loved
him, but that he was indeed still very much in love
with her. She turned, responding to the pressure of
his hand upon hers, and looked at him, smiling
sweetly. As he had done in the yard of the Swan
Inn, he fell deeply into her eyes, mesmerized as
fully as he had been in his youth.

"Will you beg him to give me a divorce, then?" Susan queried, breathing into his ear.

"Of course I will," he returned, confident he meant what he said. As though against his will, however, he found his attention torn from the elegant creature beside him, his gaze dragged back to the dais, where he saw Shalford lift Evanthea's fingers to his lips as he saluted his betrothed yet again.

Another pain rent its way snakelike through his heart, and Brandreth felt an overwhelming desire to push through the crowd and draw Shalford's cork. He even took a step forward. But his progress was prevented by Susan, who tugged firmly on his arm and whispered that if she didn't leave the crowded chamber, she was convinced she would faint just as Annabelle had.

"Annabelle?" he asked.

"Yes. Lady Elle took her into the taproom a moment ago. I vow, my knees are failing me even now." She fell into his arms. He held her closely about the shoulders as he made a path for them both to leave the parlor.

The taproom was nearly as crowded as the parlor and Brandreth decided to take the viscountess into the street. A moment later and he was standing on the cobbles of the High Street, where neither Annabelle nor Lady Elle were anywhere to be seen. The marquis's former desire to plant Shalford a facer was soon forgotten in the pretty slant of Lady Felmersham's petite, adorable nose.

Chapter Twenty-five

Shortly after arriving home, Lady Elle stood in front of the bust of Zeus, tears trickling from beneath her wrinkled eyelids. She was weeping without the least ability to staunch even one droplet as she dabbed at her cheeks in intervals of three or four seconds with a damp lace handkerchief. Her supply of current unhappiness seemed unending: Poor Annabelle had discovered a love for Shalford at the very moment Evanthea became betrothed to him, and Brandreth had eyes only for that truly despicable female, Lady Felmersham. And worse, if she did not make arrangements to pay certain of her husband's creditors by tomorrow, she would lose even the house in which she lived.

Whatever was she to do?

The eyes of Zeus returned her unwavering gaze with a ferocity peculiar to the hand of the artist who had originally fashioned the statue from hard, white marble. Thick curls, held captive by a wreath of laurel leaves, swirled about his head and hung majestically to his corded neck. Power emanated from the marked cheekbones and firm jawline, his thick brows drawn together in the semblance of a commanding frown.

Evanthea had always remarked on being comforted by the presence of the statue.

For herself, Lady Elle had been simply spellbound. Magic resided in the alcove where Zeus rested day and night, his features warmed by a glow of candlelight in the two sconces fitted to the wall on either side of the bust. But today, in the warm afternoon light, the magic seemed entirely dispelled by the troubles that had become magnified by both the events of the late morning and the appearance even earlier of two of her deceased husband's creditors. Unless she could provide these gentlemen with two thousand pounds — *merciful heavens, two thousand pounds!* — they would be forced to take severe legal recourse and demand the estate be sold to settle all outstanding debts.

"Two thousand pounds," she murmured, her kerchief pressed to her lips as though in doing so she was keeping the hopelessness of her situation in check. Her thoughts immediately turned to Brandreth and his generous offer to purchase the bust from her, but she had never truly intended to accept his offer. Her sense of honor forbade anything so mercenary. At the same time, she could not help but envision herself marching about the countryside with ragged cloths upon her feet, her woolen shawls moth-eaten and worn, her body lean and spare as she begged for her existence.

She laughed at such an absurd thought. She knew she was being quite melodramatic. Her family was extensive enough that she would never truly *suffer* as many of the poor suffered, but she would have to *beg*. She would be obliged throughout the rest of her days to *request* to reside with one of her family members or another, and to live upon the beneficence of relations who were tolerable at a distance but who could otherwise be considerably disagreeable. No, the prospect of losing Flitwick Lodge forever was daunting, indeed!

Lady Elle shuddered again, the mere thought of being beholden to anyone else bringing another gush of tears rolling down her cheeks.

"What am I to do? What am I to do?" she murmured over and over, shaking her head and continuing to dab at her cheeks as Zeus returned her gaze.

From what seemed to be a great distance, Lady Elle heard the sound of trumpets, blazing and imperious in their blasts. She looked about her in quick succession, straining to discern from what direction the herald approached. But each time she turned slightly, the music seemed to come from that particular direction, until she had made a complete circle and was once again facing the bust of Zeus. Only then did she realize that the dreamlike cries of the brass instruments were all around her.

She wondered if she was going mad and found herself enormously relieved when the blasts stopped.

Whatever did it mean? she wondered uneasily. She had the strongest prescience that an Olympian deity might be involved, but never before had trumpets resounded through her drawing room. She again regarded the bust and sighed deeply. The trumpets may have diverted her from her wretched difficulties, but only for a moment. The mere sight of the marble statue brought her unhappy thoughts tumbling about her until she was murmuring her despair all over again, "What am I to do?"

"I have always found it best to get over difficult

ground lightly," a deep masculine voice whispered in her ear. "What do you think?"

Lady Elle, who had been stunned into immobility by the man's voice as it struck her ear, slowly turned her head and gasped. "You!" she cried. "Oh, dear! Oh, my! My humble abode isn't half fine enough, merciful heavens! I—I—"

"You don't intend to fall into a swoon or a fit of the hysterics, do you?" the man returned with a teasing smile on his generous lips.

"Oh, no! I am not of such a weak constitution, Your Majesty, but I—I, oh, dear! I am amazed, actually. The likeness is near to perfection. By Jupiter, you look just like yourself . . . like your bust!"

"That old thing!" he cried with an affectionate laugh. "I wonder my darling daughter has kept it around as long as she has. It does not capture enough of my . . . *je ne sais quoi,* does it? But then, Venus has always surprised me. Her taste in art is impeccable and this bust hardly worthy of her usual fastidiousness. Having kept it in her bedchamber shows that she does have a heart, a love for me, however much she keeps it buried most of the time."

Lady Elle could hardly credit much of what she heard, though she was not surprised he confirmed the fact that the bust belonged to Aphrodite. She was particularly struck, however, by his referring to the elegant bust as a rather useless, inadequate representation of His Majesty. She was not by any great reach of the imagination an expert in matters of art and sculpture, but even she could see that an exceptionally skilled hand had crafted the statue. "This old thing?" Lady Elle murmured, stunned.

231

"Yes. If I recall correctly, I had my likeness chiseled for Aphrodite's seven hundredth birthday. She was always one of the worst of my children, her penchant for vengeance far outstripping her beauty. But she is pretty, isn't she?"

"Oh, yes, indeed, yes," Lady Elle breathed. She wondered if Zeus knew just how well she was herself acquainted with Venus and Psyche, but she feared revealing too much lest the activities of the women — particularly Psyche — became known to him.

"At any rate," he added, smiling warmly upon the bust, "I gave her the deuced thing, and ever since it has been in her bedchamber . . . that is, until Psyche stole it from her some thirty years ago, the silly chit!"

"Psyche stole it!" she exclaimed. "I knew it! Poor child! I hope you don't mean to give her a severe dressing-down. I suspect she takes things because of her acute unhappiness."

Zeus nodded. "I know. She married into the devil of a family, I fear, and that young whelp Eros, even with his brother's help, is still green! And as for Aphrodite, goodness gracious, who could ever, in her eyes, be good enough for her darling Cupid?"

"Psyche is the sweetest child."

"But hardly a match for Aphrodite."

"She does try, though. I applaud her in her efforts."

"Indeed, yes," Zeus nodded, clasping his hands behind his back and rocking slightly on his feet. He was dressed majestically in a flowing white cambric robe over which he wore a purple cloak embroidered in gold floss. A gold crown sat upon his silver hair, and in every aspect of his being he

232

was a king. "Poor Butterfly. She begged me to speak with Cupid but I knew it was of little use. Unless Eros learned through his own pain that he ought never to take his wife for granted, no words on my part would suffice to teach him the lesson. However, I do have a scheme in mind which might bring all to a happy conclusion. But first, did you know that Psyche again removed the cestus from my daughter's quarters?"

"I did not," Lady Elle responded, glancing at Zeus and wondering why his eyes were smiling so heartily. By the manner in which the other deities spoke of Zeus, she had gained the distinct impression His Majesty was ill-humored and autocratic. But he couldn't be, not when his eyes were so wondrously lit with amusement.

He further added to her growing good opinion of him by saying, "I have been thinking about the dilemma you are trying to solve, my dear Lady Elle, and I really think it would answer all your concerns—even your financial quandary—if the cestus were given to Annabelle and not to Evanthea."

"But why? Evanthea must win Brandreth back."

He lifted an imperious hand. "You must trust me but a little. The cestus to Annabelle and all will be solved! Do see what you can do!"

"Yes, Your Majesty," Lady Elle said, blinking rapidly several times. She chewed on the corner of her kerchief for a moment, thinking the situation through, then said, "To my knowledge, Evanthea does not yet have it, and I have not seen Psyche today at all."

"She was outside the inn about an hour ago. I don't believe anyone saw her. I broke the vial which contained Venus's antidote to love—the love

233

potion itself is in my possession—unbeknownst to Butterfly." He slipped his hand into the purple robes, which flowed from his broad shoulders to the floor, and withdrew the pretty glass container. He grinned at her. "So the cestus is your only hope! And now I must be going."

"I shall do as you say," she said. "But before you leave, I would like to know why—when even I can see that you are a very kind gentlemen— Psyche, Cupid, and Aphrodite positively tremble with fright at the sound of your name?"

He laughed, "Because they are my children and grandchildren. And because, though we in Olympus enjoy our immortality, the concept of maturation seems to be a difficult one when the centuries creep by and tempers grow short. Fear seems to be a requisite for keeping my kingdom in order." He flung one side of his robe over the opposite shoulder and, with a twinkle in his eye, added, "Now don't tell a soul that I've been here, and remember, if Annabelle wears the cestus, all will be well. Goodbye."

With that, he simply vanished, another blast of trumpets heralding his departure.

As Lady Elle accustomed herself to his sudden absence, she realized she was being addressed by Mrs. Brown. "Are you all right, ma'am?" the housekeeper queried.

Lady Elle turned and stared at her for a moment, her thoughts obsessed with finding Psyche. "Of course I am. Only tell me where Evanthea is at the moment."

"In her bedchamber, I believe. The house is still in quite an uproar, and the servants are wishful of trimming the withdrawing room with Miss Annabelle's ivy, roses, and muslin."

234

"Then I'll leave you to it, Mrs. Brown," she said, ignoring the wide, frightened aspect of the housekeeper's eyes. Biting her lip as she left the chamber, she wondered how Annabelle, wearing Aphrodite's cestus could possibly help her discharge a debt of two thousand pounds!

Chapter Twenty-six

Evanthea stood among the lime trees facing Flitwick Lodge, dangling her bonnet at her side, the white ribbons slick between her gloved fingers. She was staring in wonder at the front of the manor, which was being hastily put to rights by a dozen workmen—the ivy hacked away from the windows, white paint slapped upon the worn casements, and the narrow beds containing climbing roses and weeds carefully pruned and plucked as was needed. From all over the property, dead leaves from last winter had been raked up and hauled away, the grass beneath her feet had already been scythed, and at least two men were smoothing out and mending the gravel drive.

Annabelle's talent for housekeeping was evident at every turn. Once she had undertaken the formidable task of preparing the lodge for a ball, she had given herself wholeheartedly to the project, though even she admitted that she had precious little to do once she had hired sufficient servants and laborers to place at Mrs. Brown's disposal. The flighty housekeeper, for all her appearance of incompetence, knew quite well how to manage a household and how to keep two score of servants gainfully employed until the manor was ready to receive its guests.

Earlier, Evanthea quit her bedchamber, where the tramping of servants belowstairs and above, not to mention the attendant noises of the workmen as they cursed the ivy clinging to her window, had caused her to have the headache. It seemed once Mrs. Brown had so many at her command, she was determined to have every bed aired and every speck of dust obliterated from the manor before they left the premises that evening.

Sitting down upon the grass and leaning against a tree, Evanthea watched in turns first the blue sky through the green leaves above her, then, near the manor, the slow movements of a careful gardener who was working his way through the roses as meticulously as a master portraitist. Her thoughts tried to be as peaceful as the lovely setting before her, but too much had occurred to permit serenity to hold her captive.

The return journey from the George Inn had been a painfully quiet one. She had sat facing Lady Elle and Annabelle. Because she had been so consumed by what she had done in unwittingly accepting Shalford's hand in marriage, she had failed to notice until nearly the end of the journey that both Annabelle and her great-aunt had been weeping into their respective kerchiefs the entire way.

She should have been crying herself, she had thought at the time, but somehow tears refused to rise to her eyes, nor did her throat betray her with constricting pulses. She felt oddly detached from her feelings and even from the sensibilities of those who rode opposite her.

Now, as she had the opportunity to examine her heart, she felt very confused. There was a part of her that believed marriage to Mr. Shalford would be an acceptable thing, which was why, particularly given Brandreth's love for Lady Felmersham, she had not immediately taken the vicar aside and explained her misapprehension of his actions earlier, to wit, that she had thought he was offering her an escape from the heat instead of his hand in marriage.

She cringed as she remembered what followed when the ladies had climbed aboard Lady Elle's landau and Shalford had politely handed each of them up in turn. Both her great-aunt and Annabelle had made it clear by their combined expressions of unhappiness that they were horrified by the betrothal. Evanthea could comprehend Lady Elle's disappointment, since her great-aunt had for some time wished her to marry Brandreth. But Annabelle's distress had taken her by surprise, until she recalled the expression on the younger woman's face, just prior to the race, when she had watched the vicar drive down the avenue. Was it possible that Annabelle had truly fallen in love with Shalford? What a dreadful coil!

At the inn, Mr. Shalford had told Lady Elle he would call upon her on the following day to discuss marriage settlements. Poor Lady Elle did nothing more than stare at him with her eyes bulging as she shook her head. Words eluded her entirely. When the vicar begged to know if she had some objection to the union, Lady Elle burst into tears.

When Shalford had turned to Annabelle and begged her to wish him joy, she had also subsequently burst into tears. So it was left to Evanthea to bid the vicar goodbye and promise him that congratulations would no doubt be flowing his direction once all the ladies had accustomed themselves to Evanthea's loss of her spinsterish status.

She had smiled when she had said as much, hoping to lighten the moment, but Shalford had increased the ladies' tears when he had seized Evanthea's hand and said, "I am deeply honored that you accepted my hand, Evanthea. You will not regret becoming my wife. I shall devote myself to you day and night, have no doubt of that."

Evanthea had been completely overwhelmed and could think of nothing to say. Annabelle's weeping, however, threatened to bring a crowd about them out of mere curiosity at the caterwauling she had set up, so Evanthea had quickly bid Shalford *adieu,* promising him again as he drove away to dance the first set with him that evening.

But why did she feel so void of sentiment, as though a blanket had been thrown over her soul? Maybe it was *hope* that had sprouted wings and fled her heart. She didn't know, except that everything had seemed to change for her the moment Brandreth had said, *Susan, I vow I would do anything for you. Anything.* And what was she to do about Annabelle? She tried to attend to this new facet of her recent betrothal, but somehow her mind refused to apply itself. Instead, she watched the sky and the gardener in turns, her mind empty of purpose.

When Lord Brandreth recognized the pretty green silk skirts of Evanthea's carriage gown, draped on the grass from behind a lime tree, he drew his team toward her. Coming to a halt, he called her name. She seemed to be in somewhat of a reverie, since not only did she fail to hear the approach of his curricle, but she did not respond to his voice. When he called a second time, she still did not hear him and only became aware of him at last when he fairly shouted her name.

"Oh, what a start you gave me!" she cried, her brown eyes darting toward him like a frightened doe. She rose to her feet and, after crossing the short distance between them, continued, "And seeing you here, I can't imagine why I did not notice your arrival! I daresay I've been gathering daydreams."

"And what have you been dreaming about, Evanthea?" he queried, feeling as though he were speaking to her over a long chasm, a chasm created by the arrival of Lady Felmersham.

She smiled faintly. "I was thinking of my future."

"With Shalford?" he asked, searching her eyes. She lowered them immediately against his gaze, perhaps protecting herself.

"Yes, Shalford," she responded. "I don't know why it did not occur to me until today that we were well suited. Annabelle said as much even yesterday, but my heart had not been drifting in his direction at the time."

For reasons he could not explain to himself, he simply could not let her hint rest. "And what direction was your heart drifting?"

Finally, she met his gaze. "Toward a man with whom I had brangled so much over the years that I did not, until very recently, comprehend the charm he held over me. You see, he was quite the most arrogant, hard-hearted creature I had ever known, or so I believed, until he kissed me." She shook her head and glanced toward the heavens, as though seeking understanding. "It seems so silly to me now that I could have been persuaded out of my hard opinions by a mere kiss, but so it was.

240

The passion was brief, and briefly spent, however. *He* loves another and I, having had my eyes opened to the possibility of love, shan't regress. You will be surprised to know that I don't desire to remain an ape-leader anymore."

"Would you accept just anyone, then?" he asked, the former pain in his heart constricting the beating of his blood through his veins. Every confidence she had just spoken bespoke loss to him, a loss he was not prepared to endure just yet. "Shalford offered for you, pressing you hard by announcing his desire in so public a place. Surely you are hasty in your decision."

Evanthea smiled. "You know very well Mr. Shalford is not *just anyone,* and though I was overwhelmed by the circumstances surrounding his request for my hand, I vow I am pleased that he risked everyone's fine opinion of him by doing so. We shall be happy, I know we shall."

"Almost you persuade me. But did my embraces mean nothing to you?" His horses snorted at being kept standing when the stables and fresh oats were so close at hand.

"You awakened my heart, Brandreth, and for a moment I even thought . . . but never mind that. You have your own path to travel, don't you?" She looked at him intently, waiting for his answer.

"Yes, I suppose I do," he replied.

"A very difficult one and nearly unheard of in our century. Are you certain you wish to incur the disapprobation of your peers?"

"I would do anything for the woman I loved."

"And you love her?"

The pain was so great now as his gaze skimmed over the chestnut curls on Evanthea's forehead, over her creamy white complexion, straight nose,

241

and kissable lips, that he could scarcely breathe. "I do," he said.

"Then I wish you joy," she whispered, then turned to walk toward the house.

Chapter Twenty-seven

"No, no, do take it off, Evanthea!" Lady Elle cried, feeling like a traitor. "It positively ruins the lines of your gown. I know Psyche told you that Brandreth had but to look at you wearing the cestus and he would be smitten, but it is no such thing." Here she told a whisker, "For I overheard Eros telling his mother that the belt could not affect one who had already been stung by his arrow, and Brandreth has been stung, hasn't he?"

Evanthea nodded, sitting down upon the chair before her dressing table, her cheeks ashen. It was all Lady Elle could do to keep from rushing to her great-niece, putting her arms about her, and promising that all would be well. She could see Psyche had raised Evanthea's hopes to the skies and here she was taking the wind out of her eye.

For a brief moment, she even wondered if Zeus had been telling her the truth. After all, he was a vengeful deity, as most of the immortals seemed to be when crossed. Why, then, wouldn't he take delight in spoiling everything—as Cupid had tried to do—by making certain the wrong woman wore the cestus? What if Brandreth saw Annabelle first and tumbled in love with her?

But after another moment's consideration, she

dismissed her concern regarding Zeus. Never, in her entire existence—save when she had first looked into her dear Henry's laughing eyes—had she seen in a man's expression so wondrous a mixture of solid character, good humor, and strength.

No, Zeus had not lied to her.

Turning her thoughts toward Evanthea, she attempted a light note. "Why do you appear crestfallen? The cestus isn't everything and I'm sure somehow we'll come about, only you must trust me a little. In the meantime, I hope you don't intend to fall into a decline."

"Psyche seemed so certain of success," Evanthea said, her eyes full of pain as she began unbuttoning the belt. "For a moment I believed her, that Brandreth was not beyond my reach. And now you are telling me the cestus will be of no use to me. It is too much, dear Lady Elle. My heart cannot bear swinging about this way, as though it is suspended at the end of a rope and flung awkwardly through the air by whoever is nearest."

"I don't like to speak ill of anyone, my dear, but our delightful little Butterfly is not precisely the most competent of creatures." Lady Elle moved to stand next to Evanthea, sympathetic tears springing to her eyes as she helped her remove the cestus. Having destroyed Evanthea's hope of the moment, Lady Elle searched her mind for some fragment of wisdom with which she might comfort her greatniece. She thought of her love for her deceased husband and began quietly, "I don't know how to say what I wish to say to you, Evanthea, but I shall try. I have lived now for over seventy years on this beautiful, at times unforgiving island called England. I have seen loves come and go for most, but not for you and for myself, of course. Once Henry captured my heart, no one else could touch me. Ours was a true love and as invincible as I believe yours is with Brandreth." She slipped the cestus from about Evanthea's waist and, staring down into her face, continued, "Even after Henry died, I could not find a love to replace his, though I had more than one gentleman offering for my hand in marriage, let me tell you. Why do you lift your brows at me? Is it so inconceivable that a man could love me at my time of life? I vow I am quite offended. You stare at me in too much wonder for my vanity to bear. Can't you see beyond my wrinkled skin? My spirit is as young as yours and equally as appealing to a man who—"

Evanthea cut her off, her eyes wide with surprise. "You misunderstand my astonishment. Do you mean you could have been rescued from your poverty any time these past several years but refused to be?"

Lady Elle shook her head. "Silly chit! I have told you often and often I am not impoverished, for I have you and Annabelle and my ridiculous great-nephew. Real poverty, of an immaterial sort, belongs to those who have only conceit for brains, like Lady Felmersham."

"But Brandreth loves her!"

"I never said he couldn't think or behave like a gudgeon. He's a man like all the others, his head turned by a pretty face and flirtatious manners. Your father was just like him in some ways—certainly in his stubbornness—and if Psyche had not intervened, I daresay you would not even be here to ease the loneliness of my old age. He was a determined bachelor, that one."

"What do you mean? Are you telling me Psyche intervened with Papa and Mama?" Evanthea asked, apparently stunned.

Lady Elle sat down on the edge of Evanthea's

245

bed, across from her. "And nearly came to grief," she said, folding the cestus up on her lap. "She almost caused a shipwreck—or so Aphrodite believes." Realizing she could at last share the whole of the history with Evanthea, she looked down the years, her heart full of warm feelings of remembrance. "I would have so enjoyed recounting the story to you before this, you've no idea. I was wise enough to comprehend, however, that because I was the only one who ever saw the Olympian beings before now, you would not have believed I was speaking the truth. But my goodness, it seems like yesterday when George—your father—was all gobbled up with his archeological interests. He had barely a thought or minute to spare for anything resembling love. That was how Psyche discovered him and your mama. Psyche had been exploring in Greece and came upon him. She immediately became enchanted with the notion of helping him find a suitable wife. That was when she thought of your mama.

"And your mother! Remember how lively she was? It was she who insisted upon traveling through Europe by herself. Quite, quite scandalous, even though she took six outriders and three maids with her. My, my, how the tabbies did caterwaul. Much she cared. Problems arose when, very much against the advice of the Foreign Ministers along the Mediterranean, she sailed with a merchant ship traveling to Greece. One evening, as night approached, the ship was accosted by an Algerian slaver, the master of which would have been enchanted to have taken a white slave with blond hair. I've no doubt your mother would have fetched a stunning price in Algiers, though I imagine the Pesha would have tried to ransom her first."

Evanthea nodded. "This much I know. When I

was very little, Mama told me the story a hundred times . . . how the ship was fired upon and crippled, nearly sinking before it could reach safe harbor. All of it was too horrible to be believed, and the possibilities of slavery or even death unthinkable. How frightened she must have been. But where was Psyche? What did she do?"

"From what I understand, it was she who alerted the English captain to the danger his ship was in. She did so by appearing to the captain of the pirate ship and frightening him. In a moment of panic at the apparition before him, he gave the order to fire prematurely, a shot which fell into the water thirty yards short of its target, providing essential time to properly alarm the merchant captain. He returned fire, and the rest you know. To this day, Aphrodite insists that the whole business was mishandled and that had the English ship sunk, Psyche alone would have been to blame. I think she is far too strident in her opinions, but Psyche does not. She agrees with her."

Both ladies were silent a pace. After a time, Evanthea tilted her head and said, "Yesterday I realized, because of how much Psyche knew of my past, that she has been with me for a very long time. But it never occurred to me that she knew Papa and Mama."

"Yes. I believe Butterfly is quite hopeless where love is concerned, which might explain her choice of a husband." When Evanthea laughed, Lady Elle leaned forward to pluck gently at the shimmering rose silk skirts of her great-niece's ball gown. "There, that is much better," she said. "My, how charming you look in a proper gown, and your hair curling down your back so prettily. I vow if Brandreth does not take notice of you and suffer an immediate change of heart where that—that *hoyden* is concerned, I shall pronounce him hopeless—or perhaps I shall just box his ears!

"I shall leave you now, but remember this: The day is not yet over and the battle is not lost. You have only to believe in yourself and in Brandreth's good sense—however much of the moment it might be mucked up by Cupid's *poison*—and your love for him and his for you shall prevail."

"But I was responsible for his not having married Susan Lawrence in the first place. His heart is laden with anger against me for words I spoke to her many years ago."

"Then beg his pardon, for your sake. But for his, kiss him hard and remind him of what he will lose if he lets you marry Shalford."

Evanthea looked into her aunt's eyes and felt tears well up in her own. "What of Shalford?"

"I don't know, but I believe everything will work itself out. . . . Only don't abandon your love for Brandreth."

"I can't jilt Shalford. It would break his heart."

Lady Elle lifted a finger and wagged it at Evanthea. "Do you imagine he is in love with you?"

"Why else would he have offered for me?"

"I believe he was infatuated with your new eardrops and his victory over Brandreth."

Evanthea gasped. "Oh, dear. Then he, too, has erred."

"Precisely so."

"What a coil."

"Indeed."

Chapter Twenty-eight

Psyche raced through wall after wall, searching for Lady Elle and the cestus. She still could not credit that the older and usually quite responsible woman had convinced Evanthea to remove it. When she had found Evanthea in a despondent state, she had nearly screamed with vexation. The guests were already arriving and music poured from the ballroom overlooking the terrace at the west end of the house.

She raced to the entrance hall, where she found Lady Elle and Brandreth receiving guests. Where was Annabelle, she wondered, and why hadn't Evanthea been summoned to take part in the civilities? She was nearly driven to distraction and approached Lady Elle. "Where is the cestus?" she cried.

"I haven't time for you now," Lady Elle responded.

Mr. Shalford, who was at that moment telling her ladyship that he admired her brooch, said, "I beg your pardon?"

Lady Elle laughed lightly. "What did you say? Oh, I am sorry, I am hopeless without my ear trumpet. You must forgive me, Mr. Shalford." After he had repeated his compliment and received a proper expression of appreciation from her, he moved away. Only then did Lady Elle answer Psyche's question. "I gave it to Annabelle, who needs it far more than Evanthea."

"More than Evanthea! How can you say so when Brandreth has been struck by one of my husband's arrows! Without the cestus, she will lose the marquis forever!"

"And you do not believe in love quite strongly enough, my dear. Perhaps that is why you are having difficulty realizing how very much Eros loves you."

"Who loves me?" a confounded Mr. Allenby cried. He had just moved to stand before Lady Elle and seemed both stunned and pleased with the delightful information her ladyship was passing along to him. "Alice?" he queried. "I don't believe I know an Alice, or are you teasing me yet again, Lady Elizabeth. Who is she? Have I met her before?"

"Oh, Mr. Allenby!" Lady Elle cried, her cheeks feeling warm as she set about prevaricating yet again. "I have completely forgotten her name. I am not even certain she is called Alice, but I saw her go in just ahead of Mr. Sawley. I could not quite believe the sweet expression on her face as she glanced in your direction. You would do well to discover, if you can, her identity . . . er . . . at once!"

Mr. Allenby appeared delighted with this news, and after bowing over her hand, he hurried away.

"Lady Elle," Brandreth whispered, leaning near her and ignoring Felmersham's lifted brow. "To whom are you speaking?"

"Only myself," she replied, giving her hand to the viscount and smiling upon him. "Wouldn't you agree, my lord, that it is the prerogative of those of advancing years to indulge in conversation with the air?"

"I do so myself at times," he responded with a chortle. "Particularly when I have consumed at least two bottles of port."

"How droll." She then happened to glance over his shoulder and gasped. To Psyche, she whispered, "I don't like to mention it, my dear, but I believe your husband has arrived."

"My what?" the viscount cried, taken aback. "You mean my wife, don't you?"

"Did I say *husband?* How very odd." She turned to Brandreth and, with every appearance of sincerity, queried, "Have my wits gone begging?"

Psyche felt the color drain from her face as she quickly searched the square entrance hall and saw her husband, his wings batting the air in a fluttering motion that meant he was irritated, standing beside a suit of armor. "Oh, dear," she murmured, and moved away from Lady Elle. She did not at all like the expression on his face. His brows were drawn together severely as he watched her and he was not smiling, not one whit.

Nothing will ever change between us, she thought. With a flip of her skirts in his direction, she turned on her heel and headed back up the stairs, floating instead of walking. She hoped he would take offense at her attitude and leave the ball, but in this she was mistaken. By the time she reached the landing, he had caught up with her, taken her by the elbow, and plunged her at a devastatingly sharp angle downward through the staircase and out onto the terrace.

251

Here he stopped abruptly and pinned her from leaving him, taking strong hold of both her arms. "I don't intend to leave until you have given me Mama's cestus and her love potions. After that, you are free to do as you wish. I will never again question what you are about or where you go, or try to make you see the senselessness of your ways. Only give me the things you *stole* from my mother. After that, I intend to return to another palace and seek living quarters elsewhere."

Psyche had never seen her husband in this state. She did not know which she felt more keenly — a terrible dread that they would no longer live as husband and wife, that he had grown so fatigued with their silent quarreling that he would live apart from her, or a fury that even to the end, he sided with his mother against her, showing concern only for Aphrodite.

"I don't have any of them," she responded.

"Do you deny you stole them — *yet again?*"

"No. I had great need of them, particularly when you decided to involve yourself where you were least wanted. How could you shoot Brandreth just when all was but as good as settled between him and Evanthea?"

The stern, determined expression on his face wavered slightly as he released the grip on her arms. "Because I was furious with you, furious at your stubbornness and your lamentable silence and your falseness. Besides, you seemed to be enjoying yourself, breaking Zeus's law in the bargain, and I thought it might lend me a bit of amusement to see my powers inflicted upon *mortals* again."

"You despise me because I was once a mortal, don't you?"

His jaw worked strongly as he stared down at

252

her. Suddenly, Psyche remembered what the voice in the wind had said to her, that she must discover what true anger was fermenting in her husband's heart, the unspoken rage that affected his every action toward her. "Eros," she said at last, taking a small, deliberate step toward him, "only tell me this: Why are you so very, very angry with me?"

"What do you mean, tell you why I am angry?" he cried out as though deeply astonished. "I just did, or don't you think the fact that you have stolen my mother's belongings is sufficient cause?"

"No, I do not," she replied steadily. "There's something more, something you haven't told me, ever. Why when you look at me sometimes do you appear as though the only way you would be satisfied with me is if you could put your hands about my neck and strangle me?"

Cupid tilted his head back slightly as though all the muscles in his neck had suddenly become stiff. Her words seemed to strike a chord in his heart. His wings quivered in the night air as he stared at her. Unable to remain still, he whirled around, the sudden movement of his wings accidentally knocking Psyche over. She tumbled to the hard stone of the terrace, scraping her elbows and knees.

When he saw what he had done, he was beside her immediately, picking her up and cradling her in his arms. "My darling, my darling," he cried. "I didn't mean to . . . I would never truly . . . oh, my dear Psyche, whatever are we to do?"

Psyche felt her throat tighten. She slipped her hand about his neck, pulling him close and pressing her cheek against his. "I do love you, ever so much," she whispered. Tears poured from her eyes, dampening his cheek as well as her own.

"Psyche," he whispered, sounding agonized.

"Tell me, Cupid. Pray tell me what I have done to so set your heart against me that you ignore me six days out of seven? Or why it is when you come to me at night, you will not even leave the candles lit and why you scowl at me so severely? It cannot be only because I have taken something from your mother. It cannot!"

He held her close, the muscles of his arms flexing into the tender flesh of her skin and hurting her. She knew he was struggling to order his thoughts, to command his sensibilities. When he spoke, it was with great effort. "You are not a faithful wife, and though I should be more large-minded than I am, I can't forgive you. I *can't!*" With that, he slipped her off his lap and drew away from her.

She was stunned by his words. Never in her entire existence would she have expected him to have accused her of infidelity. "I? Not faithful?' Whatever can you mean?"

"Whatever do I mean? Psyche, now that I have forced myself to address the subject which lies between us like a gorge that reaches down to Hades, how can you stand there and say, 'I? Not faithful? Do you mean to lie to me? Is this what has become of the delicate, gently bred, virtuous woman I married? You steal, and you commit adultery, and you lie as well? Psyche, what has happened to you?"

"But I am not lying!" she cried. "I have never been unfaithful to you. I have never been with another man. Never!"

He lifted his chin, staring at her in cruel disbelief. "If you will not even confess your misdeed, how can I know whether I can ever learn to love you again?"

"But there has been no misdeed," she responded, her initial shock at his accusation giving way to her own anger. "And whom, pray tell, am I supposed to have seduced?"

He was silent for a long moment, condemning her with the fury in his eyes. "My brother," he said hoarsely, "as you very well know."

Psyche was not precisely stunned. Her mind seemed to work in several directions all at once. Had he seen Anteros kiss her two centuries ago, or worse yet a second time? *Merciful Olympus,* was it only last night? Had Aphrodite's doves taken flight because Cupid had been nearby and startled them? Oh, dear. Had he then assumed the worst of her?

"Anteros," she said.

"Then it is true."

Psyche blinked several times and did not at first respond. "He wished for it," she said at last. "And he kissed me, not once but twice, though two hundred years separated these harmless attentions to me."

"Harmless! How coolly you speak of your actions. Psyche, I saw you throw your arms about his neck! Anyone would have supposed you were lovers! Anyone! Not just a jealous spouse!"

Psyche straightened her shoulders and said, "I did respond to his pleas and attentiveness and to the passion of his embrace, I will not deny as much. But you heard what I told him?"

"No, I did not. As you may imagine, I did not desire to stay in order to hear or see the rest."

"He wanted me to forsake you and when I refused, he told me to deny that I didn't respond to his kisses. And I said, 'What would you expect of a lonely housewife?' Anteros knew it was hopeless and he let me go."

255

"With Mother's cestus and vials?"

"Yes."

Eros was silent for a moment, his gaze fixed on the blue bricks of the terrace. Finally, he lifted his eyes to her and continued, "Whatever may have happened last night, you cannot tell me you only *kissed* Anteros the first time, two centuries ago, for I know you were unfaithful to me then."

"How do you know any such thing?" she queried. "Did you see us together, or did someone tell you I had been with Anteros? Who was it, though I would not be surprised if your brother boasted of that which did not happen? He is just devilish enough to do so."

"He never spoke to me of it."

"Good," she said, pleased that Anteros had at least shown some sense. Still, she pressed her husband, "Who, then? Who told you I had been unfaithful to you?"

"A more credible source than my brother, but that is all I will say."

Psyche searched her mind, trying to remember the first kiss she had received from Anteros and knowing no one had been remotely nearby. Then it occurred to her that there was one person in Eros's life whom he would never credit with deception but who would most happily malign her character if she could. "Your mother!" she cried out. "Your mother told you I had an affair with Anteros. Oh, Cupid, say it is not so!"

The guilty manner in which his eyes shifted away from her told her all she needed to know. "How could she!" Psyche cried. "And how could you have believed her! I tell you now, the most that ever happened between your brother and myself was two very passionate kisses — the first of which I took pleasure in because I had found you flirting with that tavern wench in Gloucestershire, and the second because I have grown so lonely I vow if a fish looked kindly upon me, I'd take his lips willingly to mine."

With that, she brought the discussion to a close by whirling on her heel and hurrying away. She knew by the silence that followed her that Eros had chosen to remain on the terrace.

The moment she flew through the brick wall and entered the hallway adjacent to the ballroom, she was stunned to find Annabelle slinking along the wall but a few feet from her and wearing the cestus!

She approached her quickly and would have begun unbuttoning the belt, but at that moment she heard Lady Elle call to her. "Psyche!" she cried. "Pray do not! Zeus insists all will be well if Annabelle is permitted to wear the cestus!"

Psyche blinked several times at Lady Elle. "Zeus?" she queried at last, startled. "Oh, dear! Is he here? Is he quite angry? Does he know what I have been about?"

"Whether he is here or not I cannot say, since I spoke with him much earlier today. As for being angry, in truth I saw none of it. And I shan't begin to address the subject of your involvements at Old Flitwick and his knowledge of them, for I won't be so presumptuous. But I hope you mean to abide by his wishes regarding the cestus."

"Of course!" Psyche cried. "But what of Evanthea?"

Lady Elle gave her shoulders a little shrug. "I don't know precisely, but right now I am convinced it is imperative Annabelle wears the cestus!"

Psyche stepped away from Annabelle and let her

257

proceed unhindered down the hall. She then glanced from Lady Elle to Annabelle at least three times before exclaiming, "But I must know what happens!" And with that, she flew after Annabelle, who appeared to be heading toward the terrace from which Psyche had just come.

Chapter Twenty-nine

The Marquis of Brandreth had been searching for his quarry for nearly quarter of an hour. Most of the guests had arrived and were busily entertaining themselves in the ballroom, the withdrawing room, and the billiard room, but apparently not Lord Felmersham. It would seem, upon arriving, the viscount had simply disappeared. He had certainly abandoned his wife, whom Brandreth had last seen chatting easily with Mr. Shalford.

Earlier that day, Brandreth had considered the possibility that he was making a grave mistake in pursuing Lady Felmersham's wish to divorce her husband. The very notion of divorce had heretofore been so repugnant to his lordship that he did not quite comprehend how it had come about Susan had been able to persuade him on this course so easily.

He tried to retrace his steps with her, to discern when it was he had become so infatuated with her—much like in former times, but now to such a degree that he was willing to forsake every principle in order to secure her happiness and his. After searching through the stream of events, he had come to believe that his heart had tumbled at her feet right after he had become unaccountably dizzy in the inn yard of the Swan Inn. She had pinched his arm, he had looked at her, and he had been lost. He felt the back of his neck, recalling that for the briefest moment he thought he had been stung by a bee. The sensation had disappeared almost as quickly as it had begun, leaving him quite dizzy, and he had therefore decided that the race, the heat, and the company of two beautiful women had been the source of his bizarre reaction.

Now as he sought out Lord Felmersham, for the strict purpose of making known to the viscount his intention of helping his wife seek a divorce from him, he began to doubt the depth of his desire to go down such a wretched path.

But what else could he do? He had already pledged his vow to the woman he loved. As he again passed into the hallway with the strains of a country dance resounding behind him, he chanced upon Meppers.

The butler looked well pleased and neat as a pin in his formal red and gold uniform, powdered hair, and silk breeches. He bowed good-humoredly to the marquis and begged to know if he might be of service to his lordship. "Begging your pardon, my lord, but you seem in some distress."

"I have been seeking Felmersham, and the deuced thing is I can find him nowhere."

"Ah," Meppers nodded knowingly. "Follow me."

With a surprised lift of his brow, Brandreth fell in step behind the butler. Within a few minutes, they arrived at the door of the library. "What the devil—?" Brandreth queried, unable to comprehend why one of the guests had secreted himself in the library.

"Her ladyship suggested the gentlemen might be more comfortable getting up a game of whist. I believe you'll see her reasoning has merit." When Meppers threw the door wide, the marquis glanced quickly about the chamber and saw at once why Lady Elle had recommended the gentlemen seclude themselves in her husband's favorite, yet remote chamber.

There were four of them in all—Lord Felmersham, his friend Mr. Sawley, and two other bucks quite unfamiliar to Brandreth. They were all foxed, not so deeply that they were unable to discern the value of their cards, but well enough into their altitudes to be unfit company for the gently bred assemblage of women now being squired about the rest of Flitwick Lodge.

"That you, Marquis?" Felmersham called out too loudly and with a loose chortle in his throat. "Come in! Come in! But for God's sake, take that grimace off your face. You're as hapless as old Moppet here, or whatever the deuce Lady Elle calls that creature."

The viscount waved his hand toward Meppers, who rolled his eyes at Brandreth and closed the door behind the marquis. Brandreth advanced into the room, which was thick with the smells of port and snuff, the latter of which was being shared liberally among the hardened gamesters from a box in the center of the table. The white linen was now covered with messy trails of the brown powder, and at least two of the gentlemen wore patches of the same on their white neckcloths. "I had hoped to speak privately with you, Felmersham," Brandreth began. "But perhaps I ought to call upon you tomorrow."

"Whatever for?" the viscount returned cheerfully, the bulbous end of his nose a bright red as he dealt a round of cards. "Besides, I know quite well what you wish to say to me, and I think these gentlemen, who represent some of the finest of our English families, ought to hear what you have to say." A general roar of laughter accompanied this last remark.

"I think not," was all Brandreth said as he bowed sardonically toward the table and turned around to quit the room.

"One moment!" Felmersham called to him, again quite cheerfully. "If it is regarding the divorce my wife wishes, let me assure you I shan't stand in the path of love! God forbid I should appear hard-hearted!"

Brandreth was stunned and completely unable to credit what he had heard. "Susan . . . that is, Lady Felmersham spoke to you of divorce?"

"Of course. She is my wife, and however much we may not appear as though we have much interest in one another, she does keep me abreast of her latest flirtations."

Brandreth's head was reeling as he stared at the viscount, who in turn glanced at his cards and winced. "Ought to have shuffled better," he murmured.

"I don't understand you, sir."

Felmersham looked up at him and blinked, his eyes watery and red. "I said, I ought to have shuffled better." .

"No, no. You've misunderstood me. I don't understand what you said about your wife and her latest flirtations. You say she spoke to you of wishing for a divorce."

"Are you as deaf in love as you are blind, then?" he queried. "I'll grant her a divorce if she wants one. You can have no concern on that head."

Brandreth still could not believe he was hearing correctly or that the battle had been won so easily. But Felmersham had spoken clearly enough and seemed sufficiently in command of his senses to have escaped error. "I shall call upon you tomorrow, then, and perhaps we can determine the particulars."

"Wouldn't think of involving myself in anything so tedious. I shall leave it all to my solicitors. I shall want a large settlement, of course, but you can stand the nonsense—of that, my mercenary little wife was certain. Permit me the honor of giving you a hint, though. With regard to her penchant for chasing coattails, I've found it best to simply look the other way. Sawley, who the devil was that fellow she was prattling on about the entire way here? What was his name? The man who won the race today."

"Oh, the churchman. Shalford. A mere Mr. Shalford seems to have captured her fancy."

Brandreth had listened to the insulting nature of Felmersham's remarks, the tone of his voice, and the wretched indifference of his speech with a calmness, until Shalford's name was mentioned. The viscount could speak as cruelly regarding his wife as he wished, since it was obvious to the marquis that only the most disinterested and brutal of husbands could have so hardened Susan Lawrence that she would wish for a divorce. But when he cast such aspersions upon Susan's character as passed the bounds of decency, daring to intimate that already his wife's eye was wandering yet again, Brandreth could not restrain himself.

He crossed the dark chamber in three strides and, rounding the table, plucked Felmersham from his seat by the lapels of his coat. Giving the tall, thin man a hard shake, he cried, "How dare you! Apologize at once, or these *fine* English gentlemen will see you lying stretched out on *fine* English soil before the sun rises again!"

"Good heavens," Felmersham responded, blinking in surprise at Brandreth. "You've a monster of

263

a temper, don't you? Are you challenging me to a duel? Shouldn't I be the one offended in this situation? What an odd man you are."

"I love your wife, damme! I always have!"

"You have loved a phantom, then, just as I did," he said in what Brandreth could only perceive as a quite sincere tone. "But yours was the great good fortune of having escaped marriage to her. I can only recommend you escape it a second time, or by God, I'll grant her the divorce she seeks. Then where will you be?"

Something in the look in the viscount's eye, of pain and of disappointment, reached out to Brandreth and forced him to release his hold on his coat. Felmersham sank down into his chair, his shoulders slumped slightly as he reached for his goblet of port and took a long, deep draught.

Brandreth had heard too much to remain within the constricting confines of the crowded chamber. He felt nauseous and sickened by the battering he had just received. Truth had somehow reared its ugly head in the words spoken, yet not spoken, and in the terrible look in Felmersham's eye.

Once outside the chamber, the marquis let the cool, quiet air of the hallway flow over him. He breathed deeply and tried to think of nothing, so his mind might become still, but it was impossible. He should have called him out and requested Shalford to second him. But why had Felmersham looked at him with an expression he could only describe as deep pity? He had heard rumors through the years about Susan but had dismissed most of them as the habitual gossip that flowed liberally through London's drawing rooms.

Now, however, he was confronted with the possibility that perhaps he no longer knew the woman he was so intent upon making his wife, and perhaps he never had.

He returned to the ballroom, which was draped elegantly with streamers of pale pink muslin. Elegant ladies floated in and out of the chamber, dressed in their finest silks, lace, and embroidered gowns. The gentlemen held their arms tenderly, sporting black formal wear, including starched shirtpoints which had already begun drooping slightly from the exertion of dancing. Brandreth hugged the wall of the room, searching for his beloved. When he caught sight of her, he saw that she was laughing behind her fan, which she held close to her lips, and smiled mischievously into Shalford's face.

Felmersham's words and pained demeanor rolled over him again as he edged farther into the room. He could not deny that, even to his eye, Susan appeared to be flirting quite assiduously with the vicar. Her other hand came into view and he felt a shock go through him. Her gloved fingers were touching Shalford's cheek. Impossible!

The vicar immediately caught the viscountess's hand and scowled severely at her.

"No," Brandreth murmured to himself. "It can't be."

To his credit, Shalford merely bowed to her, then turned on his heel and walked away. Brandreth's esteem for the vicar rose to a new pitch. He knew in his heart he could not fault him. The blame lay clearly at Susan's feet.

Bile reached the back of tongue. He knew a desire to strike out at something, at someone. He was surprised when Felmersham's voice sounded close to his ear. "I will take her away," he said quietly. "Miss Swanbourne saved you once from this nightmare. Did you know that I took great advantage of her biting remarks to Susan that night so many years ago? I remember how she said to Susan, 'You had better take Felmersham and be done with it!' Lord, how I have regretted acting upon those words since.

"I hope you will, in time, forgive her, Brandreth. But what more could you expect from an heiress who never knew her mother, and who was petted and spoiled from the first by an overindulgent nanny?"

As he passed by, the marquis did not move to stop him. It was only after Felmersham was several feet away that he thought to offer the long-suffering husband a polite bow of acquiescence, a gesture the viscount could not see.

Chapter Thirty

Shalford had disengaged Lady Felmersham's clutching fingers from the lapel of his coat with a sense of profound disgust. For some reason the viscountess had made him the object of her flirtations, a circumstance that afforded him tremendous discomfort and no pleasure. He had heard rumors that Brandreth intended to marry her once she sought a divorce from her husband. However much he might not entirely approve of the marquis's general activities, he had always believed him unreproachable regarding the accepted dictums of his peers. Would he truly cause so great a scandal by stealing another man's wife?

Of the moment, what seemed worse was the fact that the marquis's intended wife was already flirting outrageously with another man. He wondered if Brandreth was aware of it.

Leaving the ballroom, Shalford sought relief from her ladyship's oppressive attentions by escaping onto the terrace. He moved into the deepest shadows, leaned against the cool stone, and breathed in deeply the fresh summer's night air.

The truth was, Lady Felmersham was not Shalford's only concern this evening. When he had greeted his betrothed, he could see that not only had she been crying, but that even while she smiled brightly upon him, new tears welled up in her eyes. She had tried to convince him that the cause of her *unhappiness* was profound joy at becoming his wife, but even he was not such a sapskull as to believe such humbug. He had tried to press her, but she disappeared behind her fan and her kerchief, saying after a moment that if he would but give her time, she would adjust to the shift in her circumstances and indeed would do everything in her power to make him an admirable wife. How terribly her voice had quivered and how much her general countenance had shaken his belief he had acted well by offering for her in so public a place as the crowded parlor of the George Inn.

He shuddered when he considered what he had done. In the excitement and exhilaration of having won the race, he had been overcome by a sensation of power. He had offered for Evanthea spontaneously, out of the simple thrill of having bested Brandreth in competition. His blood had been racing triumphantly through his veins, and it had seemed in so victorious a moment that he could have anything he wanted. Here, his conscience pricked him a little, for he had seen Evanthea look at the marquis for a brief moment with a longing such as he had never witnessed in her before. The thought had shot through his mind: *She loves him.* He had then dismissed the look and the thought as absurd, but the ferocity of his competitiveness with the marquis prompted him to extend his hand toward her and beg her to become his wife.

Even now, he was not certain she had ever properly understood him. And who was it that had laughed so long and so low . . . a man's ironically amused laugh? A sensation of the whole episode having been unreal afflicted him now. Was he truly engaged to Evanthea, who he suspected was madly in love with Brandreth? What the devil had he been thinking to have offered for her in the first place? That was the rub: When he had offered for her, he had not been thinking at all!

"Gregory," a hushed feminine voice called out to him.

"Who is there?" he queried, narrowing his eyes as he scanned the shrubberies all around the perimeter of the garden. He could see no one. A scattering of lanterns shone in dim pools of light but not sufficiently, it would seem, to illumine the lady who had addressed him. A tall stone statue of Artemis holding her bow, her quiver strapped to her back and a dog at her knee, stood pillarlike in the center of the garden.

A form peeped out from behind the statue, the light skirts of the lady's gown and the whiteness of her arms blending in with the light gray stone of the statue. "It is I, Annabelle."

"Annabelle?" he countered, irritated. Would she now begin to flirt with him as she always did? It was enough to have endured Lady Felmersham's cloying words and fingers, but not Annabelle. He had too many troubling thoughts bounding through his mind to tolerate her childish attempts to cajole him. "You ought not to be out in the cold night air. I daresay you are likely to succumb to an inflammation of the lungs. Where is your shawl?"

"Shalford, pray don't ring a peal over my head. I have been waiting for you and must speak with you. I promise you I will behave myself, only do come into the garden and speak with me."

Shalford knew a strong sensation of impatience, and his first inclination was to recommend she cease behaving like a chit not yet out of the schoolroom and to leave her to her devices. But there was something in the tone of her voice and in the manner in which she promised to behave herself that appealed to him. He had always believed a fine young woman resided somewhere within Annabelle's hopelessly spoiled brain and he thought someday, should the right man happen to wed her, she would become an exemplary wife and mother. Annabelle had enough spirit to manage the largest of households, one with even a dozen children underfoot. If he had had the opportunity to join a regiment, she was the sort of wife he would have wished for, much in the same manner, as a man of the church, he felt Evanthea would make a fine vicar's wife.

Perhaps for no reason, perhaps for all these reasons, or perhaps because the prospect of facing Evanthea's tears again quite revolted him, Shalford hesitated only a moment at the top of the steps. With complete disregard for how the damp grass would no doubt damage his black silk ballroom slippers, he ventured down the stairs and toward the statue.

As Annabelle stepped from behind Artemis and her dog and came completely into view, he had the impression that she was begowned like an ancient goddess herself. Her beautiful blond hair had been pulled back into a series of waves and curls, held back by bands of ribbons that shimmered like gold in the faint moonlight. Long curls hung to her shoulders and cascaded down her back, flowing with the white silk of her gown like seafoam on the crest of a wave. The ball gown was caught quite Grecianlike tightly about her waist with what he saw was a worked belt of some sort. He had never seen the belt, but it drew his eyes in an almost mesmerized manner to the soft lines of the fabric as the skirt flowed gently over Annabelle's full, feminine hips and draped becomingly to the ground.

She was speaking, he was certain of that, but he could not quite make out the words. A strange mist seemed to enter his mind, weaving through his thoughts and blocking one word out of three, until no coherent thought could shape itself in his mind. The fragments of her speech came to him as: "loved . . . long time . . . forgive me . . . childish . . . absurd . . . hope." His thoughts were equally as disjointed: "beautiful . . . the army . . . hope . . . love . . . hidden . . . discovered."

Through the fog in his mind, Annabelle's face finally came into focus before him. He saw her now, as he had never permitted himself to see her before, as the woman he loved, as the woman he had always loved but had never dared to.

"Annabelle," he cried huskily and, without begging her permission to do so, took her forcefully in his arms and kissed her hard. When the small, lithe energetic form melted into his embrace and returned kiss for kiss, the future became meticulously clear to Shalford, his heart thrilling to the new life born between them in that moment, a life that he knew would take him from the vicarage and Annabelle from the frivolity of London as surely as the kiss they shared was real.

When he released her and began to profess his love, she silenced him by affirming his thoughts as though she had read them. "A pair of colors, Shalford? I have always wanted to follow the drum, ever since I was a child. I've never told a soul until now!"

"Will there be anything we won't be able to accomplish together, my little vixen?"

"Nothing, my darling."

As Shalford again drew her against him, for the second time that day he heard a low, amused laugh, one that seemed to arrive on the wind and disappear in the same manner.

Chapter Thirty-one

Psyche stared down at the sight of Annabelle in Mr. Shalford's arms and nearly wept for joy. How beautifully and how simply were so many difficult and unfortunate circumstances resolved by the joining of these two! Now Evanthea would not be bound to marry Shalford and the vicar could finally have the career for which he was so well suited. Annabelle's fortune could take the pair of them wherever they wished to go. Psyche was certain it would not be long before Wellington had another fine officer under his command and Annabelle would see more of the world as she had always wanted.

But would Annabelle be content with the vicar? she wondered. Psyche felt rather silly when she considered how much Shalford was just the sort of man to make the lively young woman happy. Why hadn't she considered it before? But then, she had been so absorbed in both Evanthea's difficulties and her own that she had had little time to attend to Annabelle's heart.

As she watched the couple from a distance, still enrapt in each other's gaze, Psyche felt her heart melt. How beautiful the first blossomings of love were. How long ago it was that she had first felt Cupid's touch, kiss, and embrace — before she had even known who he was, when he only came to her at night and she had been told he was a deformed monster. It seemed a hundred thousand years had passed since she had first stolen a glance at his exquisite form — as she spilled oil on him because she had been so startled by his beauty! Lord, what a clumsy ninnyhammer she had been! But then they had married and, oh, how wondrous his love had been for literally countless years — until only recently, really. And how very much she longed to be loved by him.

Thoughts of their recent argument, of having learned that Cupid had been angry with her because he had believed she had been unfaithful to him, brought her own rage rising rapidly to the surface. How could he ever think such a dreadful thing of her? But then, it was true that she had kissed Anteros. Perhaps she was to blame to some degree. Why wouldn't he think the very worst of her if she would permit even a kiss to pass between herself and his brother?

She felt ill suddenly with the realization that she could not be accounted completely innocent. After all, and most particularly with the second kiss, she had given herself fully to Anteros's embrace.

"What are you thinking, Psyche?" a masculine voice whispered in her ear. "Of me, I hope!"

For the barest second, she thought Eros was behind her, leaning close to her, his breath warm on her neck. But as she turned quickly, starting at the sound of his voice, she caught sight of silver hair and the black costume Anteros habitually wore in dark contrast to his brother's. "You!" she cried.

Just as she spoke, her brother-in-law turned her firmly toward him and caught her up in a hard embrace. He did not immediately kiss her but whispered hoarsely, "Why do you struggle in my arms? When will you submit to your love for me? I have thought of little else this past day and night than of

273

the feel of you in my arms, how you responded so passionately to my kisses. Has Eros warmed toward you yet? He never will! My little Butterfly, forsake your husband tonight! Come with me! I have found a secret grotto where no one, not even my grandfather, can discover us. I will make you happy as your husband never could. Only say you will do it!"

"Anteros, please," Psyche whispered. "Do let me go. It is hopeless. I could nev—"

"How charming!" a voice intruded.

"Eros!" Psyche cried, jerking her head toward the source of the voice and seeing Cupid, in his wrath, standing with clenched hands not five yards away.

"Brother!" Anteros chimed, loosening his grip on Psyche. "It is not what you think. . . ."

When Psyche wrenched herself from Anteros's embrace, Eros responded hotly, "I'm not such a simpleton as you believe me to be and it *is* precisely what I think. How could you?" With that, he swept forward, a single beat of his wings closing the distance between the brothers before Psyche could so much as bat her eyelashes. Anteros did not have time to react. Fury had taken strong hold of Cupid, and without warning, his fist flew toward the god of unrequited love, landing upon his jaw in a stunning facer.

Anteros stumbled backward and fell hard onto the brick terrace, his own wings cushioning his fall. "You've drawn my cork!" he cried out, dabbing at his nose. "Damme, I'm bleeding all over my new tunic!"

Psyche stood watching Anteros with horror and only after a moment did she search in the pocket of her gown for her kerchief. She handed it to him and then turned toward her husband. She feared the worst, that Anteros's attack upon her virtue yet again would be construed as her own lack of loyalty and devotion. She could not speak but waited only

274

for him to condemn her. He stood mute, however, rubbing the knuckles of the offending fist with his uninjured hand.

It was only after a long moment that he tore his angry gaze from Anteros's bloodied face and look at Psyche. When he did, Psyche trembled at his expression. Fury commanded him, so much so that she took a step backward, in the direction of Anteros. Her movement caused the god of unrequited love to look up at Cupid and ask, "Why do you stare at her as though she deserves to be burnt alive? She has done nothing wrong. You most properly hit me. Don't blame Psyche for my obsession with her."

"It is not enough," Eros began, his voice strained, "that you suffer alone for my wife's infidelity."

"Infidelity? Since when is a kiss or two considered an infidelity?"

"You dare deny to me that it was not more? Liar. I know better. Far better."

At that, Anteros rose to his feet, still dabbing at his nose with the reddened kerchief. "I would call you out for that, brother dearest, but I suspect that some evil is afoot which ought to be addressed. I might have had suspect designs on a wife you seemed to have deserted, but as Zeus is my witness, I received nothing more from her than two, all too brief, salutes. Who has maligned your wife's character to you? I would imagine there are many who would enjoy speaking ill of me; I have never been popular in Olympian society. But who, having even a shred of decency, could accuse Psyche of any such misdeed?"

Psyche looked at her husband and watched the color in his cheeks fade. "Tell Anteros who," she said, all former feelings of misuse rising up in her heart. "Tell him what you told me."

Cupid lifted his chin and addressed his brother. "Mama said she saw you with my wife."

275

"Mother?" Anteros queried, stunned. A strange smile then spread across his handsome features and he began to laugh as Psyche had never heard him laugh before. "Mother told you! It is too much, too perfect! Our *dear mother* who has nothing but your interests at heart and who willingly sacrifices me at every turn, particularly if she can get you to abandon Psyche at the very same time. She dotes on you, my little gudgeon, more than any mother ought. My poor Eros," he continued, rising to his feet, "whose namesake I must share and bear for all eternity, isn't it time you grew up and left the safety of mama's apron strings? How could you believe anything she might say to you where Psyche is concerned? Your wife's beauty has been a thorn in her flesh since time out of mind. She would do anything to rid Olympus of her. But I tell you this: If you continue to side with her against Psyche, one day your wife, however virtuous she may be at present, will eventually succumb to *another* out of sheer loneliness and rage. I warn you fairly now: I intend for that someone to be me." With that, Anteros brushed past a stupefied Cupid, heading east toward Olympus as he lifted off into the night sky. Eros remained as though transformed into an immovable statue, staring blindly at nothing,

Psyche watched Anteros pass through the misty veil that shielded Olympus from view. The thought formed swiftly in her mind that never had the younger brother appeared to better advantage than now as he defended her and her honor to her stubborn husband. Her heart knew a tug of affection for Anteros that she thought could swell into something more if left unchecked. She glanced at Eros and wondered what he would next do or say.

He turned toward her as if to speak, but suddenly the beating of a hundred small wings could be heard in the sky and the next moment Aphrodite appeared in the garden, her carriage driven and piloted by an enormous flock of doves.

"There you are, you miserable thief!" she cried, signaling with a lift of her hand for the doves to come to a halt. "I want my cestus and love potions back at once! At once, I tell you!"

Psyche quailed at the sight of the goddess moved to wrath and instinctively stepped behind one of her husband's wings, seeking protection.

"Oh, it is just like you," the vengeful deity continued, descending from her chariot, "to slink behind my son's wings! What a *brave* creature you are! How could he have chosen you above all the fine, elegant, intelligent goddesses who—"

Cupid lifted a hand and, in a voice Psyche had never heard him employ before, commanded his mother. "*Silence!*" he cried. Psyche's mouth flew agape as she first stared up at her husband's profile, then glanced at Venus.

What she saw there nearly caused her to giggle, for Aphrodite had apparently been so stunned by her son's attack that she literally fell backward into her chariot. She was flailing in her attempts to right herself, kicking her gold-sandaled feet like a child who was caught in tangled bedcovers. Her gown, composed of many layers of a silklike gossamer fabric in varying shades of pale pink, blue, and lavender, billowed about in wave after wave of distress.

When she finally rose to a sitting position, the gold crown in her hair had become lopsided and sat at an awkward angle on her tangled coiffure.

"Eros," she exclaimed, sputtering and out of breath. "Whatever do you mean? . . . I have never heard anything so . . . Zeus, but what has happened to you that you must speak . . . oh, dear, I feel a spasm coming on." She clutched at her side and rolled her eyes.

"Then you had best return to Olympus at once and seek the comfort of your bed and the ministrations of Penny. As for your cestus and your love potions, I suspect that when my wife has finished with the articles she *borrowed* from your wardrobe, she will return them. You need have no concern on that head. Psyche may have erred in not begging your permission to use them in the first place, but she certainly will return them in due course. Won't you, my love?" Eros turned toward his wife and smiled encouragingly at her, taking her by the hand and drawing her forward to stand next to him.

"Yes—yes, of course I will. I meant no harm, only for love to abound here, at Flitwick Lodge." She gestured toward Annabelle, who had taken Shalford to a stone bench near the statue of Artemis and was presently holding his hand against her cheek.

Aphrodite appeared as one who had had the earth beneath her feet chipped away. Rising, she responded dumbly, "How can you speak so lightly, Eros, of your wife's thievery? Aren't you ashamed of her?" She then turned to glance in the direction of the statue and gasped, obviously horrified. "Goodness gracious Jupiter. Oh! I don't know which spectre is worse, that of a mortal female wearing *my* cestus, or a—a statue of Diana in this garden!" She pressed a hand to her breast and whispered in fainting accents, "Cupid, pray come support your mama. I fear I shall perish."

Eros sighed deeply, and possessing himself of his wife's hand, he pressed her fingers to his lips. "I'm sorry, Mother, but as much as I would like to always be your little boy, I can no longer offer you the assistance you require. I have neglected my wife because of your hold on me and because I believed your lies. . . ."

Aphrodite, who could see Cupid was not going to

278

lend her the support of his arm, straightened her shoulders. "My *lies?*" she queried in mock horror. "Why, whatever do you mean?"

"You told me that Anteros had seduced Psyche and that she had gone willingly to his bed. Do you deny having said as much?"

Venus smiled falsely and replied, "Of course I deny it. I never said any such thing. I might have *suggested* the possibility of her doing so since I saw Anteros kiss her, but I never—"

"Oh, do stubble it, Mama," Cupid interjected impatiently. "I love you very much, but I fear as a parent you leave a great deal to be desired. But what I resent most is that you have refused decade after decade to accept the very simple fact that I love my wife and that I always shall. If we have had a difficulty in the past two centuries, I have only myself to blame. First"—and here he turned to Psyche—"because I transgressed the solemn vows of our marriage by trying to get up a flirtation with a tavern wench in Gloucestershire. Will you ever forgive me, my love?"

Psyche looked into the eyes of the man she loved, able to see only a shadow of his face through the tears that swirled in her eyes. "Of course I will, Cupid, my darling."

"Good," he said, patting her hand and again pressing her fingers to his warm lips. Turning back to his mother, he continued, "And secondly, because I believed your lies, Mama—or your hints, or suggestions, or whatever you wish to call them—over the good character and virtue of my wife. For two centuries I harbored a terrible grievance against Psyche because of you. How could you? No, pray don't give me an answer. I already know the reason: You have never approved of Psyche and probably never will. But from this moment on, I vow to do better and that will mean a few changes. For one, I

279

shan't accompany you to Adonis's fete tonight. My place is with Psyche."

Venus stared at her son, her eyes blinking rapidly. "Are you abandoning me, Eros, after all we have suffered together these past several thousand years? Do you seriously mean you intend to align yourself with your wife and forsake your own mother?"

"You should never even have posed the question."

Aphrodite started to sniff, tears welling up in her eyes. "I can't believe what an ungrateful child I have spawned." She stared up into the heavens, shaking her head sadly and appearing very much the martyr. "I have sacrificed all these years to see that my son has the very best of Olympus . . . the finest scribes and teachers, slaves, even nymphs — would he ever avail himself of them? — shepherds for his flocks, musicians . . ." Her quiet wailing was brought to a halt by the steady clapping of a pair of hands.

Psyche turned to glance to her left and saw, much to her surprise, shock, and dismay, that Zeus himself was applauding his daughter. She gasped, as did Venus, who suddenly clutched the side of her carriage as though some catastrophe was about to befall her.

Chapter Thirty-two

"Excellent, my dear!" Zeus exclaimed with a wry smile adorning his lips. "I always thought you would have excelled in the theater had you been born a mortal. William Shakespeare would undoubtedly have doubled, nay trebled, the size of his audiences had only you been there to speak his lines. But I have never heard such nonsense in my life as what you are trying to cram down your poor boy's throat. It is high time you let go of Cupid's leading strings and let him become a man. His first duty is to his wife, not to you, and I am infinitely pleased he has finally recognized that fact."

"Papa," Venus breathed, dumbfounded. "I—I don't know what you mean. Of course I know that Cupid's first duty is to his wife and he may certainly do as he pleases. But I don't think it is too much to ask that he consider my sentiments, not just those of his wife."

"What humbug," Zeus responded. "You want him to behave as though he still lives in your nest, and he does not! You must realize your boy is gone!"

Venus blinked several times and opened her mouth to speak, but Zeus lifted his hand and stated, "Enough."

His daughter bit her lip. Apparently, she knew better than to try to argue with him further.

Satisfied that he had effectively silenced Aphrodite, Zeus strolled forward and moved to stand in front of Psyche. He touched her elbow and gave it a gentle pinch. "As for you, my pet," he said affectionately, "I think it time you left off stealing everything that takes your fancy. Do you understand me?"

Psyche bobbed a nervous curtsy. "Yes, Your Majesty," she said, swallowing hard. However kind he was being, he was still Zeus and she was always overawed in his presence.

"That's my girl," he said. "But there is more. I require that you return each object, secreted in the portmanteau deep within your wardrobe, to its owner with a written apology."

"Yes, sir. I shall do so the moment I return to Olympus."

"And as for the bust of myself, now residing in Lady Elle's drawing room—"

Upon these words, Aphrodite regained some of her boldness and cried out, "That bust belongs to me, Father. Don't you remember, you gave it to me centuries ago? And though I have no proof, I believe Psyche stole it from my chambers nearly thirty years ago."

Zeus slipped his hand beneath Psyche's chin and lifted it. Looking into her eyes, he said, "Truth, Butterfly. Was it you who stole the bust?"

"Yes, I'm 'fraid so."

"There, you see!" Venus exclaimed. "What a wretched child she is. Now do you understand why I have been so despairing about my son's mésalliance with this—this *mortal?*"

Psyche watched as Zeus's eyes became filled with blinding irritation. He let her chin go tenderly enough but then turned swiftly around, drew a thunderbolt from the cloudless skies by merely lifting his hand aloft, and sent it flying toward his daughter.

The bolt landed but a few inches in front of her feet, the bright flash as it struck the grassy earth sending the doves fluttering heavenward.

"Oh, Papa, I hate it when you do that. Now look at my new ball gown. It has holes in it where the sparks have burnt it up!"

Zeus shook his head at her. "If we are to speak of wretched children, you are by far the most tiresome child I have ever known. Now, do go away before I send a bolt through your carriage and you will be forced to walk to the ball tonight."

Aphrodite's brows rose in fright. By the time she batted her lashes twice, she was ensconced in her carriage. Warbling to her birds, the entire equipage was soon disappearing into the stars and heading east.

"As for the bust," Zeus continued, addressing Psyche, "I have given it to Lady Elle and to her descendants forever. Don't worry about Venus, my little Butterfly. Her bark is worse than her bite, as you must know by now, eh?"

"I suppose you are right, but she can be so persistent in her criticisms. However much I try to become inured, I find myself positively blue-deviled at times."

"Then I shall have to have a serious talk with her. You're a good girl, Psyche. Do as I have bid you and all will be forgiven."

"Thank you," she responded. On impulse, she kissed his cheek, and in return he caught her to him and gave her a grandfatherly hug.

After a moment, he released her and turned to address Cupid. "As for you, Grandson, I am very proud of you. Tonight you have acquitted yourself very well. And, with all nearly settled here in . . . where the devil is this place? Bedfordshire? Well, at any rate, let us retire to Olympus and leave these mortals to their own devices."

Psyche bit her lip. "Grandpapa," she began quietly, her heart constricting with fear lest her request anger her formidable liege, "Please permit me . . . that is, us"—she glanced up at Cupid and smiled at him—"to remain until I know what Fate awaits Evanthea. I know it was wrong of me to have come here in the first place, to involve myself in the lives of mortals," she saw the scowl on his face and hurried on, "not for mere amusement, I assure you. The truth is, I am most genuinely attached to everyone whom I try to help and most particularly to Evanthea. Please say you will let me stay."

Cupid intervened, "Forget what she says, Grandpapa. She does not know how much you dislike such entanglements. I'm sure once—"

Zeus shook his head. "It's all right, Cupid. I have known of her comings and goings for these several decades and more. I fear I am simply far too indulgent to benefit any of my relations. You see the hapless results with your mother. Good Lord in heaven, was there ever so spoiled and immature a child as she?" He sighed, turning to address Psyche, "I grant your request. You and Eros may stay, but only until all is settled. As for your life in Olympus, Psyche, you needn't tell me how hard it has been for you. And if your husband is not able to keep you well entertained, please come to me and we shall contrive something other than visits to earth. I can't let you go about mucking up the lives of mortals forever. You are bound to make a mistake at some point and then the future will be changed for the worse. You must trust me in this. No more meddling after tonight, promise?"

"Of course, Grandpapa! Never again. I promise."

"And whatever the outcome, you must return by

dawn or I shall do as your mama-in-law has suggested to me on numerous occasions: I will consign you to serving on the River Styx until you have learnt your lesson."

With that, Zeus waved a hand over his chest and simply disappeared, a deep roll of laughter sweeping away into the wind, eastward toward Olympus.

Psyche immediately forgot about Cupid and, without saying a word to him, swept down the steps toward the statue of Artemis. When she reached the bench where Annabelle and Shalford were seated and speaking in low tones, she immediately gave Annabelle a hard pinch on her posterior, forcing the young woman to leap from her seat. With deft fingers, she unbuttoned the cestus from about Annabelle's waist.

"Psyche, whatever are you about?" Cupid asked as he caught up with her. He glanced at Annabelle, who was staring in horror at the cestus dangling in the air next to her and, with a snap of his fingers, made both himself and Psyche visible to Shalford and Annabelle.

Psyche, ignoring the horror in their eyes, looked at Eros in considerable astonishment and said, "I didn't know you could do that? What other powers do you possess which you have not told me about?"

Cupid smiled at his wife and shook his head. "Let me ask you a question instead of answering yours. Have I told you lately how very much I adore you?"

Psyche gazed into his eyes and felt wondrously weak all over. Suddenly, she didn't give a fig whether or not he had magical abilities unbeknownst to her. She knew she shouldn't respond to the impulse to do so, but it was impossible. She simply drifted into his arms and let him kiss her, his wings enfolding her as they hadn't in over two hundred years.

Cupid snapped his fingers and they were once again invisible.

Annabelle tried to catch her breath but couldn't. "Lady Elle told me there were Olympian creatures fairly haunting her home, but I never thought — by her description that must have been Psyche and — and Eros. Oh, Lord, did you see his wings? And he was ever so handsome!"

"She had your belt!" was all Shalford could think to say.

"It wasn't mine," Annabelle admitted, chewing nervously on her lip. He did not notice her discomfiture, since he had begun searching the ground where the immortals had been standing before they disappeared. "Shalford, there is something I feel I ought to —"

"Look at this!" he cried, interrupting her as he pointed to impressions in the ground. Nearby was a single downy feather. He picked it up and showed it to Annabelle. "Cupid, you say? I always thought he was a tiny baby with fairylike wings."

"So did I, but earlier Lady Elle told me quite differently. I didn't believe her at the time, supposing she had merely slipped into one of her addlepated moments." Annabelle looked at Shalford and swallowed hard. "She also gave me the belt to wear, saying that it was special and would cause you to fall in love with me."

"What?" Shalford cried, a smile of disbelief breaking over his face.

"Yes, it belongs to Aphrodite, but Psyche stole it from her or some such nonsense. And it did seem to work, which has set me to wondering. Gregory, please take a hard look at me and tell me if your feelings change suddenly, disappear as it were."

286

"You mean, you think I might stop loving you because you are no longer sporting your gold belt?"

Annabelle nodded, uncertain what he must be thinking right now.

Shalford was silent, rolling the soft feather between his thumb and his finger. He glanced about him, apparently trying to decide for himself what it was he had just seen. "Are you saying then that you put on the belt in hopes of causing me to fall in love with you?"

"Yes," she breathed, grateful he was beginning to comprehend what had happened. "I was quite desperate, you see." Suddenly, she recalled the moment just before the race when she and her great-aunt and Evanthea had greeted the vicar. Annabelle remembered having experienced a stinging sensation at the time, and also that shortly afterward she had looked up at Shalford and simply fallen violently in love with him. "Oh, dear," she murmured.

"What?"

"You will probably think my wits have gone a-begging, but I believe Cupid shot me with one of his arrows, just before your race. You were staring at Evanthea — struck dumb by the sight of her — and something stung me. For a moment I actually thought I had been assaulted by a bee, but a moment later the sensation was gone. Then I looked up at you, and I vow I tumbled head over heels. I'm afraid, Gregory. What if I don't really love you, or what if your heart isn't truly given to me? What if our feelings are the false manufacturing of Cupid and the cestus?"

At that, Shalford threw his head back and laughed. "I don't give a cat's whisker why I suddenly fell in love with you, only that I did! Cupid be hanged! Your belt be hanged! Damme, Annabelle, I love you, more than I ever dreamed it possible to

love any woman. And I shall love you just as devot-
edly, just as fiercely, until the day I die. Of that I am
certain."

Annabelle suddenly forgot all about the silly cestus and the point on her posterior that still bore a
faint red mark, and she again melted into the vicar's
arms, surrendering to the warmth, love, and security
of his embrace.

Chapter Thirty-three

Lord Brandreth had listened to Lady Felmersham squawk her way from the ballroom and from the manor with a quirky twist of amusement in his heart. Her character had been revealed to him entirely during the few minutes it took first for Shalford to desert her, then for her husband to take her forcibly by the arm and to remove her from the ballroom, and finally for her own feet to carry her to the entrance hall where she and Felmersham awaited their conveyance.

She had complained bitterly about such wretched mistreatment at his hands, especially when she had not enjoyed herself half so much in weeks. She had boasted of Shalford being her next victim, had cried out that she had not even had the pleasure of jilting the marquis, then at last collapsed into Felmersham's shoulder with a sob. "Why am I so unhappy, Fel?" she had asked her long-suffering husband. "I try. I do try, but I can't seem to stop being so very wicked. Take me home. I want to see my children."

"They will be missing you sorely by now."

"Maybe they will cheer me up."

"Of course they will."

Felmersham had looked over his shoulder and caught Brandreth's eye. The marquis nodded his understanding and left the viscount to care for his wife. He had not known she was such an unstable creature. What was it Felmersham had said? That he had loved a phantom? Apparently, it was true.

He felt an overwhelming need for air and set his feet in the direction of the terrace outside the ballroom. He had so much to consider now: his own absurd behavior where the viscountess was concerned, what his true feelings toward Evanthea were, and whether he was just as unsteady as Susan to have even considered aiding her in divorcing her husband.

Lord, when he pondered the whole of his extraordinary behavior during the course of the past four and twenty hours, he was appalled and unable to explain what madness had possessed him. Even kissing Evanthea as he had, more than once, was not precisely an action of steadiness, nonetheless propriety. Really, if his life were judged upon the past turning of the earth alone, he would be accounted a poor specimen indeed!

With these self-reproaches battering his mind, he reached the terrace by way of the hallway door and drank deeply of the cool air. A myriad of stars twinkled beyond a delicate summer breeze that swept the fragrance of roses across the gardens. Moonlight on the gentle hills in the distance appeared like a fine layer of snow. The lime trees beyond the tall, ancient holly hedge swayed and danced in the soft wind.

His thoughts turned to Evanthea, and a longing swept over him so thoroughly that he gripped the edge of the terrace half-wall and strove to catch his breath. What did such a sensation mean? Was it possible he loved her, really loved her?

Finally, he took in a deep breath, and with the intoxicating rush of air came the knowledge he had been fighting ever since he could remember. The truth was he had been in love with Evanthea Swanbourne from her first Season when she had single-handedly ruined his ballroom slippers during a most unforgettable waltz. With this knowledge came a combination of giddiness and peace beyond explanation.

He thought back to the moment when he had beaten on her door and professed a love for her. He had believed some strange form of madness had possessed him then, ending only with the water that Evanthea had thrown over him. A moon madness, a bad brandy, he had blamed everything save the truth—that he was in fact very much in love her.

Why, though? She was stubborn and aggravating in the extreme. She took immense delight in provoking him, particularly by censuring the manner in which he conducted his amusements; gaming, for instance, was an especially warm theme for her biting tongue.

He sighed, thinking with great affection how different she was from every other female he had ever known. His thoughts ran abruptly to the moment in the race when he had nearly crossed the finish line, only to see her transformed by Annabelle and Lady Elle. He had always thought her pretty, however much she hid her beauty behind ill-fitting gowns, her spectacles, and coiled hair. But now she was simply beautiful.

He had seen her from a distance several times tonight and thought she looked magnificent. Her hair hung in chestnut waves past her shoulders, traversed by rose silk ribbons, her white and rose gown fitted her queenly form to perfection, and a strand of pearls bearing an elegant emerald brooch graced her sloping white neck.

Thoughts of her brought other ideas swimming through his mind, like holding her in his arms, kissing her, telling her what his true sentiments for her were.

He turned as though to act on this last notion,

when, with a deep tolling of his heart, he became aware of another horrid reality: Evanthea was betrothed to Shalford. Brandreth again clutched the top stone railing of the terrace, an acute nausea afflicting him. The thought of another man possessing her was nearly more than he could bear.

She had told him earlier that regardless of her feelings, she meant to make the vicar a good wife. He could not rely on her to jilt Shalford. She wouldn't. Not Evanthea. Once committed to a course, she wouldn't waver.

But he couldn't let her make such a grievous mistake. He knew damn well she was in love with him; she had inferred as much in their brief discussion under the shade in the avenue.

He clenched his jaw in determination. He was sorry for Shalford, but he had to marry Evanthea even if it meant dragging her to Gretna Green and marrying her out of hand. He would speak with Shalford first, but if reason and supplication did not serve, an elopement was surely requisite.

Good God! Was madness still dogging him? He had never had so many unprincipled thoughts or intentions in his life as he had had in the past two days.

Nevertheless, having finally comprehended his heart, Brandreth was determined to do all he could, first within the bounds of propriety and later outside them, if necessary, to see that his love for Evanthea and hers for him prevailed.

A faint giggling caught his ear and he recognized at once Annabelle's sweet, melodious voice. His poor cousin. Whatever was to become of her when she learned that his heart was given to Evanthea? In response to her giggles, however, the sound of a man's voice, murmuring softly to her, reached through his pity and grabbed him by the throat.

When had Annabelle found a beau with whom

she would not hesitate to secrete herself in the shadows of the shrubberies? He was shocked, then outraged that a man would dare to take advantage of a cousin whom he thought of as a sister. He was preparing to leap over the terrace wall, if necessary, and discover who was with Annabelle, when Shalford's voice struck his ear with stunning clarity, "I don't know how to address Evanthea, but I can only say that I have the profound sense she does not wish to marry me."

"Whatever will happen to her, then?" Annabelle queried. "She will die an old maid and will despise me forever for having married the man who would release her from so dreaded a fate."

"I know," Shalford responded sadly.

A smile broke over Brandreth's face and it was all he could do to keep from laughing. What irony! What beautiful irony. He grinned so broadly that his cheeks hurt. He knew now his cousin was in capable, good hands and left her to the enjoyment of her tryst.

Chapter Thirty-four

Evanthea had smiled and danced and smiled again until she thought both her face and feet might crack from the effort. She received dozens of well-wishes upon her forthcoming nuptials with a bright smile and as enthusiastic a thank-you as she could summon for one whose heart was breaking. When she was asked where Mr. Shalford had disappeared to she could only answer, with profound relief in her heart, that she hadn't the least notion. She had so badly conducted herself with him earlier that she was reluctant to see him again lest once more she burst into tears.

Poor Shalford! What a bad bride he was getting in the bargain. It would be no credit to him if, however much she might look pretty in her lace and orange blossoms on her wedding day, tears trickled down her cheeks the entire length of the church as she walked down the aisle. The worst of it was, every time she so much as thought of marrying him, tears sprouted in her eyes entirely against her will. If she thought of Brandreth in the same moment, her chest constricted so tightly she thought she might faint. Losing the marquis and marrying the vicar was a combination so painful to her that she found herself wishing the ceiling would simply collapse on her.

"Have you given your hand for the next dance?"

Evanthea turned sharply to her right and found it was indeed true. Brandreth was standing next to her, he had spoken to her. Where had he come from? Against her will, her gaze quickly searched the ballroom for Lady Felmersham but she didn't see her, which might account for Brandreth's approaching her.

Again, a terrible sensation of loss seized her as she turned her attention fully to him and looked into his gray eyes. Her stomach churned with despair as she quite absently extended her hand to him and responded, "I have no partner for the next dance."

"Excellent," he whispered, drawing her close to him by taking her hand, then her elbow, and slipping his arm tightly about hers as he led her onto the floor. Couples arranged themselves in anticipation of the waltz and he teased her, "I trust you will not ruin my slippers as you did some eight years ago."

"Oh, Brandreth, do not put me in mind of that particular night. It may seem odd, but I have been thinking of that dance nearly all day and how unkind I was to you."

"I deserved nothing less. I recall you washed my head quite severely by calling me pompous, arrogant, high-handed, and a few other morsels which have fortunately escaped me. But you mustn't fault my memory too severely. After all, a man's pride can endure only so much battering in one evening."

Evanthea felt the pain in her stomach easing up as much from the gentleness of his demeanor toward her as from the graciousness of his words. A few moments earlier, she had wondered, given the profound disposition of her heart toward him, whether or not she could ever be easy in company with him again. Her fears seemed unjustified because here

295

they were, with the strains of the waltz just beginning, and they were chatting as old, comfortable friends might.

Stepping into the dance and adjusting the flow of her movements to his, even the waltz seemed ordinary and familiar, so unlike the first waltz they had shared so many years ago.

"I have been thinking quite a lot of that night, Brandreth," she began, not quite daring to look him in the eye. "I have much to answer for—your current difficulty for one, in that in order now to win the hand of the woman you love, you must embark on a truly reprehensible and scandalous course. I blame myself for that and you were so right to blame me for your break with Lady Felmersham. I said *such* things to her, speaking out of anger because of my onerous ill opinion of you. It is no wonder she accepted Lord Felmersham's hand in marriage. Brandreth, will you ever forgive me? My curst tongue, which I have never excelled at curbing, did its mischief too well, I'm 'fraid, as you have tried to tell me only recently. If I have been tardy in expressing my regret, it is because my other fault, stubbornness, stood mightily in the way."

Evanthea was surprised when Brandreth clicked his tongue with an obvious lack of sympathy for her penitent state and said, "You are quite flawed, aren't you?"

These words, spoken so baldly, caused Evanthea to forget her desire to humble herself to him. "Not more so than you, my lord," she responded hotly. "Now, if we were to speak of flaws! . . ."

Brandreth laughed outright. "Do you know I think what I adore most about you is how readily you rise to the fly, all the while believing you are in complete command of yourself!"

"Why, you—you monster! Taunting me when I was trying so very hard to—to apologize to you."

"That's much better. I've never said this to you before and perhaps shall come to regret it, but one of the reasons I love you as much as I do is because you don't fawn over me."

Evanthea did not know quite what to make of Brandreth in this moment. He had just said *one of the reasons I love you as much as I do,* but she couldn't quite place what he meant by it. His expression was so unromantic of the moment and the statement made so matter-of-factly that she supposed he was referring to feelings of fondness as *cousin-to-cousin.* Surely he wasn't telling her he loved her, not when he knew she was betrothed to Shalford.

"I suppose I am hopeless," she responded at last, eyeing him warily. Recalling that her original intent was to make him see she had comprehended her guilt regarding the events of eight years ago, she began again, "But I want you to know I am sorry that your path with her ladyship is now so fraught with difficulty. Will you ever forgive me, Brandreth? Please say you will."

He shook his head as he turned her easily with the lilting strains of the music. "No, I don't see how I can," he answered with a frown.

"Why are you making this so impossible for me? Can't you see I've admitted I was wrong?"

"Yes, I see that. You've made yourself clear, but perhaps I haven't precisely explained my current opinion on the subject, one which has undergone a most remarkable change. You see, the wedding is off, I fear."

Evanthea knew her mouth had fallen quite unattractively agape. She closed it with an effort, her astonishment overwhelming. "It is?" she queried in a small, hopeful voice.

"Yes. It seemed once my intended began to prefer Shalford's company — though you need have no worries on that score; *he* has no interest in *her*—Felmersham decided to simply take her home."

"You mean she's gone?"

"Yes, very much so."

"You seem quite serene, but I know you loved her."

He smiled, looking over her shoulder, and answered quietly, "I believe I loved her once, but even in that I'm not certain. I was quite green, not yet out of my *salad days* when I first became charmed by her. Felmersham thought perhaps I was in love with a phantom."

"He never said so!" she cried, astonished.

"Indeed he did, and I am forever grateful to him for it."

Evanthea did not know what to say, but a frightening feeling very much like hope entered her breast and began flitting wildly about, setting her heart to beating in a dreadfully fast cadence.

She looked away from him, fearful that he might discern her thoughts, which were still useless since she was betrothed to Shalford. Instead, she introduced a new subject. "There is something more, Brandreth, that I wish to say to you. Something three days ago I would never have believed I could have said."

She felt his arm tighten about her waist. He drew her scandalously close to him as they turned and whirled about the chamber together. Smiling, he teased her, "That you love me deeply and passionately, that you always have? Is this what you wish to say to me?"

Evanthea could not breathe for a moment. She blinked rapidly at him, her eyes and mouth opened in considerable surprise. "Brandreth! I hope you aren't serious in what you say. Remember, I am betrothed to Shalford. Even though I can see by the glimmer in your eye that you are taunting me—and in a most delightful manner, I'm afraid—I beg you will desist. You have shocked me."

"Have I?" he queried. "I am beyond pleased, because it has become of the supremest importance to me that I shock you now and again. I am convinced you enjoy it above all things."

He smiled so warmly upon her that Evanthea felt her cheeks grow hot with feelings far from embarrassment. She took in a ragged breath. "You must stop," she said unconvincingly, her fingers clinging to his as he held her more closely still. She was beginning to desire he continue speaking so scandalously to her more than life itself.

But this could not continue! She was betrothed to Shalford. Hurriedly, she said, "There is a small matter of business, as it were, I wish to discuss with you."

"I hope you don't mean to introduce the bust at this moment, not when I am making such pretty love to you."

Evanthea heard herself make a sound that resembled a cross between a kitten's purr and a child's whimper. "How did it happen," she breathed, "that I have come to long to hear you say outrageous things to me?"

Her words seemed to engender similar feelings in him, for he watched her with his eyes blazing his thoughts. "If we were alone, I would kiss you, Shalford be hanged."

How grateful Evanthea was that the music protected his words from the hearing of others. How grateful she was to be on the dance floor with Brandreth and not alone somewhere with him. Oh, damn and blast, she thought with unladylike fervor, how unhappy she was!

She looked away from him and ordered her heart to slow down, bringing her wretched thoughts to a stately minuet instead of the wild waltz they were spinning. "As I was saying," she began again, "I do wish to speak to you regarding the bust of Zeus. I want you to know that I look back on my insistence that the statue belonged to me as a source of acute discomfort. You were right when you said I was being selfish in not permitting Lady Elle to peaceably sell you the bust. I withdraw my claim on it entirely and beg you will do all you can to persuade my most beloved great-aunt to relinquish it to you. I was wrong, and she has suffered more than she has needed to all these months since you initially made the offer . . . and for no other reason than that I can be miserably stubborn."

"Your sentiments do you honor, Evanthea, and I am very pleased that you have made such a generous gesture—particularly because I know how much the statue means to you. But in spite of your withdrawal, Lady Elle refuses to sell the bust to me. Even with creditors upon the doorstep, she told me as we were preparing to greet her guests that she would never sell me the bust, that her sense of honor forbade it. She did, however, say the most curious thing . . . that Zeus himself had promised the bust would go to Lady Elizabeth and her descendants forever. I told her, of course, that then you must be awarded the statue, and she pretended she could not hear a word I was saying. Of course, she had just that twinkle in her eye which warned me she was playing off her tricks again. Then she added something most curious: She said that if I should marry you, she would happily give the pair of us the bust as a wedding present."

"She did not!"

"Indeed, yes, which brings me in a rather circuitous manner to a point which I wished most particularly to address to you. Would you do me the honor of becoming my wife? I know I haven't spoken prettily, I certainly haven't fallen at your feet and begged for your hand, and I haven't told you how very much I love you and that I shall forever, but I trust the request will suffice. So I repeat, would you marry me, my most darling Evanthea?"

Evanthea could not speak, staring at him as they continued to turn easily about the throng of couples waltzing. "You can't be serious," she breathed, unhappy tears burning her eyes.

"I have never been more so than I am now."

"But — but I am betrothed! It is too late! Why are you torturing me when you know I would never jilt Shalford? Never!"

Brandreth smiled and shook his head. "I hope I don't shatter your illusions, my dear, that he is overly fond of you. I fear even now, he is being unfaithful to you."

"Whatever do you mean? With whom?"

"Come and I'll show you," he said. With that, he eased her through a maze of whirling dancers and led her onto the terrace. With his finger pressed to his lips, he bid her be silent. Permitting him to take her hand, she followed behind him as he stealthily crept toward the low wall that bordered the terrace.

Once there, Evanthea glanced down into the garden, the moonlight reflecting brightly off the statue of Diana and her hound. Near the statue, two people sat facing one another, their hands and fingers entwined. She could not at first discern precisely who they were as she squinted at them, until she heard the lady giggle. "Annabelle!" she gasped. "Whatever are you doing alone with a man in the garden?"

"Evanthea!" the gentleman called to her, the tone of his voice greatly distressed as he dropped Annabelle's hands and rose guiltily to his feet.

"Mr. Shalford?" she queried, stunned.

Chapter Thirty-five

Her voice carried easily to the couple below. Both leapt to their feet and Annabelle sprinted away from Shalford, running toward the steps, "I cannot!" she cried the whole distance. "I cannot! I cannot!"

She picked up her skirts and began quickly mounting the steps. Evanthea could hear that she was sobbing the whole way and met her at the top.

Throwing herself into Evanthea's arms, Annabelle cried, "I didn't mean to! I shan't importune him again! It was all my fault! Say you will forgive me and don't think that he doesn't wish to marry you. He is so kind and dutiful, he will make you an excellent husband! It was very wrong of me, very wrong to steal the affections of your betrothed!"

"Hush, Annabelle," Evanthea whispered, stroking her hair and holding her tight. "It doesn't matter, not one whit. You are free to love him. Indeed, quite free!"

"But then you will remain an ape-leader the rest of your life, and I can't bear to be responsible for something so horrible. It is not to be thought of!" She drew away from Evanthea, apparently prepared to martyr herself as she straightened her shoulders and dried her tears. "You shall marry the vicar. I shall not stand in your way."

Shalford was walking up the steps as Evanthea replied, "Well, I think you underestimate my chances of forming another attachment."

"At your age! Of course you won't. Who would have you but my dear, good, kind Mr. Shalford? Even with your improved looks, you've no dowry."

Evanthea could not help herself. Shaking her head, she kept herself from laughing outright with only the strongest of efforts and responded, "You do have the right of it, but I'm afraid I have lost all interest in marrying Mr. Shalford." She then spoke over Annabelle's shoulder, addressing the vicar. "Besides, how could I even think of marrying a man who goes about hugging young women in the shrubbery? It is not at all the thing, you know, my good sir, especially for one in your vocation. Indeed! I am very shocked at your *libertine* behavior."

Even in the darkened terrace, she could see that he colored quite readily. His conscience was too keen to bear such harsh teasing and she quickly amended, "As it happens, Shalford, I confess that my heart is already completely engaged and has been, I believe, for at least seven years, possibly eight." She glanced back toward Brandreth who, clearly amused by her means of conveying her attachment to him, stepped forward and took her arm in his.

Shalford's eyes opened wide. "So that's the way of it! By Jove, how splendid!"

"What?" Annabelle cried, glancing first at Brandreth, then at the vicar. "I don't know what you mean."

Shalford said, "Our dear Evanthea is to become a marchioness."

Annabelle looked blankly from Evanthea to Brandreth and back again. She seemed deeply perplexed. "Are you even acquainted with any other marquises — besides Brandreth, I mean. Who is it you intend to marry? I'm certain it isn't Brandreth,

303

because you despise one another so completely. I don't understand?"

Evanthea appeared to consider Annabelle's question carefully, then responded, "I only met one in London some few years ago. At the time I believe he was nearly seventy, so you may imagine how old he is now. And if you are inferring that perhaps I intend to marry him, rest assured to my knowledge he is already married, or rather is still married and his wife quite healthy."

Annabelle shook her head in disbelief. "You cannot mean you are going to marry Brandreth! Not when you squabble like children, hour after hour, until one is ready to have one's teeth pulled out just to get you to stop."

Evanthea clicked her tongue, "I'm afraid so."

"I don't believe it!" She addressed Brandreth. "You never once flirted with her, either, like you did with all the others. And what of Lady Felmersham?"

"The viscountess decided it would suit her best to remain married to Felmersham, as she should. I believe I fell victim to a rather absurd, youthful mooncalf infatuation, which afflicted me suddenly when she arrived here this afternoon. I realize I have shown a terrible want of character, but I intend to wed Evanthea — with your permission, Shalford."

Annabelle smiled for the first time, sniffing the last of her former tears away. "Oh, but how wonderful, and of course Gregory will give his permission and relinquish all claim upon Evanthea!" she responded brightly, taking the vicar's arm. Lifting an adoring face to his, she continued, "Won't you, my darling?"

"There can be no question, of course," Shalford said, appearing conscience-stricken to the last. "But I must, however, apologize most profoundly for having made such a mull of everything. I assure you

Annabelle has behaved admirably. It is I who importuned her. I beg you will forgive any—"

"What nonsense!" his audience chimed at once.

Brandreth added, "Your only difficulty now will be in attempting to explain to Lady Elle's guests how it was you asked the wrong lady to marry you. I suggest you put the question to my great-aunt at once and see what she advises. I think an announcement tonight—though it might shock some—of two engagements would answer, but why don't you lay the matter before her? Evanthea and I shall certain acquiesce to whatever she feels is best to do at this point."

But before Lady Elle could be consulted, Evanthea cried, "Oh, dear!"

As one, the group about her turned in the direction of her own gaze, which was fixed upon the several doors leading into the ballroom. The waltz had ended some minutes ago and a veritable crowd of murmuring, astonished onlookers was gaping at them all. A hush fell over the guests as a number of them, perhaps as many as two dozen, poured onto the terrace.

Evanthea glanced at Brandreth, a question between her brows, silently begging to know what they ought to do. He looked down at her, a terrible glint of amusement in his eye as he simply shrugged his shoulders, refusing to act. He then glanced at Shalford in an infuriatingly provoking manner and literally forced the vicar to amend the situation.

Shalford took the hint and with a muttered, yet quite friendly exclamation that he would not let the marquis forget this moment of cowardice for placing the burden of explanation solely on his shoulders, he stepped forward. "Good friends," he began, drawing Annabelle closely to his side, "I fear I made a grievous mistake this afternoon when I forced Miss Swanbourne, who has been an excellent acquaintance of mine these many years, into a most unhappy position by offering for her in public. I could not know, of course — as I have learned since — that her heart was already given . . ."

He spoke eloquently of his error, and of his discovered love for Annabelle, and of Brandreth's offer of marriage to Evanthea. Before a few minutes had passed, the crowd not only forgave him his failings, but swept down upon him and again lifted him on their shoulders. Several ladies crowded about Annabelle, demanding to know the particulars, and Evanthea thought that had the *fete* included the selection of a king and queen, the vicar and his bride-to-be would certainly have won the day.

When the terrace was emptied of well-wishers, Brandreth drew Evanthea down the steps and into the garden. He took her in his arms and said most seriously, "I know I sounded irreverent during the waltz we just shared, when I spoke of my love for you, so let me make the professions a good husband ought to make."

Evanthea looked up into his face and, with a lightness to her heart she had not felt in a long, long time, said, "Do stubble it, my love, and give us a kiss."

Lady Elle drew her head back in from the upstairs window that neatly overlooked the terrace. "You were absolutely right!" she cried as she turned back and addressed Zeus.

He laughed low and long, a sound that she knew had been filling the house for the past two days. "It was you, wasn't it . . . all along, I mean, working everything out? I recognize your laughter, which I must say I seemed to hear every time I turned around!"

He sat in a chair in her ladyship's bedchamber,

picking up an automaton from the table next to him and fiddling with it. "What fascinating workmanship! Look how all these levers move . . . curious! You are right, though. But I had to do something for little Butterfly. I knew she would never rest until Evanthea was leg-shackled to the marquis. And if the truth be known, I think I was a little bored sitting quietly on my throne in Olympus. There can be no denying that I have not enjoyed myself immensely, especially when I took on the form of a cat and broke Aphrodite's vial!" He laughed at the memory, then narrowed his eyes at Lady Elle. "There is only one last difficulty which I must see settled before I leave."

Lady Elle could think of nothing. Shalford and Annabelle would wed, as would Lord Brandreth and Evanthea. What remained undone? "And what is that, Your Majesty?" she queried.

"Your debts, of course. Or have you not considered how close you totter on the brink of disaster?"

"Pooh!" Lady Elle exclaimed, thinking her financial worries were the least of her concerns and always would be. "I'll come about somehow."

"That is precisely what I mean to recommend to you. I realize you feel honor-bound not to accept Brandreth's exceedingly generous offer regarding the bust of Zeus, but when he suggests a sizable settlement for you as part of his betrothal to Evanthea, I recommend you say *Thank you kindly* and be done with it."

Lady Elle lifted her brows and blinked twice at Jupiter. "How do you know he will do so?" she queried.

"Because he is a good boy and has a sincere affection for you. And I won't hear of his offer being rejected, do I make myself clear, Lizzie?"

How nice it was to be called by a nickname she had not heard in years. Zeus was an interesting creature, so different from the portraits of him throughout history, so much kinder than she would have dreamed possible. "Of course, Your Majesty," she replied. "Besides, in my era it is quite acceptable to receive handsome marriage settlements, even when they are unwarranted."

"Excellent," he said. "Then my work is done and I shall sleep easy tonight. What is happening out there, anyway?"

Lady Elle glanced out the window and smiled. "Brandreth has taken Evanthea in his arms and is kissing her quite thoroughly." She sighed contentedly. "I can't thank you enough. You've made an old woman very happy."

He rose to his feet, setting the automaton aside. Crossing the chamber of reds and blues, he possessed himself of her hands and said, "If I weren't immortal, Lady Elle, I vow I'd spend the rest of my days with you. What a treasure you are!"

She felt her heart quicken in a manner she had not experienced in a very long time. She smiled at him and said, "And if I weren't so old and wrinkled, and so very *mortal,* I'd almost fall victim to your charms. But thank you again, most sincerely."

He kissed her cheek and a moment later he was simply gone.

Lady Elle turned back to the window and, with tears in her eyes, watched her beloved great-niece lead Brandreth to the stone bench beside the statue. *How happy they will be,* she thought. *Almost as happy as Henry and I were.* When Brandreth again kissed Evanthea, Lady Elle sighed one last time, then turned to cross her bedchamber and left the room. She had guests to tend to, yet how very much she wished the ball was over. With a tingling of anticipation did she look forward to her next private conversation with Evanthea, so that she might hear every profession of love she had vowed only two days ago was of no interest to her whatsoever. Was it only two days ago that Evanthea had sworn she had no heart?

Lady Elle smiled to herself as she descended the stairs. How wrong Evanthea had been about herself and how delightfully well everything had been settled.

"Oh, my!" Psyche said as she leaned into her husband's shoulder and watched Brandreth salute his bride-to-be. "He is quite magnificent, isn't he? Almost as handsome and well-formed as you, my darling. Do you wonder any more that I longed to see him love a woman well? I knew once he had given his heart he would be all that could satisfy a wife."

Eros sighed deeply as he watched Brandreth kissing Evanthea. "He certainly holds her tightly, and look how she touches his hair, gripping it in her fingers as though she is afraid to let go. In this case, Psyche, I do understand your desire to intervene. They would never have discovered their love for one another; I consulted the oracle, you see."

Psyche was dumbfounded, "The oracle foresaw what would happen had I not involved myself in their lives? Oh, Eros, do you know what this means? For the first time I feel as though I belong to Olympus, not just to earth." She wept, burying her face into his strong chest, her tears dampening his tunic.

After a moment, he pulled back from her and said, "I do mean to do better by you, my love. For one thing, I think we ought to hire a house a bit further from my mother's, on the other side of the kingdom, if you wish for it."

Psyche lifted her face to him, awestruck. "You would do that for me?" she asked, her heart full to overflowing.

"I would die for you, Psyche, if that were possible. I have been such a sapskull all these decades. However, will you forgive me?"

"Easily, my love, so long as you continue to hold me and keep me enfolded within the comfort and safety of your wings."

"There is just one thing . . ." Eros began uneasily.

Psyche saw by the frown between his brows that he was greatly distressed. "What is it?" she queried.

He paused for a moment before answering. Kissing her gently on the forehead, he finally said, "Zeus has ordered me to sprinkle a forgetting dust upon all the mortals who saw you. They will have no memory of you or me or my mother or of any of the events which transpired in which we had a part."

"Not even Lady Elle will remember?"

"I'm afraid not."

Psyche looked at Evanthea, whom she could hear giggling and chatting happily with Brandreth. "If that is so," she responded in a small voice, "then I must say goodbye to her. We became such fast friends, you've no idea, and I shall miss her terribly, Lady Elle, too. Please, Eros, I must speak with her one last time. Please!"

"Of course," he said, releasing her from the cocoon of his winged embrace. "Anything, my love."

Chapter Thirty-six

Evanthea was lost in the tender search of Brandreth's lips as he kissed her again and again. It seemed once her heart had been fully and completely given, her desire was all for him and the world apart from him forgotten. Even her fingers had become entwined in his black locks, captivated by the man she loved, so much so that the mere thought of disentangling them brought a despairing sense of separation she could scarcely bear. For that reason she clung to him, and the more she did so, the tighter, warmer, and more forceful his embrace became.

She was behaving scandalously, but of the moment she did not care. She savored this time, knowing it would never come again, that a first profession of love must by its nature occur only once. Therefore she let her heart run free, her fingers drift through his hair, her own lips sweep softly over the lines of his face.

"My darling," he whispered into her hair, words that rippled through her breast like the strings of a violin at the hands of a master.

Again his lips touched hers in a tender joining.

Evanthea lost all sense of time and of her surroundings, thinking only of his embrace and the wonder of his love for her.

She did not know precisely when the voice had begun addressing her, but somewhere in the enveloping mist of her love for Brandreth, she came to a realization a woman was calling to her and probably had been for some time.

"Evanthea! Evanthea!"

Between what Evanthea determined must have been the fourth and fifth cry, she drew back from Brandreth and finally recognized Psyche's voice. "Oh, dear!" she exclaimed.

"What is it?" Brandreth asked, clearly startled by her sudden shift in demeanor.

"I must speak with you, Evanthea," Psyche whispered, laughing. "Please disengage yourself from Brandreth, if you are able! It is of the utmost importance. I've come to say goodbye."

Evanthea fixed her gaze firmly upon Brandreth's eyes, wondering how she could possibly explain to him that she needed to speak with an invisible person. "Someone is here," she began awkwardly. "Someone with whom I must speak immediately. It is a matter of some urgency, I fear."

"I don't understand," Brandreth said, first glancing about him, then asking, "Someone in the ballroom?"

"No . . . that is, yes . . . that is . . . Brandreth, I can't tell you who."

He narrowed her eyes at her. "It isn't . . . er . . . *Butterfly,* is it?" he queried.

"Yes," she responded, breathing a sigh of relief. Surely he would understand. Surely. "But how did you know?"

Brandreth drew back slightly, a frown appearing between his brows. "I can accept these flights of fancy in my great-aunt, Evanthea, but in the future mother of my children, I don't hesitate to say, I'm deeply concerned. . . ."

He broke off suddenly, as his gaze shifted to the right of Evanthea, his eyes opening wide.

Evanthea turned and saw at once that Psyche had become visible. "There you are!" she cried. "I take it Brandreth can see you?"

Psyche nodded. "I apprehended how impossible it would be for you to explain me otherwise. How do you do, Lord Brandreth? I am the *flight of fancy* you referred to, the one called Butterfly, wife of Eros."

"How—how do you do?" Brandreth responded politely, rising to his feet and bowing to her, his manners of long habit rescuing him from his obvious astonishment.

This polite gesture seemed to please Psyche immensely, for she smiled and clapped her hands, then extended them to the marquis.

Instinctively, he took them both in his, appearing stunned by the sight of her.

Smiling sweetly, she said, "I know it is unfair that I have known you forever since you have just now met me, my lord, but I am so happy to make your acquaintance at last."

"As am I," he said, smiling. "At least, I think I am. Are you real? How is this possible? I had always thought you and Cupid and the others were a myth from ancient times."

She nodded wisely, "We have been absolutely forbidden to interfere in the lives of mortals. . . ."

"But not you?"

Psyche appeared conscience-stricken as she bit her lip. "To own the truth, I am not supposed to be here and that is what I've come to tell Evanthea." She gave Brandreth's hands a squeeze and released them. Turning to Evanthea, she continued, "I have promised Grandpapa . . . Zeus, that is . . . that I will re-

313

turn to Olympus and never involve myself again here on earth."

"Oh, no!" Evanthea cried. She stepped toward her friend and slipped an arm about her waist. "Does this mean I will not see you again?"

Psyche sniffed and, placing a kiss upon Evanthea's cheek, said, "I'm afraid so."

"Oh, Psyche, no," Evanthea said, her eyes filling quickly with tears.

"Pray don't cry, or I fear I shall become a watering pot of no mean order. But don't think you shan't be in my thoughts, and every now and again I shall consult the oracle to discover how you fare." She then whispered, "I might even steal away for a brief visit once a decade, if I am able. Zeus has forgiven me this once, but he is unpredictable in his wrath. I daresay he would be furious if I disobeyed him again. But I must go now; Cupid awaits me."

Evanthea cried, "He does? But you sound so happy! Tell me, is all settled between you, then?"

"Quite magically. You see, I discovered he was angry over a lie his mother told him about me . . . that I had been his brother's . . . oh, I can't even speak the word!"

Evanthea did not misconstrue her meaning. "Do not tell me your mama-in-law would defame your character to your own husband?"

"Oh, wouldn't she just! I think she couldn't bear the fact that her darling boy loved me as he did! She has never wanted me to be his wife. Though I daresay no matter who Cupid married, she would have been equally as vindictive. But you should have heard Eros stand up to her . . . like George slaying the dragon. I was never more proud of him than in that moment, although it did help quite a bit to have Grandpapa—you know, Zeus—throwing his thunderbolts at her. He even ruined her ball gown and

314

sent her doves into such a flurry as you would not have believed!"

"I can't credit it. Then does Cupid no longer believe you are guilty?"

Psyche shook her head. "Not at all. And we are going to get a new palace, too, one far from his mother. I think we shall be happier than we ever have. Maybe we will even have children."

Evanthea could no longer restrain her affection and happiness for the beautiful immortal, and she embraced her lovingly. "I am so pleased, Psyche. And I do wish you well."

"And I, you. Goodbye, Evanthea. I know you will be wondrously content" — she glanced toward Brandreth and included him in her parting words — "both of you."

With that, Psyche sped away to join her husband. Evanthea watched Eros pick her up into his powerful arms. With his majestic white wings spread out into their full glory, he swept his wife up into the starry sky and flew eastward, disappearing from sight as a strange mist enveloped them both.

"And I had thought Lady Elle to have succumbed to the usual afflictions of the mind which accompany old age," Brandreth said, shaking his head in wonder. "And was that Cupid? Good God! I didn't know what she meant when she called herself wife of Eros! I have always thought of him as a little cherub, with pink cheeks and tiny wings."

"He is extraordinary, isn't he?" Evanthea marveled.

Brandreth drew near his betrothed and pulled her close to him. "Well," he said, "I suppose so, if one prefers *winged* creatures."

Evanthea could not resist responding with a sigh, "I always have. Indeed, it is most unfortunate you do not possess a pair of wings like Cupid's. Then I might truly be content."

"Is that so?" he queried.

"Yes," Evanthea cried, pushing him away a little. "And what of a palace? Psyche said Eros was going to find her a palace. Really, I begin to think myself ill-used since your county seat can only be accounted a meager mansion."

"You are right, of course. Staple Hall has but thirty bedchambers . . . hardly a palace!"

"Thirty?" Evanthea queried, swallowing hard. She had never had occasion to visit the marquis's country house, and though she knew it to be of magnificent proportions, she was not aware it possessed thirty bedchambers.

"Indeed, yes. But we could add a wing and fifteen more bedchambers, if you like. Or a pair of wings, and then perhaps you might begin to think of me as a *winged creature!*"

"Stop being nonsensical," she cried, laughing at him. "And tell me this much: Are you certain you will be happy with me?"

"No," he responded flatly. "But I daresay I will never be bored!"

"So much flattery!" she cried. "Do stop! I can't bear it!"

"Stubble it, Evanthea, and give us a kiss!"

Psyche clung to her husband, the night air cool against her neck as the mists of Olympus poured over them. She began to sob and could not seem to stop. Finally, Eros said, "Why do you cry, my love?"

"Because I have lost a dear friend. I shall never see her again. I just know it."

Eros was silent, his beating wings and Psyche's muffled sobs the only sounds between them as they flew over Olympus. After a moment, he said, "I know I oughtn't to tell you, but you see, when I consulted the oracle about Brandreth and Evanthea, I learned that they would one day have three daughters: Julia, Alexandra, and Victoria. It seems that a certain Olympian resident—not a goddess, but a young woman who loves to paint portraits and landscapes—flies to their rescue when two of the daughters fall in love with the same man and it is discovered that the gentleman concerned is in love with the third daughter. Quite a coil." He clicked his tongue but said no more.

Psyche looked up at him, blinking back her tears. "Tell me what I . . . that is, this *young Olympian resident* does to help them. Do I—I mean, does she really involve herself with Evanthea's daughters? What does she do?"

"The oracle was quite vague. I expect we shall never know."

Psyche bit her lip, the breeze of their flight drying her tears quickly. Her heart became light suddenly. She would see Evanthea again, and that was all that mattered. She could bear the separation now. Besides, she strongly suspected she would be involved in her own domestic concerns for some time to come, if Cupid's renewed tenderness were an accurate portent of the future.

When Eros glanced down at her and begged to know if what he had told her made her happier, she leaned her head onto his chest, holding him tightly as he gradually made his descent toward their home. "I believe it would be more accurate to say, that you've made me happy, Eros, wondrously so!"

317

THE ROMANCES OF LORDS AND LADIES
IN JANIS LADEN'S REGENCIES

BEWITCHING MINX (2532, $3.95)

From her first encounter with the Marquis of Pender-leigh when he had mistaken her for a common trollop, Penelope had been incensed with the darkly handsome lord. Miss Penelope Larchmont was undoubtedly the most outspoken young lady Penderleigh had ever known, and the most tempting.

A NOBLE MISTRESS (2169, $3.95)

Moriah Landon had always been a singularly practical young lady. So when her father lost the family estate over a game of picquet, she paid the winner, the notorious Viscount Roane, a visit. And when he suggested the means of payment — that she become Roane's mistress — she agreed without a blink of her eyes.

SAPPHIRE TEMPTATION (3054, $3.95)

Lady Serena was commonly held to be an unusual young girl — outspoken when she should have been reticent, lively when she should have been demure. But there was one tradition she had not been allowed to break: a Wexley must marry a Gower. Richard Gower intended to teach his wife her duties — in every way.

SCOTTISH ROSE (2750, $3.95)

The Duke of Milburne returned to Milburne Hall trusting that the new governess, Miss Rose Beacham, had instilled the fear of God into his harum-scarum brood of siblings. But she romped with the children, refused to be cowed by his stern admonitions, and was so pretty that he had the devil of a time keeping his hands off her.